NATURAL DESIRE, STRANGE DESIGN

'Won't you two be committing an act of desecration?' he asked Nick and Lilith with mock innocence.

'You're right,' Lilith replied. 'I suppose I'll just have to undergo expiation for it. Still, it'll liven up our first ceremony.'

By the same author:

THE RAKE
PURITY
MAIDEN
TIGER, TIGER
DEVON CREAM
CAPTIVE
DEEP BLUE
PLEASURE TOY
VELVET SKIN
PEACHES AND CREAM
CREAM TEASE

NATURAL DESIRE, STRANGE DESIGN

Aishling Morgan

Nexus

This book is a work of fiction.
In real life, make sure you practise safe, sane and
consensual sex.

First published in 2003 by
Nexus
Thames Wharf Studios
Rainville Road
London W6 9HA

www.nexus-books.co.uk

Typeset by TW Typesetting, Plymouth, Devon

Printed and bound by
Mackays of Chatham Ltd, Chatham, Kent

ISBN 0 352 33844 X

With thanks to Hilary and Penny,
for allowing me to abuse their characters

Note: this novel precedes *Deep Blue*

One

Nich Mordaunt tapped the tip of the cane to Ysabel's bottom, just firmly enough to make the soft flesh dimple. She was kneeling, her head down, her face buried in her arms, her heavy breasts squashed out on the floor, her hair spread around her in a halo of vivid green. Her knees were together, to lift the broad, fleshy orb of her bottom as high as possible. She had pulled her back in tight, accentuating her tiny waist and making her bottom seem bigger and more prominent still. An elegant Celtic tattoo on the small of her back further enhanced the exaggerated femininity of her shape, black against the white of her skin. There was no attempt at concealment, her cheeks well spread, to expose the softly puckered star of her anus, the flesh rose-pink and darkening to brown around the tight central hole. Her sex showed too, a split fig of plump flesh thickly grown with tangled, honey-blonde hair, the parting pink and wet.

'Do it,' she sighed. 'Hard. Don't spare me ... don't mind how I cry out.'

Nich gave an understanding nod. He tapped the cane to her bottom once more, made a quick adjustment of his stiff cock within his robe and lifted the cane. For a moment he paused, the cane lifted, to drink in both sight and scent. Ysabel held still, her pristine bottom raised to his cane, beautiful and passive. The thick,

1

hormonal scent of female sex hung in the air, mixed with hot incense smells and the tang of essential oils.

He brought the cane down, whistling through the air in an arc that ended at Ysabel's bottom, which it hit with the meaty thwack of wood impacting soft, girlish flesh. She grunted as it hit, an inarticulate cry of shock, pain and something more. As the cane lifted and the thin white line of the welt he had inflicted on her quickly darkened to an angry red, she set up a low, frightened whimpering.

Nich paused, once more adjusting his cock as he waited for the twitching of her buttocks and anus to subside. Again he took aim, laying the cane carefully across the meat of her buttocks, lifted and brought it down. Ysabel gave a broken, choking scream as the cane bit into her full cheeks, but she held her place, her whimpering now louder and more urgent. Nich gave a thoughtful nod, lifted the cane and once more brought it down, to add a third welt to Ysabel's now well-decorated bottom and wring a fresh scream from her mouth.

She was trembling hard, and the twitching of her anus had left a tiny sweat bubble over the hole, briefly iridescent in the candlelight before it burst. Her sex was beginning to flower, with white juice showing in the now open hole of her vagina. Nich's cane came up, and down, slashed across her bottom, to set her shaking. The muscles of one thigh went into spasm for an instant, her knee thudding on the carpet. Nich watched the fourth cane cut turn red.

Ysabel had begun to mumble, low, incoherent words spilling from her mouth, and to shake her head, to make the mass of her hair shiver in the light. Nich waited until her hand came back, suddenly, to snatch at her sex. She began to masturbate, sobbing as she rubbed herself, in an ecstasy of pain and contrition. Nich tapped the cane to her bottom, taking care to avoid her busy fingers. She gave a soft, urgent gasp. He brought the cane up, and

2

down. Ysabel screamed as it struck, full across the fattest part of her bottom, to add a fifth welt to her harshly beaten body.

Again Nich paused, watching her masturbate and trying to ignore his own, now urgent needs. Her sex was open, the hole tempting to his cock, her display too lewd to admit rejection. Contenting himself with a squeeze to the hard bar of flesh within his trousers, he once more lifted the cane to hold it above Ysabel's quivering bottom, awaiting his moment.

It came in seconds, a tightening of the muscles of her lower body, a sudden, hard contraction of her sex, a low cry. He brought the cane down with all his strength, to catch her hard across her meat right at the peak of her orgasm. Her scream of ecstatic reaction was immediate and loud, ringing out around the flat as the crimson line rose on her bottom. Her whole body was jerking, her sex and anus in spasm, her fingertips snatching over and over at her clitoris.

Nich peeled down his zip. His cock sprang free into his hand as he dropped the cane. Ysabel stayed still even as her orgasm died, keeping herself ready for penetration. Nich sank down behind her, his cock fit to burst as he pushed it to her hole and in, sliding up into her well-creamed passage as both moaned in unison. He took her hips and began to fuck, watching her whipped bottom bounce and quiver to his pushes.

He was already close to orgasm, the tightness of the sheath of hot female flesh around his cock and the sight of her glorious naked body beneath him more than enough stimulation. It started. At the last instant he pulled his cock free to empty himself over her upturned buttocks and into the crease between them. His come spattered the red welts of her cane cuts and left a long line running down to form a tiny puddle in the dimple of her anus, and he was done. He sank slowly back onto his heels with a contented sigh.

3

'Thank you, Nich,' Ysabel purred. 'That was lovely.'

'Good,' Nich answered. 'Not too hard?'

'No, just right . . . ow, my poor bum!'

She had risen to reach back with both hands and take hold of her bottom, squeezing the plump cheeks with her face set in a grimace of pain.

'There's some cream in the bathroom cupboard,' Nich pointed out.

Ysabel said nothing, but stood, slightly unsteady, and hobbled into the bathroom, still clutching her beaten bottom. Nich found a tissue to wipe his cock and settled into the worn black leather armchair in one corner of the room. Presently Ysabel returned from the bathroom, still nude, but with her bottom now a shiny ball, well creamed. She went to the couch, to lie face down, her chin in her hands, her expression set in a sleepy, satisfied smile.

'Better?' Nich asked.

'Much better,' she replied. 'I feel completely cleansed. Thanks again. You're so good at it!'

'I like to help,' Nich answered, grinning. 'Incidentally, why always six?'

'I'm not sure,' she said. 'Six just feels right. I suppose it's all this old-fashioned "six of the best" stuff. I know that's silly, and that it means I haven't completely broken away from my upbringing, but –'

'Not at all,' Nich broke in. 'Yes, your need for expiation can be seen to relate to Catholic confession, but this is not necessarily causal. See it as a human need. As for always wanting six, if that is what you need, then so be it.'

'But shouldn't we be trying to get away from Christian influence?'

'From direct influence, yes. Certainly you won't find me acknowledging the authority of a Christian priest! Still, there's no harm in drawing from Christian principle for our own rituals. In fact, I expect the remnants of Christian belief to be absorbed into paganism as it

4

grows, just as pagan beliefs were absorbed into Christianity.'

'Syncresis?'

'Exactly.'

Nich paused, glancing at his watch before he spoke again.

'Talking of religious syncresis, have you heard of Julian Blackman?'

'Vaguely. He was some sort of sixties guru, wasn't he?'

'In a sense, but there was more to him than that. Like us he was a pantheist, the first, in a sense, an extraordinary man, and from an extraordinary family. His grandfather was Sebastian Blackman, an initiate of the Golden Dawn, and his mother, Gaea, was briefly involved with Crowley in Sicily. He claims to have been fathered both by Crowley himself and by a demonically possessed goat –'

'A goat? You mean his mother . . .?'

'Possibly. With Crowley it is always hard to be sure what is reality, what is myth, what is merely prurient media speculation. In any case he was born in 1921 and returned to England with his mother when Crowley was thrown out of Sicily by Mussolini. Little is known of his childhood, but he was a Desert Rat, and attended Oxford after the war. He set his cult up in forty-nine, and was so successful that by fifty-two he had purchased a run-down country estate in Leicestershire for his headquarters. The cult was drawing largely from those disillusioned by war and seeking an alternative world vision and declined in the later sixties when such concepts became more popular. Declined in a spiritual sense, that is. He continued to attract followers, and at his death in seventy-nine he was a very rich man indeed.'

'And what happened?'

'The cult collapsed. His control had been absolute, so the moment he died the others began to squabble, although his daughter, Hecate –'

'His daughter's called Hecate? Cool!'

'Yes, and she was supposed to take his place. She was nineteen, but a woman of impressive personality. As everything belonged to her, she simply had the others thrown off her estate.'

'She wasn't a believer then?'

'So it would seem, as just a year later she married a man named Gerard Chealingham, an impoverished Baronet, and settled down.'

'Pity.'

'Yes, she seems to have betrayed her principles. That's the popular story, anyhow; I suspect the truth is a little less simple. Her husband is well known to hate anything to do with paganism. Apparently he even threatened one man with a shotgun, just for putting a bunch of grapes on the altar of one of the temples within the grounds. Hecate probably just goes along with him. But consider, she named her daughter Persephone, which would hardly be the choice of somebody out to reject paganism. Also, she kept the great bulk of her father's sacaralia and his library, until now that is. The whole lot is being auctioned off at Brady and Gordon in Notting Hill this afternoon.'

'Yeah, I saw something about that in the papers. Isn't he supposed to have squirreled something away, some sort of legacy? So you're going to get some stuff?'

'Yes, as much as I can, but there's more to it than that. The article you saw was by Frea Baum who was Blackman's partner when he died, but all this talk of hidden wealth is sheer nonsense. Blackman held something back, yes, but not what most people think of as valuables.'

'What then?'

'His work books. He was possibly the leading cultist of the twentieth century, and he is known to have conducted a great many experiments, always in private. Yet the supposedly complete listing of his library is

6

pretty straightforward, banal even, other than his own major publications.'

'So you reckon he wanted to keep his real discoveries to himself?'

'It is hard to establish his true motives. He was always secretive. But I have interviewed Frea Baum myself, as well as several other ex-members of the cult. It took a bit of piecing together, but what is known is that on a winter's night in 1978, when Blackman knew he was dying, he secluded himself in his inner sanctum with three objects. My belief is that he set up some sort of puzzle. That way, when Hecate was older she would be able to take over where he left off, but only if she had the drive and intelligence to solve the puzzle. As the objects are up for sale, she clearly doesn't.'

'And you know what these objects are?'

'I do.'

Anderson Croom patted the tips of his fingers to Vicky's bottom, smiling as he felt the sleek muscle of her pert cheek. She was bent across his lap, her already indecently short school skirt turned up over her bottom, her white schoolgirl panties well down and taut between her knees. Everything showed, the whole neat yet ripe globe of her bottom, the wet, puffy lips of her sex, the pinkish brown star of her anus.

'So,' he said happily, 'who's been a naughty girl? Who's had to have her knickers taken down for a spanking? Who's got her little bare bottom –'

'Stop it!' she interrupted. 'You're making me laugh!'

'Oh, I am, am I?'

'Yes! Now get on with the spanking.'

'Gladly.'

Anderson took a firm hold on her waist and set to work, smacking his hand down on her bottom hard and fast. She immediately began to struggle, kicking her long legs in the tightly stretched panties and tossing her hair from side to side. He clung on tight, working her bottom over with ever-faster and ever-harder swats. All the while his face was set in a boyish grin of sheer delight in having a beautiful girl bent bare bottom across his lap for spanking.

In the background the phone rang. Anderson took no notice whatever, spanking away merrily as Vicky's bottom began to turn red and her cries took on a new tone. The ringing halted, but only when a polite knock sounded at the door did Anderson stop spanking her. Anderson tightened his grip as he called out.

'Come in!'

'You bastard!' Vicky spat and immediately began to struggle again, this time with real effort, trying desperately to break free and also to get her panties up.

Anderson laughed as the door swung open to reveal an old man in a formal black suit. Vicky gave a hiss of anger but went limp, resigned to the indignity being inflicted on her as it was clearly too late to avoid it. Her bottom was towards the door, her reddened cheeks on full display, with the lips of her sex and the tight, dark-brown spot of her anus clearly visible. The old man spoke, his face flushed red as he began to close the door.

'I am terribly sorry, sir. I did not realise that you were busy.'

'Not at all, Creech,' Anderson answered. 'Just spanking my tart. Who was it?'

'The vicar, sir. He wishes to know if you will be contributing to the harvest festival this year?'

'What? Tell him to go to Hell! No, don't, give him a marrow or something.'

'Very well, sir.'

The door shut with a click as Creech retreated. Anderson gave Vicky a gentle pat as she twisted to show her face, her cheeks flushed as rich a red as her bottom.

'You are such an utter bastard!' she swore.

8

'Temper, temper,' Anderson chided. 'And mind your language, or I'll send you into the pantry to suck his wrinkly old cock.'

'No!'

Anderson chuckled and slid his hand between her thighs to cup her pubic mound. His thumb found her hole as he began to masturbate her. For a moment she struggled against it, then gave in with a moan. Anderson kept his grip as he manipulated her sex and began to talk.

'Yes, that will do nicely, much more humiliating than just being made to parade about dressed as a schoolgirl.'

'No . . .' she squealed. 'Anderson, please, that's not fair!'

'Oh, but it is, and very funny. I'd make you go like this, with your knickers around your knees and a red bum . . .'

'No . . . Anderson . . .'

'Yes, Vicky, dressed up as a schoolgirl, a tarty little schoolgirl, a real slut of a schoolgirl, and down on your knees . . . your silly little skirt tucked up . . . your knickers well down . . . your bottom bare and red behind you.'

'No . . . not that . . . anything else . . .'

He was rubbing hard, his fingers working on her clitoris, his thumb moving in the wet, open hole of her sex. A shine of sweat had begun to rise on her well-smacked cheeks, making the red skin glossy. Her breathing had become deep and even. She was shivering gently to the motions of his hand. He went on.

'You'd have to show him your breasts, naturally, perhaps just with your blouse undone a little way and your bra pulled up to exhibit them nicely. I'd make you go in like that, breasts and bottom bare for him to inspect, to fondle. Or I might just give him free rein, to interfere with you as he pleased. Either way you'd end up down on your knees, kneeling to him, his cock out

9

in front of you. You'd hate yourself, but you'd do it, opening your mouth, leaning forwards, taking hold of his erect cock . . .'

'No!' Vicky wailed, utter despair, but already her hole had begun to contract on Anderson's thumb.

'And in it would go!' Anderson crowed. 'Into your pretty little mouth, for you to suck, Vicky, to suck his penis . . . your mouth full of an old man's cock, in and out . . . your tarty red lipstick smeared up and down his shaft. That's right, Vicky, sucking and sucking and sucking, like the little slut you are, until he came, right in your mouth. Imagine the taste of the spunk. Imagine having to swallow it. Imagine him making you gag so it all comes out of your nose . . .'

Vicky gave a cry, ecstasy mixed with deep shame, as she came on his hand, her sex in frantic contraction, her anus winking in time, her red buttocks clenching and unclenching. Anderson was laughing as he watched go through her orgasm, and as he finally let go of her waist he began to spank her again, heavy swats directed to the crests of her quivering cheeks. He went on, rubbing and smacking as she shuddered her way through an orgasm that broke only when she slipped from his lap.

She gave a squeak of alarm as her balance went. She twisted as she fell and sat down hard on her smacked bottom. Anderson doubled up with laughter, unable to control himself at the sight of her dishevelment and the expression of angry consternation on her face. Finally she spoke.

'You really are such an utter, utter bastard!'

'Oh, do be quiet, Vicky,' he answered as he finally got his laughter under control. 'You're becoming repetitive. Now, why don't you be a good little schoolgirl and suck on this?'

He had put his hand to his fly. For one moment her face showed outrage, and then she had come forwards, to kneel between his knees and take his cock into her mouth as it came free. Anderson gave a contented sigh, watching her pretty, painted face in its frame of fine black hair as she sucked on his penis. His cock was growing quickly in her mouth, and as she peeled his foreskin back with her lips he found himself shutting his eyes and curling his toes at the sheer intensity of the sensation.

Within a minute she had him fully erect, and had begun to lick at his cock, using her tongue on the sensitive underside and kissing at his bloated helmet. She had taken hold of him too, pulling his balls from his fly to stroke at them, and tugging at the shaft with her other hand. Soon he was gripping the chair, struggling to hold himself back, and then it was simply too much.

He snatched at his cock, grabbing the shaft as his other hand locked in her hair. Three hard tugs and he was there. Her cheeks bulged out and her eyes popped as her mouth was abruptly filled with sperm. Then he was milking himself down her throat, with a long sigh of ecstasy as spurt after spurt of semen was ejaculated into her windpipe. Even when she started to gag he held his cock deep in, enjoying the contractions of her throat on his helmet, until at last it simply became too sensitive to go on.

Vicky rocked back on her heels, gasping for air, with bubbles of sperm coming from both her nostrils. Anderson gave a contented sigh, and tried not to laugh as he watched her struggle to hold down what he had done in her mouth. Finally she recovered herself enough to look up at him. Her large dark eyes were watery, her skin red, her lower face smeared with a mixture of lipstick and spunk.

'Good?' he asked.

She nodded weakly.

'May I borrow your knickers?'

Again she nodded, and hooked a thumb into the side of her lowered panties to pull them free from one long

11

leg, then the other. Anderson took them, wiping his cock clean as she spoke.

'More?' she asked. 'Or have you had enough?'

'I'm done, I think, and I was going to nip up to London, to Brady and Gordon. It's the auction of the stuff from that con-artist, Blackman – you know, the one who set up a phony religious cult.'

'Oh, yes? What for?'

'Just a casual interest, really, but there are some rather fine silk robes I thought might make nice dressing gowns.'

'Oh, I thought you might like to belt me or something . . .'

She had stood, and now stretched, the action pushing her breasts hard against her blouse and lifting her tiny skirt over the hairless swell of her pubic mound. Her sex lips showed, the fleshy pink folds of the inner peeping out from between the twin bulges of the outer. Again she spoke.

'Don't you even want to fuck me in my uniform?'

'Well,' he answered, 'since you put it like that . . .'

Nich laid a small curse on each new person as they entered the auction room. It was becoming alarmingly full, and not with the pagans and students of the occult against whom he had expected to be bidding, but with sleek, wealthy types who didn't look as if they'd know Grimm from Herne. Obviously the rumour that the appointments of the late Julian Blackman's cult contained clues to some form of wealth had taken hold, bringing in collectors, the idly curious and even TV astrologers. Nich shuddered at the thought, chanting a quick rote of protection in his mind and giving a nervous squeeze to the bundle of ten-pound notes in his coat pocket. The rumours, as Nich knew after months of painstaking research, were true, at least in a sense. With such affluent competitors all around him, his only

12

real hope lay in being the sole person among the bidders who was aware which four lots were necessary to discover the location of Blackman's books.

A side door to the auction room opened, admitting a tall man in a striped shirt and a bright blue suit. He strode to the auctioneer's stand and looked out over the audience with a satisfied smile. Behind him came an equally smart woman bearing a clipboard and a copy of the auction catalogue.

'Good morning, ladies and gentlemen, a pleasure to see such a full house,' the man began. 'I am Peter Sedgeley, and this morning we will be disposing of a remarkable collection of artefacts relating to alternative religion. These are being offered by Lady Chealingham, the daughter of renowned cultist Julian Blackman. For those of you who are not aware of the history of these items, I will give a brief summary. Julian Blackman founded an essentially pagan cult shortly after the last war, gaining such a large following that, in 1952, he was able to purchase Brooke House, a manor in Leicester-shire, for his headquarters. The cult thrived until his death in early 1979, when it was discovered that his will made his daughter Hecate his sole beneficiary. Hecate expelled the cult. Deprived of its inspiration, premises and money, the cult quickly died out, leaving Hecate Blackman, now Lady Chealingham, as one of the country's most eligible heiresses. Only now has she decided to realise the value of her father's collection. I'm sure you will excuse me if my pronunciation of some of the technical terms is inaccurate.'

As if they'd know, Nich thought bitterly, glancing around at the rows of beaming faces, the majority of which showed expressions of clever amusement. He muttered a general curse, excluding only the auctioneer and his assistant.

'Lot one, then,' Sedgeley continued. 'A robe, in scarlet silk, complete with cowl and sleeves. It bears a

13

design of . . . er . . . of some sort, in gold thread. Do I hear fifty pounds?'

The robe sold to a fashionably thin woman in designer tweeds for one hundred and eighty pounds. Nich found his anger tempered by sadness. The robe he recognised as one worn by Blackman for his morning devotions, the design being a symbolic sun rising above an equally symbolic oak tree. It was a beautiful object, which he would have dearly loved to possess and the wretched woman was probably going to use it to show off in at parties.

The auction proceeded, the lots fetching prices Nich found alarming, increasingly so when the last of the vestments had been sold and the sacaralia began to go for even higher sums. One matchless item after another was knocked down to a group that was beginning to take on the atmosphere of a pleasure outing, with light laughter and witty remarks punctuating the sales. Nich found a knot of nervous tension forming in his stomach as the first of his lots approached. His only hope, he realised, lay in the fact that the prices lots were fetching were in proportion to their beauty and material value rather than their true significance.

The lot was a black iron spider that had originally stood on a pole at the entrance to Blackman's inner sanctum. A hideous object by any standards, its purpose had been to ward Blackman from curses and other negative emanations. Nich hoped that it would not find favour with the crowd.

'Lot seventy-one,' Sedgeley announced. 'A large iron spider, truly grotesque in the detail of its execution. Do I hear fifty pounds?'

Nich felt a lump in his throat as the spider was raised for inspection. Blackman's personal ward and a clue to the whereabouts of the master's work books and perhaps more. With luck it would be his in moments.

'How simply frightful!' a woman two rows in front of Nich giggled.

She raised her card. Nich raised his own, simultaneously trying to will her over-tight trousers to split. Nothing happened except that she again held up her card. Nich followed, raising the bidding to eighty pounds. The woman shook her head, making a deprecating gesture to her companion.

'Going for eighty pounds to the gentleman in row five,' Sedgeley announced after a pause to glance over the crowd. 'Do I hear ninety? No? Sold to the gentleman for eighty pounds. Thank you, may I see your bidder number, sir?'

Nich sighed with relief as the hammer came down and the assistant noted his number on her clipboard. The spider was his! Moreover, the lack of interest proved that no one else was aware that it formed part of the key to Blackman's true legacy. He grinned in his exultation. With nearly nine hundred pounds remaining, surely he stood a chance.

Several more lots passed, including many objects for which Nich would cheerfully have given the rest of his money in different circumstances. The bidding continued to rise, Sedgeley raising his opening call to one hundred pounds when a bronze statue of a satyr topped the thousand mark. Nich's next target was lot 83, a jade idol combining the images of the Earth Mother and the Hunter, once the central figure of Blackman's altar and an object charged with significance. At the centre of Blackman's beliefs had been the principle of the division of deity into male and female principals, equal and opposite but not opposed. The concept was represented in the idol. Despite Nich's own belief in the supremacy of chaos, the idol was an object worthy of veneration as well as part of the key.

'Lot eighty-three,' Sedgeley called out. 'A statuette, in jade, of what appears to be a small teddy bear, although when I was little none of my bears had horns.'

More light laughter greeted his remark, Nich alone not sharing the joke but instead grinding his teeth in fury.

'A charming object and beautifully rendered,' Sedgeley was saying. 'Do I hear one hundred pounds?'

Nich raised his card automatically, only to find himself in a field of a dozen bidders. The bids rose swiftly past the five hundred mark. Most of the bidders dropped out, until Nich was in competition with just three. There was a woman he recognised as a populist astrologer from one of the tabloids, also a confident-looking man with silver hair. The third was among those standing, a plump young man with a yellowing and dog-eared copy of a Dennis Wheatley novel protruding from his coat pocket.

The silver-haired man dropped out at seven hundred pounds. Still the bidding rose, past eight hundred, then nine hundred. Nich was forced to give in, but both the astrologer and the young man continued to bid. The statuette finally sold to the man for nearly two thousand pounds. Nich marked the successful bidder's appearance with puzzlement. He did not have the look of a pagan, nor a collector, and it was hard to see why he would be prepared to pay so much if his interest was no more than casual. Even if the man was prepared to sell, Nich knew he could not hope to match the price.

Nich meditated while the remaining statues and carvings were sold off, only turning his attention back to the auction when the first item of jewellery was held up for inspection. The third object he needed was a plaque of twisted gold and garnets in a design entirely devoid of symmetry. It had no significance that he knew of and appeared to be intended solely as part of the key. It had been worn as a necklace by the young Hecate Blackman. His sole hope of success, he realised, lay in the fact that as an *objet d'art* it was quite tasteless. He waited as the smart young woman took over the auction, announcing herself as Felicity Chatfield.

'Lot one-o-four,' she declared. 'A necklace of gold, fourteen-carat plated, and set with garnets. A highly distinctive design.'

16

'Apparently,' the man to Nich's left whispered conspiratorially, 'old Blackman's daughter used to perform their weird rituals wearing that and not a stitch besides.'

'Nonsense,' Nich replied tersely, 'that would be unthinkable. She would have had several other pieces of jewellery as well, to a total of either seven or thirteen.'

'Oh,' the man replied uneasily. 'Well ... right ...'

Nich answered with a grunt, raising his card to catch the opening bid.

To his dismay the bidding rose more swiftly than ever. The bizarre design of the piece had evidently caught the crowd's imagination rather than repelled it. On turning to scan the room in alarm, he discovered that the bulk of bidders were male and characterised by expressions of lascivious guilt. Clearly the image of naked female pagans was a more powerful draw than artistic taste. In moments the price had risen beyond Nich's reserve, and when the necklace did go it was to the same fleshy young man who had brought the statuette, for well over a thousand. With a strong sinking feeling, Nich realised that he might after all not be the only one to understand the importance of the two items.

Two times out of three he had failed, yet the final lot was the most important and the one least likely to fetch a high price. Consisting of the notebooks and papers cleared from Blackman's study, it could surely only be of interest to a serious student such as himself. The notebooks, he was convinced, contained the instructions for combining the three objects to reveal the location of the books. Without them his task would be next to impossible, but with them and the spider it might just be possible to solve Blackman's puzzle.

The lot he needed was the final one, and he was delighted to note that the level of bidding dropped when the auctioneer reached the books and then dropped again, more sharply, for the collection of pictures and prints. The crowd began to thin as unsuccessful bidders left and eager buyers went to queue at the reception desk. Nich treated himself to a hand-copied Paracelsus; a Golden Bough, worn but complete; a framed print of the Leicestershire house; and several disturbing drawings done by Blackman himself.

With only four lots left the auction was briefly interrupted by a late arrival. A tall elegant man with an air of self-assured ease, Nich noted at a glance, moving his catalogue to allow the man to take the vacant chair to his right. Another collector probably, Nich decided, but not a very serious one or he wouldn't have turned up when the auction was nearly over.

'Thank you,' the man said quietly. 'I fear I am rather late. Have the vestments gone?'

'They went first,' Nich replied. 'There are only a few odds and ends left.'

'What a shame,' the man replied casually. 'I had my eye on Blackman's robe for the vernal rites. Oh, Anderson Croom, by the way.'

'Pleased to meet you,' Nich replied with sudden enthusiasm tempered by fresh alarm. 'Nich Mordaunt. Yes, with it I might have allowed myself an ascendancy next equinox. It went for around four hundred, I think.'

'Oh, I doubt I would have paid that,' Croom answered. 'The blue silk would have matched my eyes though. It would have made a marvellous dressing gown. Still, I can live without it.'

Nich looked at Croom with horror, his initial impression of a kindred spirit fading as rapidly as it had come.

'Oh, well, I suppose I'd better get something,' Croom continued, oblivious to Nich's glare of outrage at his intended use for Blackman's blue silk robe. 'It would be a pity to have an entirely wasted journey. Not one-five-one though, very dull, tarot cards.'

'Lot one-five-one,' Felicity Chatfield called out. 'A set of hand-painted cards, possibly a sort of tarot. Worn but believed to be complete. Do I hear twenty pounds?'

Nich raised his card, unable to resist the prize and reasoning that the box of oddments would fetch only a few pounds.

There was desultory bidding from the remaining TV astrologer, but Nich secured the cards for 45 pounds, leaving him with a comfortable sum.

'Lot one-five-two, the final lot,' Felicity announced. 'A box containing books and papers belonging to the late Julian Blackman. Do I hear ten pounds?'

'That sounds more interesting,' Croom remarked, raising his card.

Nich raised his in turn, confident that Croom's rather casual interest would not last. A large man in the front row joined in, quickly raising the bidding past the level Nich had hoped to buy for.

Croom continued to bid, obviously enjoying the process as much for the fun of the thing as from any desire to own the box. Nich countered furiously, the sinking feeling in the pit of his stomach growing as the bidding approached the sum of his remaining money. The large man dropped out with only ten pounds to go, leaving Nich with the bid.

'Oh, why not,' Croom murmured and raised his card.

Nich found himself faced with the choice of backing down or placing a bid in excess of his reserves. Having already taken his overdraft to the limit to obtain sufficient money for the auction, he realised that continuing to bid would be futile and slumped back in his seat, watching the precious box knocked down to Croom. At least he would be able to bargain, he reflected, offering his books and prints against the apparently far less valuable box.

As Nich left the auction room he found the queue at the desk already stretching back the full length of the corridor and halfway down the stairs. Croom came up behind him, reading his catalogue and giving an occasional rueful shake of his head at some missed prize.

Nich considered the man. Above average height and lean but relatively broad-shouldered, Croom's physique gave the impression of fitness contrasted with languor, lethargy almost. This later impression came from the way he carried himself, as if amused and slightly bored by the world. A mop of hair of the deepest brown and the relaxed set of his boyish good looks added to the image.

Despite a pang of antagonism towards the air of upper-class conceit which Nich found in Croom, the man's very lack of seriousness raised his hopes of being able to trade purchases. Croom was evidently a collector but appeared to be motivated largely by vanity and a love of beautiful objects. Surely, then, he would exchange a box of tatty old notebooks and papers for Blackman's original artworks?

'Perhaps you'd like to make an exchange?' Nich offered as Croom joined the queue behind him. 'I bought several drawings, actually signed by Blackman himself. I'm prepared to offer them in exchange for the box.'

'That's very generous,' Croom replied, 'but given that the true value of even one drawing far exceeds that of the box, I can hardly accept your offer. It just wouldn't be right.'

'No, no, really, I don't mind at all,' Nich answered, trying to keep the desperation from his voice.

'Thank you, but no,' Croom continued. 'You see, the truth is that this sort of quasi-religious gobbledegook fascinates me. I mean, what could have inspired Blackman's followers to believe such arrant nonsense? I suspect his notebooks contain the answers.'

'Arrant nonsense?' Nich echoed, aghast. 'Blackman was a master, a . . . a paragon . . . The depth of his knowledge was astounding, his reasoning . . .'

'Come, come,' Croom laughed. 'Blackman was one of the most skilful frauds in history. Damn it, he read philosophy at Oxford, where he had something of a reputation as an atheist. He was at my own college, as it happens, at the same time as my father. Not only that, but he served in North Africa during the war. Surely you can see that he picked up a lot of his concepts in Egypt?'

'Certainly ancient Egyptian theology played an important part in his beliefs,' Nich replied hotly. 'So did others. His awareness of basic polytheistic verity transcended any single set of beliefs! He was a genius!'

'Yes, a genius at extracting money from the gullible.'

'No! Look at the richness and complexity of his rituals! Have you read his *Compendium of Religious Symbology*, or his *Understanding of Natural Magic*? No fraud could achieve such complexity, let alone so great a depth of understanding. Besides, he was devoted to his followers!'

'Why then did he leave his entire estate to his daughter?' Croom asked condescendingly.

'How was he to know that Hecate would betray her principles?' Nich retorted with growing anger.

Croom merely laughed, walked over to the door of the hospitality suite and signalled the barman, leaving Nich fuming in the corridor.

Felicity Chatfield lifted her cup of coffee and walked across the auction room to where Peter Sedgeley was beginning to rearrange things for the afternoon's auction. The morning had gone well, in fact considerably better than had been anticipated. In addition to their normal client group of collectors and specialists there had been a fair number of minor celebrities from the media and entertainment fields. One man in particular had caught her eye, a latecomer who was in fact a fairly regular bidder. Until that morning, though, she had never been able to put a name to his face.

'Did you see the guy who turned up late?' she asked Sedgeley as she reached the table on which he was stacking catalogues.

'Yes,' Sedgeley answered, 'he's a regular. Crome, or Croom, I think his name is.'

'Anderson Croom,' Felicity replied. 'He's in this month's *London Girl*, there's an article on the fifty richest single guys in the Southeast. He's in it.'

'Oh, yes?'

'Yes, I've got it somewhere. Hang on.'

Felicity left the room and fetched the magazine, flicking through the pages until she reached the article she wanted. Sure enough, there was Croom, as handsome and dapper as in real life, photographed in Piccadilly.

'Here it is,' she told Sedgeley when she returned. 'They rate him London's twenty-fourth richest bachelor. He must be loaded! Apparently he inherited his fortune from his parents and doesn't work at all; lucky so-and-so.'

'It's all right for some,' Sedgeley answered.

'You're just jealous,' Felicity chided him gently. 'Apparently he even employs a butler! He drives a Bentley, and has expensive tastes in wine, food and clothes; he collects books and valuable curiosities and is not currently romantically linked to anyone in particular.'

'In which case he's undoubtedly gay,' Sedgeley remarked. 'Don't get your hopes up.'

'No, no,' Felicity insisted, 'by that they just mean that he isn't engaged to a celebrity or anything. In the "Hot Tips" section it says he leads an exciting and varied night-life. That's how they say he's forever dating different girls when the magazine doesn't want to risk being sued for libel.'

'There we are, then,' Sedgeley stated. 'He's an unprincipled seducer. Not the sort of man a well brought-up girl like you should be associating with.'

'Oh, I wouldn't mind a go,' Felicity answered.

Two

Anderson Croom gave a contented smile as he lowered the glass of Armagnac from his lips. He and Vicky had just finished a light dinner of partridge stuffed with truffles and served with French beans and wild rice, washing the delicacy down with a bottle of Volnay. Miniature Sussex Pond puddings had followed, made with a kumquat and served with a half of old Sauternes. They had then retired to the drawing room for his post-prandial glass of brandy. Creech had brought in the Armagnac. Croom took a moment to savour the fragrance of the tawny liquid and then looked up at his butler.

'Tell me what you think, Creech,' he said. 'There was a curious man at the auction this afternoon, name of Mordaunt. He's some sort of religious crackpot, bright-red hair, wears entirely black, barring some peculiar jewellery. He was desperately keen to get his hands on a box of old notebooks I bought, even offered me some moderately fine drawings in exchange. It made me wonder if there wasn't something in this rumour of old Blackman having salted away something really valuable. Vicky thinks it's a wild goose chase.'

'Of course it is,' Vicky broke in. 'If there is anything it'll turn out to be some healing crystals, or crap like that.'

'I don't think so,' Anderson insisted. 'Consider what we know. Blackman took the total wealth of a couple of hundred people, which bought the house, kept the cult going and paid for all the fancy goods that were auctioned off this morning. I would bet that he still had plenty over, even allowing for his daughter's inheritance.'

'That is somewhat conjectural, if I may say so, sir,' Creech answered.

'Dead right,' Vicky agreed.

'So it might seem,' Anderson said, 'so it might seem. However, I spent this afternoon going over old Blackman's notes. A lot of it's in cipher, but only a simple transposition with occult symbols for letters and numbers. I worked it out in an hour or less. Looking at what I found, I feel that we are on solid ground.'

'Indeed, sir?' Creech said.

'Indeed, Creech,' Croom continued. 'It appears that he was concerned to safeguard a measure of his inheritance from legal challenges made by cult members once they discovered that Hecate was going to inherit the entire estate. She was nineteen at the time, remember, yet he stipulated that his notes were not to be given to her until she reached twenty-one. His assumption must have been that she would then read them, learn how to combine three of the artefacts she had inherited and so find the cache containing the remainder of the inheritance.'

'Sure,' Vicky put in.

'Would it not have been more practical to leave clear instructions, sir?' Creech asked.

'Apparently not,' Croom continued. 'Blackman trusted neither his lawyers nor anybody else. Possibly a reflection of his own character.'

'Most likely, sir.'

'In any case, he seems to have misjudged his daughter's character, as she evidently never read the notes. Some of the papers were still sealed with wax when I brought them back this morning. Black sealing wax marked with a thing like a bear, if you please. Now, it seems logical to assume that the value of the hidden inheritance at least equals that of the first inheritance, otherwise why bother? Do you agree?'

'Not an unreasonable assumption, sir.'

'Not unreasonable at all. So, if we allow for inflation and so forth, the cache must be worth several hundred thousand pounds –'

'In old one-pound notes,' Vicky interrupted.

'No,' Anderson insisted. 'The volume would be enormous, and bear in mind that this was under ten years after decimalisation. Blackman would have invested in something that would retain its value.'

'Bollocks.' Vicky laughed. 'If he thought she'd get the stuff in three or four years, he'd have gone for the simplest thing, cash.'

'Inflation was high,' Anderson pointed out. 'So were taxes. My bet is gold, that or diamonds, maybe half a million pounds worth, maybe a million.'

'If I may say so, sir,' Creech stated, 'your reasoning appears somewhat optimistic.'

'Not you as well!' Anderson answered. 'Look, damn it, it makes perfect sense . . .'

'Sure!' Vicky laughed.

'Do you remember what happened earlier, Vicky?' Anderson demanded.

Vicky went abruptly red, her face briefly showing shock before settling into a pout.

'If I may say so, sir,' Creech put in quickly, 'even if all you say is true, it seems a great deal of effort to go to when you have no need of the money . . .'

'So you admit there is some?' Anderson broke in.

'I admit it is a possibility, sir,' Creech went on.

'Then I want it,' Anderson said. 'At least I want to try. Look at it this way. We already know the location of one of the artefacts, a large iron spider which is mentioned in the notebooks and with which Nich

Mordaunt left this morning. I assume he was outbid for the other two, a jade thing like a mad teddy bear and a preposterous necklace, as they're in the catalogue but he didn't take them. All I need to do is find out who bought the teddy bear and the necklace and offer them more. Then I can bargain with Nich, or pinch the spider.'

'You're going to get arrested,' Vicky said. 'I tell you, it's either a load of new-age crap, or this Chealingham woman will have had the lot years ago. Why not be sensible . . .?'

'Because I don't want to,' Anderson insisted. 'The only things that keep me going nowadays are food, wine and tormenting you. I can't do that all the time, can I, or I'd be as fat as an ox with my cock worn down to a stub. I get bored.'

Nich walked briskly up Queensway, the tails of his ankle-length black greatcoat flapping behind him. He had made a deliberate effort to look smart. Black jeans, a black polo-neck jumper, polished black boots. Even his jewellery had been kept to a minimum, a ring with an eight-pointed design in crimson enamel, the chaos symbol and his personal ward. Reaching the premises of Brady and Gordon, he paused only long enough to utter a simple incantation for luck and then pushed open the door.

'Good morning, sir. How may I help you?' a cheerful voice greeted him.

Nich immediately recognised the woman who had spoken as Felicity Chatfield. She was sitting behind the reception desk, as neat as she had been the previous day, in a crisp white blouse with her golden hair carefully arranged on top of her head.

'Good morning,' Nich replied. 'I was at the auction yesterday and I was wondering if you could help me?'

'Certainly, sir. There is some remaindered stock if you would be interested in meeting the reserve price?'

'Remaindered stock?' Nich repeated. 'Yes, I'll take anything you can let me have for, let me see, I can probably go to one hundred and fifty pounds.'

'Twenty pounds would be more realistic,' Felicity said quietly with a smile and a glance down the corridor. 'It was lot thirty-four.'

'Thank you,' Nich replied. 'That's extremely kind of you.'

'Not at all sir,' Felicity continued. 'Between you and me, both we and the seller will be glad to get rid of it. It is rather bulky, after all.'

Nich passed over a twenty-pound note, delighted at the thought of another item from the Blackman collection for only twenty pounds, regardless of what it was. If it had been lot 34, he reflected, it would be a vestment of some sort. He signed a collection note, half of which Felicity passed to a brown-coated warehouseman who took it with a grunt and threw Nich an odd look.

'I was really hoping to find out who the purchasers of one or two of the other lots were,' Nich continued, emboldened by Felicity's open friendliness. 'Some of the items were of great personal value to me, you see, and I was hoping to make offers for them when I can get a little more money together.'

'Personal value?' Felicity said, her eyes widening slightly before she recovered her composure. 'I'm afraid we can't release the names of buyers, sir. It's our policy.'

'Please,' Nich continued, 'it's really important.'

'I'm sorry, sir,' Felicity replied firmly, 'but we never give out the names of buyers. It causes all sorts of trouble, you see. You really should have spoken to them after the auction.'

'I had to wait for the last lot,' Nich pleaded. 'One was gone before I got out, and the other . . . wouldn't see reason.'

'I'm sorry, but it's out of the question,' she insisted, her voice taking on a new edge.

Nich focused his eyes on her, willing her to perform the simple act of bringing up the relevant information on her computer screen. Felicity stared back, equally obdurate, her pale-blue eyes unblinking and her mouth set in a firm line. After a long moment Nich gave up.

'Very well,' he said, stepping back from the desk. 'I suppose you'd be sacked if you let me know and any complaints were made, but I'd like to see whoever's in charge. What about the man who was here yesterday?'

'Mr Sedgeley is in no more of a position to take such a decision than I am, sir,' Felicity responded in a tired voice. 'Mrs Green is the manageress, but I assure you –'

'I'll see Mrs Green, then,' Nich demanded.

'Mrs Green is in a meeting, sir,' Felicity replied.

'I can wait.'

'Mrs Green will be unavailable all day, and in any case she wouldn't give you the information you want.'

'I'd like an appointment to see her, then. Tomorrow morning.'

'It's Saturday tomorrow, sir. We're closed.'

'Monday, then.'

'Mrs Green is going on holiday on Monday, for a fortnight.'

'Who will be in charge then?'

'Mr Sedgeley.'

Nich threw up his arms in disgust and strode out of the door.

'The warehouse door is to the left, sir!' Felicity's voice followed him.

Nich walked around to the side of the building, seething inwardly at Felicity's stubbornness. He was also at a loss to understand why his piercing gaze, normally so effective, had failed to work on her. Lack of belief, he suspected; atheists and the like were always harder to work on. In the alley that ran down the side of the auction house he found a tall double door with the surly warehouseman leaning against the side and smoking a cigarette. Nich handed over his half of the collection note, reflecting that at least his morning had not been totally wasted. The warehouseman took the note and threw Nich another strange look. Nich ignored him, being used to such responses.

'It's in here, mate. You want to bring your car up?'

'I don't have a car,' Nich replied, following the man into the warehouse. 'I can manage.'

'You're a bleeding sight stronger than you look then, mate! Here we are, lot thirty-four, one Victorian commode chair, mahogany with brass and leather fittings.'

'This isn't what I bought,' Nich said, staring in horror at the chair. 'I bought lot thirty-four, from yesterday's auction. Robes of some sort, I'd imagine.'

'No, mate. Says here, in black and white. Lot thirty-four, one Victorian commode chair, mahogany with brass and leather fittings.'

'Yes, yes, I know what it says,' Nich snapped, 'but I'm telling you, it's not what I bought. There must be some sort of mistake – yesterday's auction was of religious clothing and artefacts, there weren't any of these, these . . .'

'Religious stuff?' the warehouseman queried. 'That was the lunchtime one, that was. No leftovers from that, sold like hot cakes that did. No, yesterday afternoon was Victoriana. Mainly chinaware an' that.'

Nich stared aghast at the chair. It was large and solid, made of dark wood, with the lower part enclosed by panels, each carved with a fat cupid. There was a hole in the seat, revealing the china bowl within. Alarmingly, each arm, the back and the lower legs were fitted with broad leather straps and heavy duty buckles.

'I'll move it outside for you, shall I then, sir?' the warehouseman was saying.

'No, I don't want it,' Nich protested as the man picked up the commode.

'You paid for it, mate.'

Despite his protests Nich quickly found himself standing outside Brady and Gordon with the chair beside him. A woman with a miniature poodle gave him a look of alarm and stepped pointedly into the road. Nich turned to look down the street, wondering desperately what to do.

'Trouble with the bowels?' an amused voice sounded from behind him.

Nich turned to find Anderson Croom standing on the pavement with his mouth set in an open smirk and a magnificent bunch of lilies in his hand.

'Is it meant for some pagan ritual?' Croom enquired. 'If so, I confess I'd be interested to see it.'

'No, it is not. I ...' Nich began then stopped, unwilling to endure any more of Croom's sarcasm.

'It was a mistake,' he said with cold dignity.

'That's what they all say,' Croom answered him. 'Brady's deliver, you know – or if you really don't want it, I'll give you a fiver?'

Nich nodded, angry humiliation tempered by relief as he accepted the note from Anderson.

Anderson entered the auction house with his customary boyish grin spread even more widely across his face than usual. He had dressed carefully, with his ivory silk shirt open at the neck and a suit of fine, dark blue wool under his camel-hair coat.

'Good morning, how may I help you?' Felicity greeted him. 'What beautiful flowers.'

'I ... er ...' Croom began with carefully calculated shyness. 'They're for you. My name's Anderson, by the way, Anderson Croom. Look, I know this is terribly forward of me, but I was wondering if you'd like to come out for a spot of lunch?'

'I ... I'd love to,' Felicity answered, accepting the enormous bunch of lilies with both arms. 'I must put these in water, they're beautiful! I'm Felicity, Felicity Chatfield, but you must know that – you were at the auction yesterday morning, weren't you? I remember, because you turned up late. And you're in *London Girl*, aren't you, in that article about . . . I mean . . . not that . . .'

Croom acknowledged his identity with a modest gesture as Felicity began to blush.

'I'm off in half an hour,' Felicity continued. 'I know a lovely Italian café . . . oh, I'm sorry, you must think me terribly pushy, but it's not every day I get bought such beautiful flowers and asked out to lunch.'

'It's my pleasure,' Croom assured her easily. 'The café sounds delightful. A dish of Parma ham and sun-dried tomatoes would be just the thing. Shall I come back in half an hour?'

'Yes, well . . . no, actually. I mean, would you mind staying here?'

'Certainly, a pleasure.'

'I'm sorry to make a fuss, but there was a strange man in here just now trying to get addresses for other buyers, which we're not allowed to give out. He got rather cross, and he doesn't seem quite sane to me.'

'The fellow outside? With the peculiar chair?'

'Yes, that would be him. Is he still there?'

'He was when I came in. He was at the auction yesterday afternoon too – a Satanist, I imagine.'

'At the auction? Oh . . . A Satanist? Do you really think so?'

'Undoubtedly. Just look at the way he dresses, and that weird jewellery. I'd stay well clear of him, if I were you.'

'I shall,' Felicity replied with a slight shudder. 'I'm glad you're here. We've got a security bell, of course, but . . .'

Croom smiled brightly and settled himself with one elbow on her desk, looking forward to the prospect of talking to her until she could leave for lunch. By one o'clock they were chatting as if they had known each other for years, Croom having carefully manipulated the conversation onto topics that interested her and also allowed him to show off his knowledge.

'Actually,' Felicity remarked as she got to her feet, 'would you be terribly kind and wait here for a second while I go and powder my nose? There's no one else on the desk this morning because it's Friday.'

'Certainly,' Croom replied, 'but lock the door first. I don't suppose I'd be very good at giving people the details of the next auction.'

Felicity locked the door. Croom waited until the precise staccato clicks of her heels had faded up the stairs, then seized his opportunity and slid into her chair in a single, smooth motion. A keyword search on the computer quickly brought up the data on the auction, revealing the card numbers of the successful bidders. Croom hastily flicked through his catalogue, finding Lot 83, the statuette. It had gone to bidder 92, a Percy Forbes, who lived in Battersea. He hastily scribbled the address onto Felicity's pad of sticky notes.

Again he searched the database, to find that Lot 104, the necklace, had also gone to bidder 92 even as he caught the distinctive click of Felicity's shoes on the stairs. Hastily adjusting the computer and chair, he tore off several sticky notes and crammed them into his jacket pocket. As he moved away from the desk a movement caught his eye. He looked up to find Nich Mordaunt's scowling face peering in at him through one of the glass panels in the door.

Felicity returned to find Anderson Croom lounging elegantly in the armchair, his expression breaking into a brilliant smile as she approached. She smiled back, hoping that she hadn't been too forward in accepting his invitation to lunch. His approach had been a nice blend of shyness and charm which she half suspected had been put on for her benefit. Asking for a lunch date also showed an appealing touch of consideration, avoiding the possible embarrassment of her accepting an evening date and then finding that they weren't really that keen on each other.

Physically he was nothing to be sniffed at either. He was tall, certainly over six feet, with broad shoulders and a finely chiselled face. *London Girl* had been quite wrong in placing him twenty-fourth among London's most eligible bachelors. In her book he came a firm first, even if he wasn't the richest. What the magazine hadn't shown was his wonderful eyes, of a pale blue-grey and with a vivacious glint. Nich's eyes, she remembered with a shiver, were an unnatural green, the colour of virgin olive oil.

Croom rose to greet her as she approached and took her arm as they left the auction house. She accepted without hesitation, guiding him to the café. As they crossed Queensway she noticed the black-clad figure of Nich standing nonchalantly in a shop doorway and pretending to read a magazine.

'There's that man!' she told Croom.

'Just ignore him,' Croom replied calmly. 'He'll probably go away.'

'I doubt it,' Felicity replied. 'He seems pretty determined.'

'Then tell him that you don't have the names and addresses he wants. Say they were casual bidders whose data you didn't keep.'

'But we keep everyone's data,' Felicity objected. 'We won't give out a bidder's card without a name and address. Besides, I as good as told him that we had the information but just wouldn't give it to him. Never mind, though, this afternoon I'll be able to ask Peter to the take the desk.'

'Very sensible.'

They reached the café and ordered lunch, Felicity unable to keep herself from glancing over her shoulder, Croom laughing and talking. There was no further sign of Nich during their meal, but Felicity was unable to shake the feeling that he was nearby. Her opinion of Anderson Croom improved over the course of lunch, his ability to make her laugh being particularly attractive. When he had walked her back to the auction house she readily accepted his suggestion of dinner.

Arriving at Brady's in time to see Croom collect Felicity, Nich hung well back in the shadows, the rapidly gathering dusk making his task easier. His confidence increased as the couple went into a pub and downed several drinks, Felicity drinking gin and lime, Croom pints of real ale. Nich watched through the thin, clear glass line in an etched window, observing a flush grow on Felicity's cheek as she poured gin into herself.

Leaving the pub, Croom and Felicity walked north, now arm in arm and laughing unrestrainedly. They chose an Austrian restaurant, Nich taking a seat in a café across the road and sipping coffee while he watched Croom order up steins of the thick white Tyrol beer, which Felicity accepted with enthusiasm. Unfortunately the man who had taken Croom's coat had hung it in a cloakroom behind the bar, robbing Nich of a chance to go through the pockets.

Ordering a plate of olives and bread, Nich watched Croom and Felicity carouse, she becoming merrier by the minute, he equally cheerful but apparently unaffected by the drink. They finished the meal off with tiny glasses of some colourless spirit, Croom tossing his back, piling several notes onto the bill and leaving without waiting for change. As they left, Nich watched Croom slip his arm around Felicity's narrow waist, letting his hand stray for just an instant onto the curve of a buttock. She made no protest, simply throwing

Croom a look of mock reproach which was answered with a wicked grin.

Nich scowled and left the café, putting coins on his plate to cover the bill. For a moment he thought they might get a cab, possibly losing him, but was relieved to see them turn west towards Notting Hill Gate. He followed at a safe distance, watching as they went into a pub, emerged, and went into another. When they left it was closing time, and Nich followed easily, merging with the crowds.

Croom now had his arm firmly around Felicity, and was showing a lot of attention to her bottom, patting her through her coat and giving her cheeks the occasional squeeze. Felicity responded with giggles and playful remonstrance, clearly drunk. Nich was grinning as he came behind, north and west for the best part of a mile before they stopped at a tall red-brick apartment block.

Felicity fumbled the key into the lock, giggling as Anderson's hand stroked her bottom through her coat. The door finally opened, slamming behind them as they went in. She felt drunk, and ready for sex, a feeling which had been building slowly since the moment he walked into the auctioneer's. There was no question in her mind that it was going to happen, it was just a question of how.

They moved quickly up the stairs, Felicity's nervousness growing with every flight. It seemed to take forever to get the door open, and when she had, she found herself babbling meaningless chit-chat and shaking hard. There was a bottle of wine in the fridge, and she went to open it, nearly dropping a glass.

When she came into her living room it was to find Anderson on the sofa, at ease, watching her with unashamed admiration. He patted the place at his side.

Nich gazed up at Felicity's building. A light had gone on in one of the upper flats. Fourth floor, left side, Nich noted as he moved away.

As he had hoped, a narrow mews led down the rear of the apartments, black-painted fire escapes zigzagging down the back of each building. Nich calculated which flat belonged to Felicity, waiting until the coast was clear and then swinging himself up onto a car and then to the roofs of the mews houses. A catlike balancing act along the top of a high wall, a pull up and he was on the fire escape, climbing in a low crouch until he was level with Felicity's lighted window.

Laughter and the chink of glasses came from within. Nich stole forwards, to peer through a chink in the curtains. Felicity and Croom were easily visible, in a tangle on the sofa, kissing. Both were half dressed. Felicity had her blouse off and one small pink tit peeping out from over the cup of her bra. Croom had his trousers and underpants well down, and was in the act of guiding her hand to his cock.

Nich scowled as he watched Felicity's slim, neat fingers placed firmly on Croom's bulging genitals. She giggled and began to tease him, stroking his balls with her fingernails. Croom's cock quickly began to grow, yet he seemed thoroughly in control, clutching a glass with one hand and stroking her breasts with the other. Felicity was more passionate, quickly taking his cock in hand and tugging at the shaft to bring it to full erection. Croom's response was to take her firmly but gently by the hair and ease her head down to his crotch, to make her take his penis in her mouth. She took it, and began to suck.

Soon, Nich was sure, they would go to the bedroom. He waited, watching.

Anderson gave a sigh of pure contentment as Felicity began to suck on his cock. Sliding his hand around the curve of her bottom, he began to inch up her skirt. Her response was to push her bottom out, drunk and eager for his touch, all her inhibitions washed away in a tide of drink. He smiled to himself as her skirt came high, to expose the bulging seat of her tights, filled to capacity with soft, neat bottom. She cupped his balls as he began to stroke her cheeks through her tights.

He was watching her suck, delighted by the image of his thick, heavily veined cock in her pretty mouth, with her eyes shut in pleasure and her yellow curls tumbling around her face and over his balls. As her skirt came right up, he glanced over to admire her bottom. For all her slim figure she was quite big, fleshier than Vicky, and more cheeky – ideal spanking material.

The temptation was strong, just to get it all down and give her bottom a good roasting before he took her to bed. Spanked girls were often better behaved in bed, ruder, more pliable to his needs. Or she might be shocked, even put off, ruining what looked like an excellent night ahead. He held back, contenting himself with slipping a hand down the back of her tights, to feel the silky back of her panties. She managed a soft purr around her mouthful of cock and began to suck harder. Encouraged, he hooked his thumb into the waistband of her tights and pushed them down, baring most of her sweet cheeks and the smooth blue seat of her panties.

Again he began to stroke her bottom, teasing her crease, pushing the panties in a little deeper with each stroke, close to her anus. She just pushed her bottom out further, and when his hand cupped her sex she began to move it, rubbing herself on him in her eagerness. For a moment he masturbated her through her panties, his fingers pushed into her cleft, to feel the wet openness of her sex through the material. Still she sucked, more eagerly than ever, masturbating him into her mouth and wiggling her bottom.

Suddenly it was just too much. She had to be willing, and he no longer cared if she wasn't. He pulled up his hand, took a firm hold of the seat of her panties and hauled. She squeaked as she was lifted, bodily, her panty crotch tight in the groove of her sex, and deposited across his lap. He held her by the panties, her lovely bottom up high, her lush cheeks spilling out to the sides, helpless and ready for punishment. He gave her an experimental pat.

'What . . . what are you doing?' she squealed.

'I'm going to spank your bottom,' he answered with relish.

'No! Hey . . . Anderson!'

He just chuckled and began to spank, even as she began to struggle, wriggling and wiggling in her taut panties as her bottom bounced to the slaps, and squeaking with every one. Her protests were real, if half-hearted, and filled him with a cruel delight. He smacked harder, to make it hurt more, so he could watch her kick, to see her shake her head and wobble her breasts about in her pain.

'You pervert!' she hissed. 'Ow!'

There was a catch in her voice, as if she was about to burst into tears, a response that filled him with sadistic glee. Still he spanked, harder and faster, and as her bottom began to turn properly red he began to laugh. She gave an angry hiss, smacking out at him, but he simply hauled her panties tighter still into her sex, pulling her close to leave her soft, naked belly rubbing on his erect cock as he beat her. Both her boobs were out, jiggling to the smacks, and as the anguish and pain of her grunts and squeals died slowly to noises of arousal he realised he had won.

Nich watched in mingled disapproval but also pleasure as Felicity was spanked. The disapproval came from Croom's rough handling of her and failure to ask permission. The pleasure came from a deeper conviction that, after the way she had refused his request, she was only getting what she deserved, and yet more from the beauty of her bare red bottom and her helpless sexual response.

38

He could see her sex too, her lips squeezed out by the taut line of blue panty material pulled up between them. She looked ready, wet and puffy, and he had no doubt that there would be little resistance when the time came to fuck her. His own cock was stiff in his trousers, and he was wishing he could plunge it into her ready hole, as he had so often done to Ysabel after her canings.

Croom stopped, suddenly. Felicity went limp, panting, making no effort to rise. Her hair was a bedraggled mess, pulled out from its neat style to shield her face, but as she turned he saw that her cheeks were wet with tears. She said something. Croom chuckled, gave her bottom another pat, then quite casually whipped down the little blue panties he had pulled so tightly into her bottom crease. Her sex came on show, the slit wet and pink between the thick, golden-furred lips.

She got up, slowly, rubbing at her sore bottom, but making no attempt to cover it. As she turned sideways, Nich saw that her face was set in sulky pout. Again she spoke. Again Croom merely laughed, as he pushed his trousers and pants off his ankles. Felicity's pout grew sulkier still. Croom stood, gave her bottom a last, firm swat and followed her as she waddled from the room with her tights and panties clutched at the level of her knees.

Nich had moved back out of the line of sight, and waited until he was sure his prey had retired to the bedroom. As he peered into Felicity's living room a new elation rose in his throat. Croom's coat, jacket and trousers lay on the floor, thrown haphazardly down in his haste to undress, and left.

Drawing a slim blade from his pocket, Nich went to work on the window catch. It came easily, and the window slid up in silence. A moment later he was through, his nose twitching at the smell of sex and wine. From the bedroom he could hear moans and grunts of passion, Felicity clearly having overcome her resentment at being spanked. Grinning maniacally, he went to Croom's clothes and began to look through them.

Nich searched to the sound of Felicity's fucking. The camel-hair greatcoat proved blank, as did the outer pockets of the jacket. The inner jacket pocket, however, yielded a pen, a bulging wallet and a clump of yellow sticky notes, one of which bore an address in Battersea. The expression on his face grew demonic, wild glee filling him as he jammed the notes into his own pocket.

Felicity's moans and grunts had risen to screams, accompanied by the rhythmic squeaking of the bed. In a mood of near-berserk euphoria, and feeling invincible, Nich crept silently to the door. There was a small hall, with another door directly opposite, the bedroom, into which he could see.

They were on the bed. Croom had put Felicity on her knees, her pink bottom raised, still in her tights and panties but otherwise nude, with her little tits swinging to the rhythm of the fucking. She was shaking her head, her eyes tight shut, her mouth open, each thrust drawing a choking scream from her mouth. Triumphant, thoroughly aroused, yet still vengeful, Nich levelled a curse at Croom. Immediately Croom stopped.

'No!' Felicity wailed. 'I was nearly there!'

'The condom's burst!' Croom answered.

'Oh, no! Quick, do something!'

'I am. I'm trying to get it off!'

'You didn't come, did you, not in me? Did you?'

'No.'

'Good, I . . . Ow! No, not that . . . not up my bum!'

'You don't want to get pregnant, do you?'

'No, but . . . Ow! No, Anderson, that hurts . . . Not up my bum, I said!'

'Sh . . . just relax, push out, as if you were on the loo.'

'You dirty pervert! That's disgusting!'

'No, it's not . . . it's wonderful . . . oh . . . I'm going in . . . oh, that is good . . . you are so tight . . . so hot . . .'

'You filthy, perverted . . .' Felicity gasped and broke off with a grunt as her anus gave.

'Yes, I know,' Croom puffed, 'but it feels good, doesn't it . . .? So good. There, you're sloppy now, so I'm going to push it right up. Hold on.'

He grunted. Felicity gasped as her rectum filled with cock and he had begun to pump into her, moving as before, with his hands locked firmly into the soft flesh of her hips. She began to moan, then to grunt and sob. Her hand went to her sex and Nich realised that she was masturbating as she was buggered. Keen to watch her climax, he hung back from retreat, only to change his mind as Felicity began to scream again and a sudden, sharp pounding began from the flat below.

Chuckling to himself, he retreated, to let himself out of the window, levelling a final curse at Croom as he went. As his foot contacted the iron gridwork of the fire escape he heard Croom's grunt of ecstasy, followed by a yet shriller, louder scream from Felicity. The knocking from the flat below grew to a furious crescendo in perfect time to the lovers' orgasms as Nich fled.

As he descended the fire escape in great bounds he found himself unable to suppress his mirth, first grinning and then breaking into open laughter as he reached the street. Cackling his glee to the low, orange clouds above London, he set off into the night.

Three

Anderson Croom awoke with an unpleasant taste in his mouth. He lay for a moment with his eyes shut, allowing the events of the previous day to run through his mind. A broad smile spread across his face as he reached the end of his train of thought, turning and opening his eyes to admire the golden cloud of Felicity's hair where it was spread across her pillow.

Swinging his legs out of bed, he got to his feet, shivering slightly in the cold morning air. A glance at Felicity's bedside clock showed that it was approaching ten. He yawned and stretched, shaking his head to clear the groggy feeling and moving slowly into the kitchen. As he left the bedroom he noticed that the living room window was open, accounting for the cold draught.

The kitchen proved to be a neat as the rest of Felicity's flat, done in pine with marble worktops, with an array of labour-saving devices lined up against the wall. He looked hopelessly at her cafétiere, wishing that Creech was there to show him how it worked. Hesitating to experiment with the machine, he turned to the refrigerator. There was orange juice, and he poured a tall glass. A good swallow helped to clear the taste from his mouth and make it easier to think.

As he left the kitchen the draught from the window made him shiver. He couldn't remember the window being opened, in fact, he was sure it hadn't been. He remembered Felicity's eagerness for sex, the hungry way she had sucked at his cock, her dismay as she found out she was going to be punished, and her pained reaction to the spanking. At no time had they paused to open the window. It had been far too cold; indeed, even now there was a thin coating of frost at the corners of the panes.

On sudden impulse he put down the glass and reached for his jacket, his hand going immediately to the inside pocket. His pen was there, his notecase, but no sticky notes. He emptied the contents out, checking and double-checking, only to reach the same sickening conclusion.

'Damn!' he cursed aloud. There could be only one explanation. Nich had followed them somehow and stolen the notes, maybe even while he'd been having sex with Felicity just yards away.

Plotting feverishly, he decided that the first thing to do was ensure that Felicity didn't realise what was going on. He shut the window and slid the latch into place, noting the fire escape outside and the tell-tale mark on the paint of the latch. Nothing else appeared out of place and a quick check of Felicity's handbag showed that nothing obvious had been taken. Amateur! he thought scathingly. If the roles had been reversed he would have copied the addresses down and shut the window behind him. As it was, he could remember the addresses anyway and was now aware that he no longer had time to spare.

He peered quickly into the bedroom to check that Felicity was still asleep. Going to the phone, he dialled his own number. Creech answered, and he had quickly arranged to be collected at the door of Felicity's flats in an hour. Satisfied that he had done all he could for the time being, he replaced the receiver and went back to the bedroom. Felicity was still asleep, the covers pulled tightly around her, with only her hair showing, and one

43

foot. He bit his lip, aware that it would be best to simply leave, but tempted by the sight of her gentle curves beneath the duvet. His cock was turgid with morning blood, and he knew it would take only a few swift tugs to bring himself to full erection.

To think was to act, and he quickly slid himself beneath the cover, pressing to the warmth of her body with his cock in the crease of her bottom. He began to rub. She gave a little groan and put a hand back, attempting to push him away.

'Not now . . .' she moaned.

He ignored her, pulling himself closer, to take her firmly in his arms as he began to nibble at the back of her neck. Again she groaned, and began to wriggle in his arms, trying to get away, but only succeeding in squirming her bottom against his cock. He sighed with pleasure and pulled her tight against him, one hand pressed to her sex as he rutted in her bottom crease. She gasped as his finger found the moist flesh between her sex lips.

As he began to masturbate her she abruptly ceased to struggle. He chuckled, and moved down, still rubbing her as his cock probed between her thighs. For a last moment she resisted, then her leg had come up. His cock-head found her hole, tight, yet moist. She gave a little squeak of pain as he pushed, but then he was in, the taut mouth of her sex pulling on his foreskin as he forced himself up.

'You're an animal . . . a real beast,' she gasped, but she was sticking her bottom out and her leg stayed up until he was fully inside her body.

He adjusted the pillow to make himself more comfortable, took her by the hips and began to fuck. Her bottom felt wonderful in his lap, soft and bouncy, with her sex so tight it was hard to tell which hole he was in. He smiled at the memory of how he had buggered her, the bitter, disgusted complaints as her anus was forced, and the way she had given in and masturbated as it was done to her. On sudden impulse he twitched the duvet away, exposing her bottom, with the little fleshy cheeks squashed to his belly.

'Hey! It's cold!' she protested.

He ignored her, admiring her bottom as he fucked her. She was a little bruised from her spanking, the crests of both cheeks showing dull marks, and her anus appeared each time he drew back. It was a delightful sight, too good to resist, and he felt his cock jerk in the onset of orgasm as her buttocks spread once more. Quickly he pulled out, to jerk at his juice-smeared shaft.

'No . . . Anderson!' she managed, but too late as his come spurted over her naked bottom, splashing both cheeks.

He finished off, milking himself over her bum cheeks and between them, splashing her cleft and the now rather red little hole at the centre.

'Do you have to?' she complained as he rubbed the sperm over her anus with his helmet.

'Yes,' he said emphatically.

'You are really disgusting, you know that, don't you?' she asked, twisting her head around as he finally pulled back.

'True,' he admitted, 'but you do have such a delightful bottom. You're very round, aren't you?'

He had reached out to squeeze a bottom cheek, fondling for a moment before wiping the sperm he had touched on her hip. She gave a resigned sigh and rolled face down, away from him.

'Could you at least clean me up, please?' she asked.

'Certainly,' he said, reaching for the pack of tissues beside her bed. 'But don't you want to come? I don't mind give you a lick, or whatever you fancy.'

'No . . .' she answered. 'No, thank you.'

'I'd better sort myself out, then,' he went on. 'My man's picking me up in forty minutes or so.'

'But it's Saturday. Aren't you going to stay? I thought we could go shopping or something?'

'Sorry,' he interrupted, 'got to go, but we'll meet up again soon, I expect. I rather enjoyed last night.'

'I bet you did,' she sighed.

Nich awoke to a feeling of urgency. His body ached from the exertions of the night before, both following Croom and indulging his passion with Ysabel when he had returned to her flat. She was still asleep, and every instinct was telling him that he should be too, yet he forced himself to rise.

He dressed quickly and swallowed a glass of milk, kissed Ysabel and left. The morning was cold and dank, with a touch of fog still hanging in the air. It took a moment to get his Triumph started but, once he had, his thoughts quickly cleared and he began to ponder his options.

Forbes was obviously the fat young man who had bought the jade idol and the necklace. He had to have some knowledge, either pagan or occult, yet it was hard to see him as a serious practitioner. The same was clearly true of Croom, for all his claims of atheism. No unbeliever would go to such lengths.

He began to ponder whether or not his curse had been effective. Croom's condom had seemed to burst instantly, or might even have done so before the curse was uttered. Not only that, but by fucking Felicity's bottom hole Croom had quickly deflected any effect the curse might have had. It tied in well with the ring he had noticed on Croom's finger, apparently an ordinary signet ring, but in black onyx, the stone to deflect negative energy.

Attaching mystic significance to certain stones might be a relatively modern fad, he considered, yet it was certainly widespread. Blackman had been keen on the idea, indeed had been responsible for much of the lore of stones now generally accepted. For Croom to be wearing a stone of such obvious significance yet not to be a believer seemed to be highly improbable.

He turned his mind to the problem of retrieving the idol and necklace. Croom seemed rich, and would doubtless offer money. Nich could not hope to match the price, when he had not even been able to meet the bids Forbes had made. Outright theft was always an option, but something to be avoided if possible. That left reason, the force of his personality and an appeal to Forbes' fascination with the pagan. If Forbes proved to know about Blackman's books, then everything changed, and he could bargain.

The address was 7A Cork Street. The street proved to be a double line of two-storey houses, their red-brick faces running exactly parallel to the far end. He slowed the bike, reading a number, 284, and sped up again. As he neared the halfway point a car turned in at the far end, an old-fashioned Bentley of a model seldom seen except at weddings. He was immediately sure it would prove to be Croom's car, but as he drew closer he made out the lined face of an elderly man at the wheel. With a sigh of relief he pulled the triumph up between two cars. No. 7 was little different from any of the other houses, the door painted a rich green with two bells beside it. He pressed the upper, and turned sharply at the sound of a voice behind him, an arrogant, upper-class drawl. Croom was standing behind him, the silver-haired old man beyond.

'It really isn't the thing to break into ladies' flats, you know, Nich, old boy,' Croom stated. 'It's just not done.'

'And I suppose sexual assault and anal rape are "done",' Nich retorted.

'I'm sorry, you've lost me,' Croom enquired. 'How is that relevant?'

'You know damn well what I . . .' Nich retorted and broke off at the sound of footsteps on the stairs within the house. 'Do not think of reporting the events of last night, Croom!'

'I wouldn't dream of it,' Croom answered. 'A frightful bore, the police. So you actually pinched the notes from my pocket while Felicity and I were making love? You've a nerve, I'll say that for you.'

'Making love?' Nich queried. 'I'd hardly . . .'

He broke off again as the door swung open, to reveal the face of the fat young man from the auction, who immediately gave a nervous glance to Nich's black motorcycle leathers.

'Mr Forbes?' Croom enquired, pushing forward. 'Good morning, I'm Anderson Croom. Don't listen to this fellow, he's a Satanist, and a burglar into the bargain.'

'I am neither!' Nich retorted. 'Mr Forbes, please listen –'

'What is it? What do you want?' Forbes broke in.

'I wish to offer you a considerable sum of money,' Croom said quickly, 'in return for a couple of items I believe you purchased at the auction yesterday, at Brady and Gordon's.'

'I did, yes, but –'

'Splendid, may I come in?'

'I have more to offer you!' Nich said hastily. 'What you truly seek, Mr Forbes, arcane knowledge! I have the spider, Mr Forbes.'

'What?' Forbes demanded. 'Look, I . . .'

'Excuse me, sir,' Creech put in gently from behind Nich. 'I realise this is somewhat unexpected, but it would be greatly to your benefit if you could spare us a moment.'

'Exactly,' Croom agreed, pushing in at the door. 'We won't be a moment, I assure you. No, not you, Nich, you haven't been invited.'

'Nor have you!' Forbes pointed out, but Croom was already inside the door, his arm around the baffled young man's shoulders.

Nich followed, Creech also coming behind, up the stairs and into an expensively furnished flat. Nich quickly took in his surroundings, polished wood, cream-coloured leather, a deep-pile carpet, expensive electrical equipment, with not so much as a hint of pagan influence. Only as his eyes lit on the bookcase did he realise just how basic Forbes' interest was, and how lascivious. All five shelves were crowded with books, a few reference works, financial publications, and four solid rows of paperback novels, all of them occult thrillers and supposedly factual accounts of witchcraft and satanic ritual.

'. . . I would be happy to go to two thousand pounds,' Croom was saying.

'I paid nearly four!' Forbes answered. 'And anyway . . .'

'Five, then,' Croom answered, drawing his notecase from his pocket. 'I assume you'll take a cheque?'

'No, I . . .' Forbes began. 'Look, really . . .'

'Mr Forbes,' Nich interrupted. 'Do you recall the orgy of witches at the climax to *Black Naked*?'

'What's that got to do with anything?' Forbes demanded.

'My girlfriend's coven performs a similar ritual,' Nich answered. 'Nude.'

Forbes' fish-belly complexion changed to a rich pink. Nich went on quickly.

'The true ritual is considerably more sensuous. We pagans consciously seek to throw off the mantle of Christian repression and prudery –'

'Six thousand,' Croom cut in.

'I . . . I . . .' Forbes stammered. 'I don't have them, that's what I've been trying to say.'

'Oh,' Nich answered.

'I . . . I sent them to my girlfriend . . . they were a birthday present,' Forbes went on.

'Your girlfriend is a pagan?' Nich asked.

49

'Where does she live?' Croom demanded.

'Look, I'm sorry, but . . .' Forbes said, only to be cut off once more by Croom.

'I'll pay seven thousand, and I'll buy your girlfriend another present, something with a little more artistic merit – at Tiffany's perhaps, or Harvey Nichols. Is this her?'

He had crossed to a sideboard, on which a photograph of a young girl with striking blonde curls had been given pride of place. She was snub-nosed and freckled, her features impish, especially her large grey eyes, which seemed to sparkle with mischief even in the photo. Forbes quickly followed Croom, reaching out a protective hand for the photo.

'Don't trust him an inch, Mr Forbes!' Nich warned. 'And definitely not with your girlfriend! Now, if she wishes to learn more of pagan ritual, or of the occult, I would be more than happy to oblige.'

'Well, yes,' Forbes said, 'we are interested . . . after a fashion. It all seems so much more . . . more exciting than church.'

'I know exactly how you feel,' Nich assured him. 'Many people come to recognise the essentially negative nature of Christianity and seek a more positive, fulfilling system of worship. Your girlfriend . . .?'

'Tabitha,' Forbes supplied. 'Tabby. She's my fiancée . . . sort of.'

'Tabitha,' Nich echoed, 'is Aramaic, of course. Yes, even from her photo I can see that Tabby is more appropriate, expressing a catlike vitality –'

'Excuse me, Mr Forbes,' Croom cut in, 'as I was saying –'

'This man,' Nich cut in quickly, 'is not to be trusted. Now look, I have considerable influence among pagan groups, and I would be glad –'

'Eight thousand pounds!' Croom stated.

'I'm really not interested,' Forbes answered him, his voice suddenly a great deal stronger. 'I'm a floor manager at Isaac Goldman, Mr Croom. My bonus this year was one hundred and fifty thousand.'

'No great sum,' Croom answered him, and stopped at a cough from Creech.

'I am Nicalo Mordaunt,' Nich went on hastily, 'Nich, more generally. You may well have come across my name?'

'Yes, I have,' Forbes answered. 'You write in some of the magazines, don't you?'

'Yes,' Nich confirmed, then hesitated, wondering if he could afford to take Forbes into his confidence, or if he might already know.

'Do you know anything about Frea Baum?' he asked.

'No,' Forbes admitted. 'Is she a witch?'

'Yes, and no,' Nich said cautious. 'Look, get rid of this idiot and I'll give you a few pointers in the right direction.'

'Gladly,' Forbes answered, and turned to Croom. 'Would you mind leaving, please? Now.'

'I really think ...' Croom began, only to stop as Creech once more cleared his throat. 'Very well, as you insist, but I warn you, Nich here is an unscrupulous Satanist and –'

'Could you just leave, please?' Forbes demanded.

Croom gave a curt bow and made for the door, leaving Nich smiling happily.

'Damn!' Croom cursed as the door of 7 Cork Street slammed behind him. 'He would have to be a bloody banker, wouldn't he!'

'It is of limited consequence, sir,' Creech said.

'It damn well is not!' Croom retorted. 'How in Hell's name ...?'

'What I mean to say, sir,' Creech said firmly, 'is that we have Miss Ferndale's address. I successfully copied it from Mr Forbes' telephone book while he was otherwise engaged.'

51

'Miss Ferndale? Tabitha? Good man! We'll get to her while Mad Nich's talking bullshit with that idiot Forbes. Where does she live?'

'Devon, sir. Ferndale Manor, near Chagford.'

'A manor? Splendid!'

'I think it is a hotel, sir.'

'Oh. Fair enough. Home then, for some clothes and to book a room. After that, Devon. I don't suppose I'll need you.'

'Yes, sir. And Miss Victoria, sir?'

'What about her? I can hardly bring her, can I? OK, so this Tabitha girl might be bisexual, but it's hard enough –'

'I was simply pointing out, sir, that she feels somewhat neglected. You did, after all, promise to try out your new chair when you spoke to her this morning.'

'True,' he admitted. 'I did.'

Tabitha Ferndale's reflection looked back at her from the mirror. She caught up her hair in both hands, first piling it on top of her head in a heap of golden curls, then sweeping it back, then arranging it so that it fell around her shoulders. No style made any difference; the fact remained that the necklace didn't suit her, not even set against black velvet, normally the perfect material to enhance gold. She doubted it would suit anybody. It was too big, a great vulgar plaque of gold plate twisted into bizarre arabesques with no symmetry at all and decorated with big, flat cut garnets set at odd angles. Also, it was punctured by oddly shaped holes and little cavities which added nothing to the design.

It was, she reflected, just the sort of stupid thing Percy would buy her. It was expensive but in bad taste, as were all his numerous presents. The hideous little idol he had sent down with the necklace. The silk dress on her birthday: awkwardly short and tight, and a yellowish-green that made her complexion look sickly and was one of the few colours that didn't suit her dark-gold hair. The 'artwork' consisting of four bricks and a piece of old lead pipe; supposedly highly meaningful but looking like something pinched from the rubble of a dismantled public convenience. There were also two enormous pottery Dachshunds with soulful expressions and a solitary tear running from each eye. Each was worse than the last, but she had never had the heart to tell him to get lost, only once losing her temper, when he had asked if she'd like vouchers for cosmetic surgery to enlarge her breasts.

She took the necklace off, the twists and prongs of gold catching in her curls and increasing her annoyance with it and, by extension, Percy. It simply wasn't fair, when most of her friends had nice boyfriends, or at least good-looking ones, but she got saddled with a buffoon. Other men were put off by his referring to her as his fiancée all the time, or else didn't feel able to compete against the extravagance of his presents.

Then there was his obsession with the occult, which she was sure was nothing more than an excuse to get her to take her clothes off in the hope of persuading her to have sex. She might have gone along with it if he had managed to make it seem exciting instead of just sleazy. He always did, ever since the day the summer before when she had foolishly agreed to let him take her out and ended up giving him a drunken blow job in the back of his car. Since then he had simply assumed it meant they were together, and she had never had the heart to tell him otherwise.

She sighed as she once more adjusted her hair. It had to be done. He had to go, and what she needed was someone from outside the stifling confines of the circle of friends she had known since school, somebody with a bit of flair, somebody exciting. The phone message handed to her by Linda at the hotel reception had suggested her luck might be about to change. It had been from a Mr Croom, saying that he would make an offer for both the necklace and the idol, and asking her not to let them go before he had done so. He had also reserved a room for the night.

Anderson Croom slowed the Bentley, his headlights illuminating a sign by the side of the narrow Devon lane. FERNDALE MANOR it said in gold letters on a field of deep green, followed by the information that it was a hotel and four gold stars. He had driven down at a leisurely pace, stopping at his house for lunch and at the Royal Hotel in Chagford for tea.

As he turned the car in between the high granite gateposts, the drive opened out in front of him, a ribbon of tarmac curving gently between two rows of full-grown oaks. Ahead were the lights of the hotel, a substantial building that might no longer be a manor house but clearly had been during an earlier era. Anderson parked between a 7-series BMW and a Mercedes and got out of the Bentley, stretching in the cold air to revitalise his circulation. The main door bore an illuminated sign, a discreet brass plaque with the word RECEPTION picked out in black. Anderson made towards it, pushed open the heavy oak door and stepped into a panelled hall reminiscent of the one in his London club. After glancing approvingly at his surroundings, he gave the bell on the desk a sharp tap, summoning a young woman in a smart green uniform.

'May I help you, sir?' she enquired in an accent with just a hint of Devon in it.

'Anderson Croom,' he announced. 'I have a reservation, and I believe Miss Ferndale is expecting me.'

'Miss Ferndale is in the bar, sir,' the girl said, indicating a double glass door through which a warm yellow light and the sound of convivial laughter were coming.

Anderson crossed the hall and pushed open the door, to enter a long room carpeted in the same deep green and furnished in wood and brass. Opposite him a long bar occupied two-thirds of the wall, stopping at open double doors beyond which he could see tables set for dinner. To his right an elderly man in a blue blazer was reading a paper; his companion, a white-haired old lady in a dark-red dress with lace at the collar, sat drinking tea.

Turning, Anderson saw the source of the laughter he had heard. Three people sat in an alcove. One was Tabitha, even prettier and more vivacious in the flesh, her face set in a smile of pure mischief, her hair a glorious riot of dark-gold curls, her gently curving figure enticing beneath a plain blue dress. The second was a bulky young man with a ruddy complexion and the same yellow curls cropped close to his head. The third . . . was Nich Mordaunt.

Fighting back the urge to rush over and denounce Nich as a Satanist, Anderson put on a cheerful expression and walked slowly across to the group. Tabitha was the first to look round, the mischievous glint in her eye making Anderson wonder how the conversation had been going prior to his arrival. He favoured her with his brightest smile, receiving a giggle and a faint blush in return.

'You must be Anderson Croom,' she said, Nich and the third man immediately looking up. 'I'm Tabitha, this is my brother Mark and I think you already know Nich.'

She broke into giggles, and he realised that she was drunk. Anderson took her hand and kissed it, shook Mark's bearlike paw and threw Nich a smile and a glare. Tabitha giggled again as she filled her glass from the half-empty wine bottle that stood in the centre of the table before calling to the barman for another glass. Anderson took the seat nearest to Tabitha and allowed her to fill the new glass to the brim.

'You'll be glad to know I've held off, so you should be thankful to me,' Tabitha said as Anderson took a sip of the wine. 'Nich here wanted me to give him the frightful necklace and the silly idol you're both after. I wouldn't, not until after you'd had a chance to make your case.'

'Thank you, that was thoughtful,' Anderson replied, desperately trying to work out his best approach. Tabitha seemed friendly, flirtatious even, but it was impossible to know what Nich had told her. What, for that matter, did she know about Nich? Knowing that to say nothing would be the worst thing he could do, he decided on a moderately honest but light-hearted approach.

'I suppose you know this fellow is a Satanist?' he asked casually, indicating Nich.

'Pagan, please,' Nich interjected.

'Oh, yes,' Tabitha said. 'We know all that. I phoned Percy to see what was going on, and he told me. He told me to give Nich the things, too, which is one reason I didn't.'

'I see,' Anderson said, trying to hide his satisfaction at the discovery that the relationship between Percy and Tabitha was obviously not everything it had been made out to be.

'So why do you both want this stuff so badly?' Tabitha asked, folding her hands in her lap and putting on a mock-serious expression. 'Nich wouldn't tell me, but if you do, I might just give in to you.'

Anderson allowed his eyebrows to raise a fraction at the implication of her words, then leaned back to consider. Tabitha was obviously relishing her control of the situation and already fairly drunk. If he, or Nich for that matter, took a high-handed or impatient approach she was bound to favour the other. He would just have to play along, which might not be such a terrible fate, bearing in mind her coquettish personality and trim curves. Telling her the truth was obviously not a good idea.

'It's not that exciting, really,' he began with a modest gesture. 'Nich and I both collect occult pieces, that's all, and both the necklace and the idol are unique. I was too late for the auction, you see, and your boyfriend outbid Nich.'

'Don't call him my boyfriend,' Tabitha said, making a face.

'I thought you were engaged?' Anderson asked

'Only in his dreams,' Tabitha replied.

'Ah-ha,' Anderson said cryptically.

'So,' Tabitha continued, 'you barge in on Percy and chase all the way down here just to get this rubbish for your collections?'

'Yes,' Anderson admitted. 'There's a lot of history behind them too.'

'Me too,' Nich added, 'but I would have put them to proper ritual uses, not just stuck them in a display case.'

'What are their proper ritual uses?' Tabitha asked in fascination. 'Percy just gave me some crap about girls having to be in the nude when they wore the necklace, or else it would be bad luck or something.'

'The details are complex,' Nich began in a didactic tone, 'but essentially the necklace is a piece of regalia appropriate to female celebrants during rituals that involve earth magic. It is worn in association with other pieces of regalia and without robing . . .'

'So the wearer would be nude?' Tabitha asked.

'Of course, other than the regalia,' Nich answered. 'Nakedness is an essential element of all earth-magic related rituals. The association between nudity and impropriety is purely a product of centuries of Christian repression. We all . . .'

'Hang on,' Tabitha put in. 'Percy was trying to get me to wear it in the nude for him. Do you think he's really into this stuff?'

'No, just sad,' Anderson answered. 'I, of course, as a rationalist and a collector, simply want it because it is unique.'

'It still seems a lot of effort to go to,' Tabitha said.

'Not in the least,' Nich insisted.

'Well worthwhile,' Anderson added.

'They're both crazy!' Tabitha said to her brother.

'Oh, I don't know,' Mark replied. 'I'd cheerfully go up to London for a rugby ball signed by the British Lions or something like that. It's just a question of what you collect.'

'Precisely,' Anderson agreed, grateful for Mark's unexpected support.

'Why wouldn't you tell me, then?' Tabitha asked Nich.

'My interest is rather more genuine than his,' Nich replied sulkily.

'Men!' Tabitha remarked. 'Right, well, I think the necklace is vulgar and the idol thing is creepy. I certainly don't want either, so you can have them. Who wants which?'

'No, no,' Nich said immediately. 'They must be kept together.'

'Absolutely,' Anderson agreed.

'Together?' Tabitha queried. 'OK, so the question is, which of you gets them?'

'Only I can put them to their proper use!' Nich declared.

'I will happily double any sum he offers,' Anderson said calmly. 'No, I'll triple it.'

'Boys, boys,' Tabitha said, clearly enjoying herself. 'Don't squabble. Let's have a bet, winner gets the stuff.'

'Good idea!' Mark agreed.

Anderson turned to Nich and was met with a scowl. For a moment he considered making a firm offer of money, but stopped himself, sure that it was the wrong line to take with Tabitha.

'Very well,' he said, trying to sound enthusiastic. 'I accept.'

'Nich?' Tabitha asked.

'All right,' Nich answered. 'We'll play cards, poker. I have a pack in my pocket as it happens.'

Anderson watched as Nich placed the cards on the table, noting the complicated design of plants, animals and abstract symbols printed on the reverse of each.

'Hang on a minute,' he protested as Nich began to deal. 'This card's got a chicken with three heads and the one on this card's only got two!'

'It's a cockatrice,' Nich hissed but gathered the cards in and returned them to his pocket.

'I've got a pack in my car,' Anderson offered.

'Undoubtedly bent,' Nich said.

'Speak for yourself,' Anderson answered hotly.

'Boys, boys,' Tabitha said again. 'Cards are boring anyway. Be original. I know, there's that army game, where you have to toss off on a biscuit . . . no, I've got it, whoever'll give the other a blow job gets the stuff!'

Anderson and Nich exchanged a look. Both shook their heads.

'Chickens!' Tabitha giggled.

'I know,' Mark put in. 'We play a great game down at my rugby club. You can drink pints, one on one. Anyone who takes more than ten seconds to down a pint is disqualified, otherwise the last man to be sick is the winner!'

'Not in the hotel bar, Mark,' Tabitha protested. 'Mummy would be furious!'

'Oh,' Mark replied, sounding deeply disappointed. 'I suppose you're right, but we could go outside . . . I know. how about a beer race? Each man buys six pints and lines them up at one end of the pitch, piling all their clothes at the other. They race up and down, drinking a pint at one end and putting something on at the other. The first to finish is the winner. It's hilarious!'

'We don't have a rugby pitch,' Tabitha pointed out.

'We can go out on the bowling green and turn the spotlights on,' Mark suggested. 'No one'll see.'

'There was already frost on the ground when I came in,' Anderson remarked.

'Oh, you can keep your shoes on,' Mark offered generously.

'He's only had one glass of wine, this is my fifth or sixth,' Nich objected.

'Easily remedied,' Tabitha stated, filling Anderson's glass to the brim and passing it up to him.

'It would hardly be fair,' Anderson remonstrated as he took the glass. 'Nich is wearing casual leathers, no more than four or five items in all, excluding boots and socks, and all easy to put on. I, by contrast, am properly dressed, including a shirt with cufflinks and collar studs. Also, counting my cravat, I have six items.'

'Give Nich your cravat, then you'll have five each,' Mark said. 'You don't have to be smart, just dressed.'

'I . . .' Anderson began.

'No more arguing,' Tabitha declared firmly. 'We play Mark's rugger-bugger game or it's off. Mark, be a sweetie and fetch my coat and another bottle of wine, a red one this time.'

Mark rose and hurried from the bar. Anderson and Nich exchanged looks again, only this time of sympathy.

Nich stood naked and shivering in the white glare of the bowling-green spotlights. Croom was beside him, also naked. Mark Ferndale stood to the side with a whistle. Tabitha was seated on a concrete step that led to the path between the high yew hedges that surrounded the green. Her hand encircled a wine bottle, the other a glass into which she was pouring a generous measure. She was dressed in a thick coat with a luxurious rabbit-fur collar, the hood up. Ice crystals glittered on the grass.

At their end of the green stood two piles of clothing. One, next to Nich, piled at random and black but for a cravat of apricot silk. The other, by Anderson, neatly folded and piled with the items he would need first at the top. At the far end of the green two rows of pint glasses stood like obese sentries, six in each row, and every one full to the brim with dark ale.

'OK,' Mark announced, 'The rules are: One pint and one article of clothing at a time. No spilling of your opponent's pints or stealing of clothes. Any spilt beer marks a five-second penalty, to be marked with my whistle. OK, then, on your marks! Get set! Go!'

Nich dashed for the far end of the bowling green. Reaching it, he grabbed a glass, to hurl the contents down his throat with beer pouring from the sides and down his chest. Despite his efforts Croom finished first and turned, only to have the smooth soles of his elegant shoes slip in the frost. As Croom measured his length on the rock-hard ground Tabitha burst out laughing, no longer a girlish giggle but a full-throated roar of delight. Stifling his curses, Croom got up, to stagger on as Nich snatched for his underpants.

'Tabitha?' a voice called out. 'Good heavens!'

Nich turned. A woman in her early forties, blonde, compact, and essentially an older version of Tabitha, stood in the entrance to the green, her eyes round with surprise. For a moment the tableau held, then Nich gave a stiff bow from the waist and took the single step necessary to reach his clothes. Anderson extended a hand to the newcomer.

'Good evening. Mrs Ferndale, I presume?' Anderson managed with as much aplomb as he could muster. 'I'm Anderson Croom.'

'Then for heaven's sake put some clothes on, Mr Croom,' she answered, with a doubtful glance towards his cock and balls. 'Tabitha, Mark, what are you doing?'

'Oh, nothing, Mummy,' Tabitha said in full face of the evidence. 'Just mucking about.'

'Well, for heaven's sake, stop it,' Mrs Ferndale demanded, her voice showing more resignation than genuine anger. 'What would your father say? What if there was an inspector around and you were seen? We'd lose at least one star, maybe two.'

'I do a spot of that occasionally,' Croom remarked as he struggled to get his trousers on over his shoes.'

'You are a hotel inspector, Mr Croom?' Mrs Ferndale said, her tone of maternal admonition vanishing to be replaced by one of genteel friendliness tinged with worry.

'Not professionally,' he admitted, 'but I do a little criticism for Clermont Guides, wine lists mainly. It's strictly on an amateur basis, of course. They find me valuable for the more out-of-the-way places, although I sometimes think old Clermont only does it to keep me amused. He was a great friend of my father.'

'Clermont Guides? Mr Clermont an old friend of your father?' she replied. 'Have you seen our wine list? No? But you must. I do hope you stay for dinner. Do call me Elizabeth, by the way.'

'Delighted,' Croom managed as he pulled his shirt on.

'Would your friend enjoy dinner as well?' she continued, eyeing Nich doubtfully.

'I . . .' Croom began.

'I should be honoured,' Nich said quickly, extending his hand to Mrs Ferndale. 'Nich Mordaunt.'

'Pleased to meet you,' Mrs Ferndale answered as she took his hand.

The red enamel eightfold symbol of his ward ring glinted in the bright white light. She gave it a curious glance before speaking again.

'Do come inside. Aren't you both frightfully cold? Now, Tabitha, you know you're supposed to be wait-ressing, and Mark, you promised to help out on the bar while the golf club's in. It's a busy night, Mr Croom, and my husband's up in London, so you must excuse me if I deprive you of Tabitha's company until after dinner.'

Croom made a gallant gesture to convey his resignation, offering his arms to both women.

'Give Mark a hand with the beer, there's a good chap,' he said as Nich stepped forwards towards Tabitha.

Half an hour later, Nich found himself seated in the dining room and feeling distinctly out of place. The other male diners were dressed in suits without exception. The conversation was loud and ran to golf, cars and social gossip. Separate waiters brought a menu and a wine list, Nich studying each in turn and regarding the prices with horror. The wine that Tabitha had been quaffing with such abandon cost fifteen pounds and was the second least expensive. She was about, and had now changed into a waitress's uniform in the hotel green, complete with apron and lace cap, but was serving a group of tables on the far side of the dining hall.

Looking around, he saw Croom approaching, dressed in full black tie, from brilliantly glossy shoes to the perfect bow of black silk at his neck. His expression suggested an amused disdain for the other diners, one eyebrow rising as he caught sight of a man in a brown suit. The waiter greeted him and motioned him towards Nich's table. Croom took the seat, threw another scornful glance around the room and spoke.

'I suggest a truce for the duration of dinner,' he offered as he picked up the wine list. 'Tabitha seems to have rather taken the situation out of our hands, and as she is not serving our table neither of us has a chance to gain an advantage. I see little point in arguing, either; it would merely spoil our digestion.'

'So be it,' Nich replied after a moment's hesitation.

They fell silent, Anderson studying the wine list. Nich returned to his perusal of the dishes on offer, immensely thankful that dinner had been offered on the house.

Croom was also studying his menu, and appeared absorbed in it. Nich took the opportunity to study the signet ring, which was clearly visible. The symbol, he noted, was a face with acanthus leaves flowing from the mouth and ears, a green man: not a common heraldic symbol, but an ancient pagan one. His last doubts dissolved. The ring was clearly Croom's ward. For a moment he considered, then spoke.

'I suspect, Mr Croom,' he began, his voice soft and low, 'that you and I have more in common than is immediately obvious.'

'That seems unlikely,' Croom replied, not taking his eyes from the menu.

'You clearly know that Blackman's true wealth remains hidden,' Nich continued, ignoring Croom's remark, 'and also what is needed to find it.'

'Absolutely,' Croom replied cheerfully, 'and I intend to have it, all of it.'

'Don't you believe in the sharing of such treasure?'

'Certainly not, filthy communist idea!'

'Knowledge, Mr Croom, should be available to all.'

'Knowledge, maybe; money I prefer to keep to myself.'

'I fear you overestimate the commercial value of Blackman's books.'

'Books? Oh, for heaven's sake, don't give me that! You know as well as I do that Blackman has stashed away some serious loot.'

Nich didn't reply and, for a moment, there was quiet as each man considered the other.

'Mr Croom,' Nich said after a while, 'I have the spider, you have Blackman's notebooks. Tabitha is merely playing games with us, and her decision may go either way, but if we agree to share, we ...'

'Absolutely not, sorry. I think the pheasant will be good, if it's properly hung, although I am tempted by the duck. What are you having? I hope it's game of some sort, because they have a ninety-seven *les Amoureuses,* young admittedly, but rather tempting.'

'Mr Croom,' Nich snarled, his teeth grating together, 'if you could please be serious for one moment. I know that you are not the spoilt, self-indulgent, parasitic wastrel that you pretend –'

'Steady on,' Croom broke in. 'I'm perfectly serious. A claret would be completely inappropriate, or were you thinking of a Rhone? The Cote-Rotie –'

'Look,' Nich interrupted. 'I know that you are aware of the true significance of Blackman's life's work and that you intend to make use of it, just as I do. Neither of us can succeed without what the other has so, although I detest the idea, I am prepared to work with you. What do you say?'

'My answer is simple,' Croom replied. 'I intend to take Tabitha to bed, enjoy her thoroughly, and in the morning she will give me both the necklace and the bear thing in gratitude for what will undoubtedly have been the best sex of her young life. As for you, if you wish to avoid a night of frustration, I suspect that you might find her mother pliable, or possibly the girl on reception if you prefer something a little more tender. Linda, I think her name is.'

Nich could find no words to reply and turned his attention back to the menu with a furious scowl.

Four

Anderson sipped at the glass of Armagnac he had ordered to finish off the meal and watched the room. A last few diners remained at their tables, but most had left. In Tabitha's section of the room she was bending to return the credit card of an elderly couple. The pose left her uniform skirt rounded out by the shape of her bottom and he smacked his lips in anticipation.

'Beautiful,' he remarked. 'I can hardly wait to see it bare.'

'Don't think to awe me with your false confidence,' Nich answered him. 'She has yet to decide and, in any case, I don't recall her inviting you to bed.'

'She had us strip,' Anderson remarked. 'You don't really suppose that was for the sake of the competition, do you?'

'Well, yes . . .'

'Naïve as well as religiously deluded, I see. She had us strip, Nich, old fellow, partly to see if we were any fun, and partly to get a look at our bodies, cheeky little brat that she is.'

'And if so, what makes you think she will choose you?' Nich demanded.

Anderson merely laughed and swallowed the rest of his brandy. Tabitha was coming towards them, and he greeted her with his warmest smile.

'Back to the bowling green, then?' he asked.

For a moment she looked surprised, then spoke.

'You would, too, wouldn't you?'

'We have a game to finish,' he said calmly.

'You must be mad!' Nich cut in. 'It must be minus four out there by now.'

'Anything to oblige a lady,' Anderson said, and patted his lap.

Tabitha glanced at the last of the diners, at Nich, hesitated, then sat down. Anderson smiled as the softness of her bottom settled onto his leg, and let his arm circle her waist.

'I'm not sure we need to go out again,' she said softly.

'Well, I'm game,' Anderson said, 'so if you're backing down, Nich?'

'Absolutely not!' Nich snapped.

'Never mind the silly necklace stuff,' Tabitha said. 'We'll play in the morning. You're both staying, aren't you?'

'No,' Nich answered. 'I don't have a room. I'd hoped . . .'

'He'd hoped to be sharing your bed,' Anderson put in.

'That's a bit cheeky!' she answered.

'I said nothing of the sort!' Nich declared. 'In fact, only a moment ago Croom here was boasting about how he was going to take you to bed, and making crude remarks about your figure.'

'That is really beneath you, Nich,' Anderson answered. 'Fair enough, Tabitha is a very beautiful girl. Your response to her is only natural, but to try and blacken my name –'

'Don't quarrel, boys,' Tabitha said, cutting him off. 'That really wasn't very nice, Nich, was it?'

'But I didn't . . .' Nich began and trailed off. 'Tabitha, can't you see that he's just trying to seduce you?'

'Yes,' she answered.

'She's not some silly little girl, you know,' Croom added, 'she's a grown woman, with her own mind.'

'Thank you, Anderson,' Tabitha answered. 'Are you coming, then?'

'But . . . but what about the necklace and the idol?' Nich demanded. 'You're not going to give them to him, are you?'

'Have one each, or we'll work something out in the morning,' Tabitha said. 'Honestly, you and your silly collecting.'

'Exactly,' Anderson said, rising as she did, still with his arm curled around her waist.

He threw Nich a grin as he began to steer her towards the door.

'What am I supposed to do?' Nich demanded.

'Get a room,' Anderson answered him. 'It's only a hundred and eighty.'

'Linda will sort it out for you,' Tabitha added.

'One hundred and eighty pounds, for one night?' Nich asked.

'Well, you can't sleep down here, you'll freeze!' Tabitha replied.

Nich made a gesture at once dignified and resigned.

'I know,' Tabitha continued, 'you can have Anderson's.'

'I . . .' Anderson began in automatic protest.

'Don't be mean, Anderson,' Tabitha said firmly. 'Give Nich the keys. After all, you won't be needing them.'

'But my suitcase, my . . . my dressing gown!'

'You won't be needing those either. Now be nice, or I might change my mind.'

Catching the tone in Tabitha's voice, Anderson realised that magnanimity was the only course open to him. Taking the keys from his pocket, he threw them to Nich, who caught them, favoured Anderson with a grin and faded towards the main staircase. Anderson turned and followed Tabitha through the door, his misgivings quickly dissipated by Tabitha's rear view as she climbed the narrow, steep stair in front of him. Her skirt showed a fair bit of stocking-clad leg, and her bottom rounded out the seat beautifully, filling him with the urge to smack it.

'I feel a bit tipsy, Anderson,' she confided. 'Give me your arm.'

Anderson hastened to assist, curling his arm around her waist and kissing her. She responded for a moment, then pulled away.

'Not here,' she breathed. 'Upstairs. Would you like me to wear the necklace?'

'No, no,' Anderson replied. 'I'd rather you wore your uniform, or at least some of it; perhaps just the apron and the little cap.'

She giggled and patted his cheek playfully. He pulled her close and kissed her again, this time open-mouthed, their tongues meeting briefly before she pulled away. When she did, it was to lead him upstairs, suddenly full of energy, but stumbling on the stairs in her drunken urgency. Anderson followed, up two flights to a long corridor, all the time admiring the shape of her bottom and the way her cheeks moved under her skirt. By the time they had reached her room he had decided to spank her, and to Hell with the consequences.

They were kissing immediately, mouths wide, tongues together. Tabitha began to pull at Anderson's clothing, tugging at the buttons of his shirt, then his trousers. He held her, lifting her skirt as they kissed. She gave no resistance, and in a moment it was up and the soft roundness of her bottom was in his hands, her full cheeks encased in big, lacy panties. He squeezed appreciatively as his fly was peeled down, then gave her an experimental slap.

'Sh!' she admonished as she pulled his cock from his pants. 'Hmm, you are big, I thought . . .'

'It was damn cold, you cheeky girl,' he answered and planted another firm slap on her bottom as she began to

69

tug on his cock. 'In fact, I think I know what you need . . . a good spanking.'

'Oh, no, you're not going to get kinky on me, are you?'

'I'm afraid so. Sorry, Tabby, but after that little episode on the bowling green, you deserve it.'

'Why can't you just fuck me?'

'I will, after I've spanked you.'

'No!'

She had continued to tug on his cock as they spoke, and he was fully erect in her hand. Again he smacked her, harder, the sound ringing out in the quiet of the room.

'Ow, my bottom!' she squeaked. 'Don't, Anderson. It's too noisy, and Mummy's room is right opposite!'

'So you do like it? And you've had it before, haven't you?'

'No! I didn't say that!'

'As good as . . .'

He folded her in his arms and lifted her by her bottom, feeling her cheeks through her panties as he carried her. She squeaked, and wriggled, but let him do it, taking her to the bed. She spoke as he turned her over across his knee.

'No, please, Anderson, it's too noisy! What about Mummy?'

'Mummy is still downstairs, as you very well know. Now come on, young lady, bum up, and let's have these pretty knickers down.'

'Anderson!' she wailed as he turned her skirt up properly, to expose the full expanse of her bottom, the cheeks bulging out the lacy panty seat, plump and tempting.

He ignored her as he took hold of her waistband, and she gave a sigh of resignation as her knickers were peeled slowly down. Anderson chuckled as her bottom came bare, full and golden and cheeky, her cleft deep

70

and high, her meat tucking nicely down to her thighs. Settling the big panties level with the tops of her stay-ups, he began to stroke her bottom.

'So,' he said, 'tell me who did it to you before, and maybe I'll let you off.'

'You're nothing but a dirty little boy,' she reproached him.

'I know,' he answered, and pulled her bottom cheeks apart to show off her anus, a neat dun-coloured star of tiny crevices leading to a little brown hole, firmly closed.

'Hey!' she protested. 'That's dirty!'

'Do you think so? I'd have said you'd wiped rather well.'

Instantly she lurched to one side, trying to get off his lap, but he had been ready, and had caught her firmly by the waist, hauling her back into spanking position.

'You dirty bastard! Don't you dare, don't you . . .' she yelled, and broke off with a squeal of pain as his hand landed full across the meat of her bottom.

Anderson laid in, hard, landing spank after powerful spank across Tabitha's bottom, each one squashing out the flesh of her cheeks and drawing a fresh squeal of pain and shock. She fought crazily, scratching, writhing her body and kicking her legs up and down in the trap of her lowered panties. Anderson held on, and only spanked the harder for her struggles, his teeth gritted in delight and determination as he beat her. She was trying to speak, but she couldn't, forced to gasp for breath as the slaps hit her in a furious rain.

Still he spanked, harder and harder, the slap of palm on girlish bottom flesh ringing out around the room in time to her howls. His cock was still hard, rubbing on her hip as she bucked and thrashed in his grip. She was showing too, as her cheeks danced, the dark spot of her anus and the pouted rear lips of her sex revealed by every smack and every frantic kick. The temptation to fuck her was growing overwhelming, but he forced

71

himself to hold back, spanking and spanking despite the sting in his hand.

Finally, with her bottom a glowing red ball, glossy with sweat and rough with goose pimples, her struggles began to die down. He kept on spanking, a little less hard, the smacks aimed at the meatiest part of her cheeks, over her bumhole. She began to moan, the kicking of her legs slowed and stopped. Her thighs came wide, to show off her sex, her bottom began to lift to the spanking. He stopped, still holding her firmly in place.

'You . . . you utter bastard!' she gasped. 'Look what you've done to me!'

'I know,' he said happily as he cupped a hand under her sex.

'No!' she squeaked, but he had already begun to masturbate her, and the protest broke off in a low moan

'So,' he said, 'who was the lucky man who taught you how nice it is to be spanked?'

She shook her head, her golden hair quivering to the motion. He rubbed harder, until her moans began to change to grunts, then stopped.

'Well?'

'No . . . just make me come, you . . . you . . .'

'Language, language, Tabby. There's a nice big hairbrush on your dresser. You wouldn't want me to have to take that to you, would you now?'

'No . . . please . . . it hurts like Hell!'

'So you have had it used on you, I guessed as much. Who is it? Percy? I bet he loves it!'

'No! Not Percy . . . I haven't! Not ever!'

'No? I can just see it, with those little goggle eyes of his feasting on your bum as your knickers come down . . .'

'No . . . he doesn't . . . I'd never let him!'

'Who, then?'

'No, I can't . . .'

'Who? Now, or it's time for the hairbrush.'

72

'No ... just rub me off, will you, you pig!'

'Temper, temper! OK, if you want a proper beating, but I warn you, you won't be able to sit down in comfort for a –'

'OK!' she gasped. 'Pig ... bastard ... it was Mark. He used to like to spank me ... just for fun ... you know, if I was cheeky with him or something.'

'Your own brother? Tut, tut, Miss Tabitha. Did he take your knickers down?'

'God, you're a dirty bastard! No, he ... yes, some-times ...'

'Oh, dearie me! Going bare-botty across big brother's lap, how that must have felt!'

'It's just a game, that's all!'

'But a pretty humiliating one for you, I'll bet. What else? Does he make you suck his cock afterwards.'

'No! He hasn't done it for ages, anyway.'

'Strange chap! If I had a fat-bottomed little tart like you for a sister, it would be knickers down every evening for her, and cock-sucking for afters.'

'You pig!'

'I know. Now, come on, my girl, titties out and we'll see about that fucking, shall we?'

He released her. She gave no resistance, letting him move her around and into a kneeling position on the bed, her red bottom stuck high and her knees planted as far apart as the lowered panties would permit. She even lifted herself on her elbows as he began to fiddle with her front, pushing his hand down under her apron to undo her buttons. Within her uniform blouse her breasts felt fat and warm, each a full globe of girl flesh with a stiff nipple at the tip, pushing out the material of her bra. He pulled them free, and out to either side of the lacy white apron, to leave them dangling under her chest. Her hair had come loose, but the little cap was still attached among her curls, adding one more deli-cious touch to her dishevelment.

'Beautiful,' Anderson remarked. 'There's nothing quite like a girl in uniform, especially one who's been thoroughly interfered with.'

'I . . . I don't let every man do this sort of thing to me,' Tabitha said, her voice sulky, yet hoarse with passion.

'I bet you don't,' he answered as he climbed onto the bed behind her.

She was ready for cock, her sex open and juicy between her thighs, the smell of her thick in the air. He put his helmet to the wet, mushy flesh, between her lips, to rub on her clitoris. She moaned and stuck her bottom up, the reddened cheeks spreading to show off her anus and open hole of her sex. He dipped his cock in briefly, sliding it up her until his balls met her sex. Reaching down, he cupped them firmly and began to rub his scrotum in the groove of her pussy. She moaned again, louder. He began to fuck her, pushing in with short, hard jerks, and all the while rubbing at her. She began to wiggle on his cock.

'You . . . you are so dirty!' she panted.

'Dirtier than you think, my girl,' he answered, and stuck a finger in his mouth.

Tabitha turned her head, puzzled, then shocked as he took his spit-wet finger from his mouth and put it to her bottom hole.

'No . . . not my bum!' she moaned, but her ring had already begun to open, his finger slipping deep into the hot, moist cavity of her rectum.

She gave a low, despairing sigh as he went back to fucking her, still using his balls on her clitoris and pushing in with short, hard jerks, all the while feeling around up her bottom. It took moments. He chuckled as he felt her holes tighten, once, twice, and then she was coming, gasping and sobbing into the bed as her vagina went into spasm on his cock and her anus twitched and pulsed on his finger. He kept moving inside her, until she finished with a low moan.

74

'You . . . you can come in me, I'm safe,' she managed.

'Thank you,' he answered, gripped her firmly by her anus and sex and began to push.

He had already been close, and as he jammed himself deep into her rear it started, a great wave of pleasure, tinged with regret at the realisation that with just a little more restraint he could have buggered her as well. Then he was coming, spurt after spurt of semen erupting into her sex, until it burst from the mouth of her hole, to splash over her pussy and his balls.

Only when he had milked the last drops of come into her body did he stop pushing, and withdraw his finger from her bottom hole. Even then he held himself deep inside her, his eyes fixed on her disarranged clothing, her spanked buttocks and her penetrated sex. At last his cock began to go limp and he withdrew, to sit back on the bed, thoroughly content. Tabitha got up slowly, shaking her head as their eyes met. Anderson grinned back and stood to walk to her basin.

'You are such a pig,' she remarked. 'Look at my bum!'

'True,' he answered, 'but I bet you won't forget that in a hurry.'

She threw him a sulky look and turned back to the mirror. She had twisted herself around, so that she could see her bottom. Both cheeks were an angry red, and already blotchy with bruising. Her face set in a petulant *moue* as she inspected herself, with the little green skirt held up in one hand as she stroked at her cheeks. Anderson blew his breath out, promising himself that he'd bugger her just as soon as he could manage another erection.

Tabitha waited as he washed, then took her turn. He began to undress, then paused, one cufflink pushed half through a button hole. On the mantlepiece was a squat jade figure on an ebony stand, which could only be the idol Nich and he were after. The necklace was there too, the ugly design unmistakeable from the catalogue. It had been thrown carelessly down on her dresser.

'Can you lock the door?' he asked.

'Oh, don't worry about that,' she answered. 'Mummy isn't likely to come in, and she wouldn't mind all that much anyway. I just said that so you wouldn't spank me.'

'I fear you were simply too lovely to resist,' he answered, 'and, you must admit, you enjoyed it in the end.'

Tabitha just gave her head a despairing shake as she began to dry her hands.

'No,' Anderson went on, 'I wasn't thinking of our privacy. I was thinking of Nich. He's just not to be trusted.'

'What, you think he'd sneak in and pinch the stuff?'

'He'd certainly be tempted. Back in London, he stole some papers from my pocket while ... while I was asleep.'

Anderson moved to the mantelpiece and lifted the statuette to inspect it. It resembled a child's teddy bear, but only superficially. The face was not really ursine but combined the characteristics of human and deer in a clever blend. The eyes were little cabochon-cut stones, either fine garnets or rubies. Antlers protruded from either side of the head, worked in silver. The body of the statuette was squat and round-bellied, suggesting both the pregnant female and obese male forms. The chest likewise, might, or might not, be considered to represent breasts. Each limb, as short and plump as the body, had been carved in a restful position, giving the figure a dignified manner akin to that of a meditating Buddha. The beast sat on a short base of polished ebony, which concealed any further clues to its gender.

'There isn't a lock, I'm afraid,' Tabitha said, 'but he doesn't know this is my room, anyway.'

'He can find out, no doubt,' Anderson stated.

'Maybe we could swap rooms with Linda and take the stuff in with us. And her door locks.'

'That seems a little unfair on Linda,' Anderson answered, 'unless she enjoys being accosted by Satanists in the early hours.'

'Mark will be in with her,' Tabitha told him.

Nich lay in the impressive four-poster bed of the room Croom had reserved. The mattress was just right, and he was propped up on three ample goose-down pillows, yet still he found it impossible to get comfortable, or to concentrate on Blackman's biography, which he had brought down as reading matter.

It was impossible not to think of Croom, and in particular of him in bed with Tabitha, and probably having sex even as he struggled to bite down his own frustration. Then there was the idol, and the necklace, both of which she was sure to give to him after a night of lovemaking, or which he might simply take.

The tang of defeat was strong in his mouth, and even meditation and the placing of an elaborate curse on Croom had failed to dispel it. He wanted to act, but it was hard to see what he could do without risking disaster. He had discovered which her room was, from a drunken Mark Ferndale, on the pretext of wanting to play a trick on Croom. The temptation to try a raid was growing with the minute, yet he was sure Croom would have taken precautions. Finally he abandoned the idea and contented himself with going through Croom's belongings.

Anderson woke to absolute blackness and a dry feeling in his mouth. Reaching out, he touched the reassuring shape of the necklace. It lay where he had left it, next to his mobile phone, the idol immediately beyond. With the door and window locked he felt fairly secure. Nich had no way of knowing which the right room was, yet after what had happened at Felicity Chatfield's flat it was hard to relax completely. As his eyes adapted to the feeble moonlight filtering through a gap in the curtains, he found he could make out the elegant curve of Tabitha's body under the covers. She made a contented noise in her sleep, moving slightly with a rustle of bedclothes. Anderson smiled to himself, reaching out a hand to stroke her curls.

A drink of water was an urgent priority, as well as a visit to the loo. Annoyingly, there was no sink in Linda's room. Raising himself onto one elbow, he slipped noiselessly out of the bed. Vague shapes could be made out in the dimness and he remembered a dressing gown hanging on the door. Moving carefully to avoid the clothes, shoes and so forth scattered on the floor, he made his way around the bed. He found the dressing gown and slipped it on. It was tight around his shoulders, indecently short and, if he remembered rightly, pink. It would have to do, he decided, turning the key in the lock and easing the door open without a sound.

The corridor was even darker than the room, a blackness relieved only by the faintest of glows from the light above the fire door. Anderson paused, trying to work out where the bathroom would be. To one side was the fire door and the stairs, to the other, the main part of the top storey. With his hands extended to feel for hazards, he made his way slowly along the corridor.

A faint, resonant snoring came from behind one door. Mark's room, Anderson deduced, unless of course he had gone to sleep in the bath, which seemed at least possible from the state he'd been in. The next door was open, Anderson poking his head in to find a long sitting room, the curtains open to show the upper branches of frost-covered trees illuminated yellow by the outside light. His heart jumped as he made out the outlines of two dachshund dogs apparently asleep on the broad window sill, but stilled again as he realised they were only china. Moving back, he continued down the corridor and into a little square hall. If it was the entrance hall to front of the flat, he reasoned, then he had probably come too far.

Turning around, he trailed his fingers along the wall, finding a door which opened under his hand to reveal the welcome shapes of bathroom fittings in the dim moonlight. Closing it quietly behind himself he groped for the light switch, found a cord and pulled it, only to be greeted by the whine of an extractor fan. In the utter silence of the night it sounded like a jet engine at full blast, and Anderson hastily pulled the cord again to shut the noise off. He waited a moment, expecting Tabitha's mother's voice at any instant, then restarted his search, finally finding the switch and turning on the lights. As he had feared, the dressing gown was pink.

Two minutes later he was back in the corridor and less than certain of what to do. He realised that he should have trailed his hand along the wall from Linda's room and counted the doors, but it was now too late. How long had the corridor been? It was hard to remember, but the living room occupied most of the far side and had to be twenty-five, maybe thirty feet long. Anderson paced the distance out and stopped, listening for Mark's snores. There was absolute silence.

It had to be the next door on the left, he decided, running his hand along until he found a lintel. The door opened, the room for some reason just as black as the corridor. He took a pace forward, extending his arm for Tabitha's wardrobe. His hand met empty air, so he took another pace, catching his shin on what felt like an iron bar.

'Shit!' he swore softly, clutching at his leg.

'Eh?' a soft, female voice asked sleepily.

'Jesus, my shin!' Anderson exclaimed.

'Is that you, Mr Croom?' the voice asked.

79

Anderson froze, immediately realising that Tabitha would hardly address him by his surname when they had made love just hours before. The voice was the same though, perhaps a touch deeper.

'Elizabeth?' Anderson said, realising that there was only one possible excuse for being in Mrs Ferndale's room in the early hours of the morning.

'Mr Croom, you really shouldn't be here!' Elizabeth Ferndale admonished him, but without rancour.

'I know but . . .' Anderson managed, deciding that the little-boy-lost act represented his best chance of not leaving Ferndale Manor in the back of a police car.

'I'm a married woman,' she said, 'and you're half my age!'

'It's just that . . .' Anderson answered, hamming it up for all he was worth, 'I . . . I just couldn't help myself. You're so . . . so lovely.'

'Thank you, Mr Anderson, but really . . .'

'I'm sorry, I shouldn't have come up,' he answered.

'No, you shouldn't,' she said softly, 'but now that you're here I suppose you'd better come into bed.'

There was the sound of bedclothes being pulled back, an invitation that Anderson found impossible to resist. Tabitha, after all, was asleep, and the mother's refined poise was likely to make an interesting contrast to the daughter's mix of bouncy enthusiasm and sulky acceptance of his excesses. Slipping the dressing gown off and kicking it under the bed, he reached forward as a soft hand found his thigh.

The hand moved quickly up to his cock, taking hold as he slipped into bed. He pulled up her nightie, to take hold of her breasts. She began to masturbate him, cradling his head to her naked chest and whispering gently to him as his cock grew in her hand. He found a nipple, suckling her eagerly as he let his arousal build and his hands explored her back and bottom. Her flesh was soft, less firm than Tabitha's, less youthful, yet every bit as feminine.

Anderson's cock rapidly grew stiff but, as he tried to mount her, she pressed back, gently pushing him onto his back. He went, happy to relinquish control for a change, and allowed her to mount him, her panties pulled aside, riding his penis, face to face, so that he could reach up and play with her breasts. They were bigger than Tabitha's, and heavier, but similar in shape. As he began to caress her hardened nipples he thought of how the girl he had just fucked had once fed from those same breasts and found himself grinning in the darkness.

She had begun to moan and shiver, and to rub her sex in his pubic hair, when he remembered what he had promised himself with Tabitha. Deciding that if not the daughter, then the mother would do, he took hold of her waist and eased her off his cock. For a moment she resisted, then let it happened, lying back on the bed as he got to his knees.

'Roll over,' he whispered.

'Oh, Mr Croom!' she answered, with a trace of her daughter's giggle in her voice.

She did, with a sigh as she turned her bottom up. Anderson quickly pulled down her panties, and spent a moment caressing her, wondering if he dared give her a spanking. The answer was clearly no, with Tabitha so near, and he contented himself with a couple of firm swats to each cheek before lifting her by the hips. He caught the smell of her sex as her buttocks spread, then he had moved close and rested his erection between them.

The cleft of her bottom was wet with her own juice, and for a moment he contented himself with rutting in it, before putting his cock head to her open vagina and pushing in. Well up her, he took hold of her nightie, pulling himself into her, deep and firm, regular pushes, until she had begun to moan in ecstasy. Slipping a hand under his balls to her sex, he began to masturbate her. She gave a purr of pure joy in response.

He knew he could hold off, and continued to fuck her and rub her sex until he felt the first of her contractions. Immediately he stopped, and slid his cock slowly from her hole. She let out a low, disappointed moan.

'You haven't,' she sighed, 'not yet! You can do it in me, darling . . . it doesn't matter.'

'Thank you,' he answered, 'that's a very sweet offer . . .'

As he spoke he had transferred his cock to her bottom crease. Taking her firmly by the hips, he let it slide down the juicy cleft to her anus.

' . . . but I think I'll bugger you,' he finished, and pushed.

She gasped in shock and tried to move, but he held her firmly in place.

'Mr Croom, no!' she hissed. 'I don't . . . I won't . . .'

She broke off in a grunt of pain as he pushed again, her ring spreading out over his helmet.

'Just relax,' he said quietly, 'and up I'll go, and it won't hurt at all. It will be lovely, as I'm sure you know, Elizabeth?'

Her answer was a sob and a tightening of her anal ring. He held on, his cock pressed firmly to her bottom hole, the wet flesh squirming against his helmet as she struggled to hold herself tight. Again he pushed, and abruptly she gave in, her anus opening to him like a flower, to take his head and close once more on the neck.

'There's a good girl,' he sighed. 'Thank you, that is lovely.'

Her answer was a broken sob, but he felt her anus flare on his prick. He pushed once more, closing his eyes in ecstasy as the flesh of his foreskin squeezed past the constriction of her ring. She was wonderfully tight and, whether it was her first or not, she was obviously not buggered regularly.

Now that he was in, she said nothing, accepting her buggery with the same quiet understanding she had shown to him at first. Then, as he pushed the rest of his cock bit by bit into the hot, slimy cavity of her rectum, she began to make extremely unladylike grunting noises, to his delight.

She had given in, but he kept his hold until his full length was up her bottom, with her ring pushed in around the very base of his shaft. When he did let go, it was to once more slip his hand under her belly, to find her sex. He began to masturbate her, all the while moving his cock slowly backwards and forwards in her straining bottom hole, pulling her ring in and out with each movement.

At once her grunting became louder, more animal. He rubbed harder, full on her clitoris, waiting for the moment her anal ring began to contract on his erection. It came, and he began to slam into her, his belly slapping against her bottom, his hands locked in her nightie and busy with her sex, her ring pulsing, his cock a hard rod in the sloppy cavity of her rectum. Abruptly she was sloppier still as he came up her bottom, his cock squashing in his own sperm as they cried out in mutual ecstasy, coming together.

Mark Ferndale lay in the dark, staring upwards. He had woken to the pressure in his bladder, and for all that his head was spinning with drink and he simply wanted to collapse, he knew he had to go to the loo. His cock was also rock hard, and almost painfully sensitive, making him think of Linda.

She had come upstairs with him, and kissed him good night with all her usual passion, only to refuse to let him into bed on the grounds that he was too drunk. It had left him extremely frustrated, but he passed out before he'd had the chance to masturbate. Now the urge was stronger than ever, but after a few experimental tugs at his cock he realised that the loo had to come first.

Cursing under his breath, he swung his legs out of bed. It was cold, his window wide open in an attempt to reduce the inevitable hangover, and he quickly pulled his dressing gown on. Pushing out into the corridor, he made his way to the bathroom. Just holding his cock as he urinated left him in an agony of need, and he was so stiff he had to hold his shaft down to aim.

Once he'd emptied his bladder the temptation to masturbate into the loo was overwhelming, but the moment he began to tug at his erection thoughts of Linda intruded. She was just yards away, probably in nothing but a baggy top and her panties, soft and warm.

He had to go to her, to make his urgency plain, to fuck her, or at the very least persuade her to suck him to orgasm. She would do it, he knew, if he pushed hard enough. She might be resentful about it, he would probably end up having to buy her something pretty special, but she would do it, and that was what mattered.

Back in the corridor, he made for her room, clutching his erect cock through his dressing gown with one hand and steadying himself on the wall with the other. He found the door, pushed in and groped for the bed. His hand settled on the swell of her hip, and with the feel of her flesh the last of his uncertainty disappeared. Throwing one knee up onto the bed, he found her head and pressed his penis to her mouth.

She gave a muffled groan and tried to pull away, but he held on, rubbing his cock head against the softness of her lips. He reached down, to squeeze her nose, pinching her nostrils firmly together to force her to open her mouth. She gave a grunt of annoyance, struggling, then she had given in, her mouth had come open and she was sucking his cock.

Mark sighed, as much from relief as pleasure, as his cock was engulfed in the warm wetness of her mouth. She was impatient, sucking hard and rubbing her tongue on the underside of his stretched foreskin, obviously keen to get the unwelcome blow job over with. He knew that a few swift tugs would bring him to orgasm in her mouth, but he wanted to feel her in his arms, to explore her breasts and bottom.

He pulled the duvet back, groping in the darkness for her body. To his surprise he found that she had turned onto her back, her thighs wide. His fingers found her sex, as wet and slimy as if he had already come in her. He gave a happy grunt as he realised that she had been waiting for him, and masturbating. A moment later he was on board her, between her thighs as she welcomed him. His cock found her hole and pushed up, easily, deep into her body. He began to pump, the dizzying sensation of orgasm already rising up in his head.

She moaned beneath him, bucking her hips against his and wriggling herself on his cock, something she had never done before. He pushed in harder, grinning as he fucked her, then with his teeth gritted as his orgasm overtook him and he filled her sex with sperm. He stopped, collapsing on top of her. Again she moaned, this time in disappointment, then spoke.

'I . . . I thought you were going to be rude with me again? If you're going to threaten to do a girl up her bum, at least go through with it!'

Mark froze. The voice was not Linda's. As senses other than sheer lust penetrated his alcohol-sodden brain, he realised that the body beneath him was not Linda's either. He groped for the light switch as a dreadful possibility rose up in his head. He found it. Yellow light flooded the room, and his worst fears were realised as he found himself looking down at his own sister, in whose pussy his cock was still firmly wedged.

Anderson Croom came to an abrupt halt as light appeared beneath the door he was approaching. For a second there was silence, then a scream – Tabitha's. He hesitated, puzzled, then stepped forwards, even as the door was flung open. Mark Ferndale staggered out, lost his balance and sat down heavily in the corridor. Tabitha appeared, naked and wild-eyed, her face the colour of a tomato, and not much different from her bottom.

'Idiot!' she yelled at Mark. 'Moron! You fucking, drunken halfwit!'

'I . . . I thought you were Linda!' Mark stammered.

'Well, I'm not, am I!' Tabitha screamed. 'Do I look like Linda, you . . . you . . .?'

'What's the matter?' Anderson asked.

'This idiot got into bed with me!' Tabitha snapped. 'I thought it was you, and . . . and . . . Jesus shit, you're a moron, Mark!'

'I don't see it was all my fault!' Mark retorted.

'You . . . you didn't . . .?' Croom asked.

'Yes, I fucking did!' Tabitha screamed.

Croom put a hand to his mouth, struggling to hide his laughter under the pretence of a cough. Tabitha was glaring at Mark, her fists clenched, her mouth tight. Another light went on behind him and a voice spoke – Elizabeth Ferndale.

'Tabby? Mark? Whatever is the matter?'

Anderson moved quickly past Tabitha into Linda's room. He snatched for the necklace and idol, bundling both into his jacket with feverish speed. Tabitha answered her mother, in a voice breaking to tears, as he grabbed his mobile phone.

'It's stupid Mark, Mummy! Anderson and I had gone into Linda's room because . . .'

'Anderson and you?' Mrs Ferndale queried as Croom made a random snatch towards the clothes on the floor.

'Yes,' Tabitha answered, 'we . . .'

Croom didn't hear the rest of the sentence. He had pulled open the window and swung himself out. He winced as his feet touched the ice in the gutter that ran between the parapet and the slates of the roof. Scrambling along towards the fire escape, the conversation behind him was lost. Then he caught Elizabeth Ferndale's voice again, an angry demand for him to come back as his hands grappled for the icy ladder that led from the roof to the main fire escape.

Below him the grounds of Ferndale Manor were faintly illuminated by the ghostly light of a half-moon, ice glittering over every surface. He reached the ground, stubbing his toe on a milk crate as he hobbled out from the delivery bay where the fire escape came down. Above him a window slammed open, the light flooding out onto the frozen lawn. Glancing up, he saw two heads outlined against the light, each with curly blonde hair, one with an arm raised and holding what appeared to be a dachshund.

Anderson broke into a run as the pottery dog exploded on the ground, showering him with shards. For an instant he glimpsed the head, a large, tear-streaked eye staring up at him accusingly. An inarticulate scream came from behind him, followed by another crash as the second dachshund impacted on the packed gravel of a path. He made the corner of the building, to find the first flush of dawn creeping into the eastern sky.

He made the Bentley and stopped, gasping for breath. He looked warily back, but there was no sign of pursuit. As he lifted the bundle of clothes in his hand to look for the car key he found that as well as his jacket he was holding only two other items. They were his apricot silk cravat and the little green skirt that went with Tabitha's waitress's uniform. He managed a wan smile as he found the key.

Five

Vicky sat was where he she had been since Anderson left her on Saturday, tied into the commode chair in the garage, at the centre of the concrete floor. The straps allowed only just enough give to let her to wriggle her limbs and keep the circulation going, and she was stiff and dizzy with fatigue and cold, her bare skin prickling with goose pimples. Despite the function of the commode, he had not made her strip nude, but left her topless, a pair of white panties her only garment, a piece of calculated cruelty that had been preying on her mind from the start.

His last words had been to tell her to call for Creech as soon as she wanted to be released, but that the cost would be sucking the elderly butler's cock. She had held off, even in the morning, her mental resistance never breaking. Her physical resistance had not been so easy to control, and shortly after dawn she had wet herself, pee spurting into the gusset of her panties to leave them hanging wet and dripping beneath her. Still she had refused to give in, and at last she had heard the Bentley return, bringing her a sense of relief and longing which had left her shaking her head in need.

The panties were now plastered to her stubble-covered sex, and hung heavy beneath her bottom. Her pussy and the sensitive area beneath her bum itched, an agonising sensation that she could only relieve by squirming her bottom in her dirty panties. She was desperate to be released, yet also desperate for the orgasm she knew would be the reward for her torment.

For an hour nothing happened, with her feelings of frustration and the need for help growing by the minute. Then he came, an overwhelming sense of dependence flooding through her as the garage door swung up, to leave her shaking with need. He gave a pleased smile as he approached her, then wrinkled his nose in distaste. She looked up, her vision hazy, her head swimming. He reached her, ducked down to inspect her panties and gave a cluck of amusement as he discovered the wet part sagging beneath her bottom.

'So you never did call for Creech?' he said.

Vicky managed a feeble shake of her head.

'Brave girl. The water held out, I see.'

She nodded.

'I bet you're hungry though?'

Again she nodded.

'Interesting,' he remarked, 'that you would endure so much discomfort rather than suck a man off. I thought you would have been screaming for him the moment you realised you couldn't hold your bladder.

'No,' she sobbed, at last finding her voice.

'And as for actually peeing in your knickers, really! How did that feel, when you were trying to hold it, and when it came out?'

Her response was a broken sob as she hung her head.

'Look at me,' he demanded.

Her head came up, slowly. She felt dizzy, and her eyes wouldn't focus properly, her mouth was slack, and she could feel drool running from one corner, but it didn't seem to matter. Anderson reached for the water vessel he had attached to the top of the chair and put the hose into her mouth. She sucked greedily for a moment, then released it.

'You do know he'd have set you free anyway, blow job or no blow job?' he asked. 'He might even have refused to accept it. Nice fellow, Creech, not an ounce of cruelty in him, although I'm sure he'd love to pop his cock in that pretty mouth if you were to offer, but not like this. You understand that, don't you?'

She nodded.

'So you were prepared to sit there, for as long as it took, in your wet knickers, rather than let him see your tits? I don't believe it, Victoria.'

She could find no response. He went on.

'What I suspect, Miss Potty Knickers, is that you rather wanted it this way, not because you couldn't bear the thought of him, but because you wanted to end up like this, and you wanted me to see you.'

For a long moment she stayed still, then gave a single, miserable nod.

'So, what shall I do with you?' he chuckled. 'What would you like me to do with you?'

'Anything . . . anything you want,' she mumbled, her words scarcely audible.

'Anything?' he said. 'Now that's not strictly true, is it, Vicky? It's not true, because you are going to want that greedy little cunt seen to, aren't you?'

She nodded.

'And you'd like it seen to the way you are, I suspect?' he asked. 'Tied up in your pissy knickers, so that you can feel what you've done in them hanging around your bottom as you come, and think about how you felt when it all came out.'

She gave the tiniest of nods, a barely perceptible movement of her head. Her emotions were burning in her head, her arousal rising with a power she could do nothing to prevent. Croom laughed aloud.

'Please?' she said softly.

'Of course,' he answered, 'but first, as I had to drive up from Devon this morning in nothing but my dress jacket and a waitress's' skirt, I intend to soothe my ruffled feelings by pissing all over you.'

'Oh, God,' she sighed.

'Oh, God is about right,' he answered her. 'I didn't even get breakfast! Mark you, Creech was damn quick with the old bacon and eggs when I got here. I adore that dry cure bacon he gets, don't you? And two goose eggs, wonderful. There was a whole jug of coffee too, and a glass of orange juice, so I expect I can manage a good pint of piss.'

As he spoke he had overturned a large zinc pail and climbed onto it, placing his crotch at the level of the top of her head. He took out his cock, Vicky's eyes following the motions, fear and need, disgust and excitement all building together in her head. As he peeled the foreskin far enough back to show the tip, she hung her head.

'In the face, Vicky,' he ordered.

She looked up, reluctantly. Her face set in utter misery, in no way put on, despite her now desperate need to be urinated on. He squeezed his cock, letting the pressure build up, and her sense of anticipation. She was shaking, her breasts quivering, the muscles of her stomach twitching. Still he waited. She shut her eyes tight, expecting the gush of hot fluid in her face at any instant. Nothing happened. Her lip began to tremble, her feelings growing stronger, and stronger still, until she broke and began to babble.

'Do it! Do it . . . just do it, you bastard!'

'Open wide.'

Her mouth came open. He let go, urine spraying from his cock, full into her open mouth. Immediately she went into a coughing fit, bubbles of pee and mucus exploding from her nose, then a gush of yellow fluid erupting from her mouth, down over her chest and into her lap. It stopped, his stream cut off, holding himself back until she had stopped gagging. She caught her breath, and he let go once more, now over her head, the pee splashing onto her crown and running down her long black hair, to plaster it to her skin.

91

He was laughing as he urinated over her, and playing with his stream, moving it over her body, in her hair, her face, over her breasts and into her crotch. When he moved back to her face she opened her mouth again. He filled it, hot urine bubbling into her mouth and over-flowing, the taste overpowering, the scent strong in her nostrils. She knew he would be watching in delight as his urine bubbled out around her lips and ran down over her breasts. She swallowed of her own accord. Immediately her stomach jerked in revulsion, and as she fought down her sick his laughter grew shriller and louder still.

'What a slut!' he crowed as his stream finally died, to trickle out into her lap. 'Imagine drinking my piss! I adore you, Vicky, there is simply no girl on earth quite so filthy!'

She didn't answer, but hung her head again as he shook the last few drops of urine over her from the end of his penis.

'OK, cunt time,' he announced as he climbed down from the bucket.

She kept her eyes tight shut, as his pee was still dripping from her fringe and both her eyes were wet. Her sex twitched in anticipation of his touch, and again as he put his hand to the slippery flesh of her tummy, moving slowly down to the rim of her panties. She winced as he peeled the sticky material from her sex, and gasped as he thrust his hand down the front. As he began to rub her, she caught the fleshy slapping of his cock being tugged to erection.

'What do you want, Vicky?' he whispered. 'Being tied and left, being pissed on, sucking Creech?'

'What . . . what you said before,' she gasped. 'About my panties.'

'Dirty bitch,' he said. 'So, did you do it on purpose, or couldn't you help it?'

'Accident,' she managed. 'This morning . . . I . . . I couldn't stop it.'

'I bet you tried, though, I bet you tried really hard. It must have hurt, but I bet it hurt your pride more than your body. Didn't it, Vicky, when you realised it was really going to happen, that you had to scream for Creech or do your business in your knickers?'

She gave a hollow moan and pushed her belly out onto his hand. She felt her panties move as they tugged against her skin. He began to rub harder with his whole hand, making her bottom wobble. She moaned, abandoning herself to the inevitable, her misery and humiliation soaring with her arousal as she concentrated on the obscene feel of her wet, sticky panties. Orgasm hit her suddenly, her sex tightening, her anus also, as her muscles went into spasm. Then her control had gone completely and she was jerking and writhing in her ecstasy, her bottom bouncing on the commode seat, her whole sex in frantic contraction, one thigh hammering on the hard wood, her arms twitching in her straps, her pee-soaked breasts and belly quivering to her motions.

At the very peak of her ecstasy she opened her mouth in a long, agonised scream of raw emotion. Immediately it was stuffed with cock, and before she could even respond he had come, giving her a mouthful of salty, sticky sperm to add to her woes. A second peak rose at the added degradation, sending her whole body into a series of uncontrolled jerks that died slowly with her orgasm. Anderson gave a pleased chuckle as she went limp in the chair. She sat still, not daring to open her eyes, letting her exhaustion wash over her as the terrible tensions of her bondage slowly faded. Finally she managed to speak.

'Are you . . . are you going to let me go now?' she managed.

'Yes,' he answered. 'After all, I have to get the Bentley in here.'

He quickly unbuckled her arms and, as she rubbed at her sore wrists and gave her pussy a desperately needed scratch, she heard the sound of a tap running into a bucket. It stopped, and the next instant a pail of freezing water had been emptied over her head. Immediately she went into a fit of gasping, shivering, then coughing, but when it had finally died down she managed to open her eyes.

'Better?' Anderson asked. 'I trust that lived up to your expectations.'

Vicky merely nodded, unable to even begin to try and describe her feelings. He gave a self-satisfied smile and ducked down to unfasten her legs. Both came loose, but she stayed still, waiting until he had found a pair of scissors in a tool box. Carefully, he snipped the panties, one side, then the other. For a moment they stuck to her, then fell into the commode with a splash.

'Thank you,' she managed. 'May I have a towel, please?'

'I think plastic would be a better idea,' he answered, reaching to a shelf for an oily sheet. 'Then it's bath time for you, I think, young lady. Don't worry about Creech, he's washing the car.'

Vicky took the sheet without comment, feeding it between her legs as she rose. Anderson watched as she limped slowly from the garage with the plastic sheet clutched between her thighs.

Smiling happily, Anderson Croom walked to where the Bentley was parked in the driveway. Creech was applying polish to the already gleaming green paintwork. He looked up as Croom approached.

'Ah, Creech, what's for lunch?'

'Grouse, sir,' Creech answered, 'barded and served with field mushrooms, runner beans and wild rice. I have selected a Cornas eighty-eight in accompaniment, from Juge.'

'Excellent. Vicky's in the bath now, but I'm sure she'd appreciate a plate of bacon and eggs.'

94

'Very well, sir.'

Creech applied a final touch to the Bentley's bonnet and turned for the house. Croom spent a moment admiring his reflection in the great car, then turned to follow, only to stop as a black Triumph motorcycle turned into the drive. He recognised it with a shock, then the rider had removed his helmet to reveal Nich's brilliant-red hair and foxlike face.

'What are you doing here?' Anderson demanded, stepping forwards.

'I came to return your suitcase, as it happens,' Nich answered. 'Your address is attached.'

'Ah ... well, thank you, although I dare say the Ferndales would have forwarded it, once they'd calmed down a little. Did you get my dress trousers? It's just that my links were in the pocket, and they were my great-grandfather's.'

'Yes, and everything else.'

'Good for you, whatever your real motives. I suppose I'd better try and be a reasonable host, then. I think Creech has a bottle of Cornas breathing. Would you care for a glass?'

'I'm driving, thank you.'

'Suit yourself.'

'What exactly did happen at Ferndale Manor?' Nich asked suspiciously.

'Oh, it all got rather complicated,' Croom sighed. 'And it wasn't really my fault at all. I had Tabby, but got lost trying to find my way back to the room after going for a pee. I accidentally went into her mother's room and, of course, what could I do? Then –'

'What did you do?' Nich asked.

'I buggered her, as it happens, but –'

'You sodomised Mrs Ferndale, directly after having sex with her daughter?'

'Yes, but that wasn't the real problem ... or, at least, I'd probably have got away with it for a while. Tabby and I had moved to Linda's room to keep the idol and the necklace safe, and while I was otherwise engaged that idiot Mark came in with a raging hard-on and fucked his sister.'

'Her brother? He fucked her?'

'Yes. She thought it was me, of course. Oh, and you'll be glad to know I gave Tabby a damn good spanking. What a brat, eh?'

'You spanked her?' Nich demanded. 'Against her will?'

'Not entirely, but enough to count it as a proper punishment, I'd say.'

'You can't do that!'

'Why not?'

'It's outrageous, totally unacceptable . . .'

'I must say, you take a damn high moral tone for a Satanist . . .'

'I am not a Satanist! I am a pagan, a pantheist as it happens. The difference is as –'

'Pagan, Satanist, pantheist, it's all one to me, and rubbish from start to end. Don't you believe in spanking girls, then?'

'The use of pain as an erotic stimulant must always be subject to the consent of the receiver.'

'You sound like you're quoting from some sort of manual! There's nothing wrong with spanking a girl's bottom, Nich. OK, so they have to get over a bit of pain . . . and perhaps a bit of indignity, but they soon come to like it. Well, most of them.'

'That is simply not the issue! These things must be discussed, in advance.'

'Discussed? Don't be a fool! There's no use in asking a girl if she likes to be spanked when she's never tried it. She's sure to say no, if only because most modern girls are too damn precious to surrender their dignity. The only sensible thing to do is spank them, and if they squeal, let 'em go, as the old saying goes.'

'I didn't notice you letting Felicity Chatfield go.'

'She didn't squeal, not really. She put up a bit of a fight, naturally, but they always do. That way they retain some of their precious dignity – not a lot, true, but some. It's when their knickers come down that they really hate it, often more than the actual spanking, so I can always tell when they want to lose before I even lay a slap in.'

'Your attitude is intolerable! How can you be so arrogant?'

Croom merely shrugged and went on.

'There are naturals, certainly, girls who've always known what they want, but they're few and far between. Besides, it's so much more fun to take a girl's knickers down and spank her when she's going to get in a state over it. A very few never quite lose their innocence. My girlfriend, Vicky, for instance. She really understands her own sexuality, but she still squeals like a stuck pig when I spank her. I'd introduce you, only she's in the bath. Most girls need a bit of training, or at least a nudge in the right direction.'

'How can you say that? Women must be allowed to develop their own outlook, without interference . . .'

'Oh, what nonsense! Everyone needs to be taught. Sex is life's greatest pleasure, yet to learn how to fully enjoy that pleasure necessarily involves a little pain; the loss of virginity, all the stresses and strains of adolescence and, in this case, a girl's first spanking. Left to their own devices, damn few people would ever get to experience more than the most banal sex, girls especially.'

Nich drew his breath in before he spoke again.

'Your attitude is curiously dark for an atheist.'

'My attitude is sensibly masculine, untainted by political correctness.'

'I can see the virtue in a primitive expression of masculinity, yes, indeed, it is an element of many pagan creeds, yet –'

'So what are you after?' Croom cut in. 'As if I need ask.'

'Hmm . . . I had intended to appeal to your better nature, but it is becoming clear that you do not have one. So instead, I will appeal to your rationality. I have the spider, without which you can do nothing. We should work together and share Blackman's legacy.'

'Absolutely not.'

'Then you will have nothing, and Blackman's great work will be left to rot. Think, Croom, of what it might contain, and of the disadvantages to the Yah religions if we uncover it!'

'The what?'

'Christianity and so forth.'

'Oh.'

'Well?'

'Sorry. For one thing, I suspect the cache to be in gold or possibly gems, and for another I am well on my way to working out how to find it, spider or no spider.'

'What?'

'I may as well tell you, I suppose, as it can make no difference. The apparently asymmetrical design of the necklace is deceptive. Blackman's notes are both verbose and vague, but it is a map of sorts. There are seven little notches, patterned in what becomes an extended octagon if you allow for an eighth point a little way clear of the necklace. Your spider, I take it, is a typical arachnid, with eight legs?'

'How did it go?' Ysabel asked as Nich collapsed onto her sofa.

'A disaster!' Nich retorted.

'Oh . . . sorry. Do you want a coffee, a beer?'

'Coffee, please. Anderson Croom got the necklace and the idol too. Worse, he's getting near to solving the puzzle.'

Ysabel rose to make coffee, Nich still talking as she entered the kitchen.

'I even offered to make a deal, to share Blackman's books. He wouldn't go for it. He's convinced it's just money, or so he says.'

'Maybe he is?'

'No. He's covering up. He's a Satanist, I'm certain of it. Not in the modern sense, but more in the tradition of the Hellfire Club. Indeed, he seems to model himself on that period in many ways. How many people have a butler nowadays? And his vanity! His attitude to women is hardly modern either. He likes to dish out spankings, unexpectedly, and the more his victims hate it, the more he enjoys it.'

'Oh, yes?' Ysabel queried.

'Yes,' Nich stated emphatically. 'He did it to Felicity, from the auction house, and to Tabitha Ferndale as well. He seems to think it's funny!'

'How do you mean, funny?'

'As in it makes him laugh to see a girl's pain and distress as she's spanked.'

'A genuine unreconstructed male chauvinist pig! I suppose he can get away with it because he's rich.'

'Partly, yes. Mainly he gets away with it because he only does it when they're already having sex.'

'Wow, what a shock!'

'No doubt.'

'So what are you going to do?'

'He has to visit the Blackman estate, spider or no spider – and, being a toffee-nose, I imagine he can wangle himself an invitation. When he's there, he will need to have everything with him. We need to be there too.'

'And how are we going to get invited to a country estate?'

'What we need to do,' Anderson Croom stated thoughtfully, 'is to secure ourselves an invitation to Brooke House. Doubtless everything will then become clear.'

'Do you think so, sir?' Creech asked, turning the idol in his hands.

'Yes,' Anderson answered confidently.

Creech raised one doubtful eyebrow. For an hour they had been studying the idol and the necklace, with Blackman's notebooks spread out on the table. Beyond Anderson's conviction that the necklace was some form of map, they had achieved nothing. Blackman's notebooks contained instructions, in cipher, including the information that the thorax of the spider should be placed over the cup. Although the seven grooves showed clearly how the spider would sit, it was impossible to be sure exactly how the beast's thorax would go. Nor did any feature of the necklace resemble a cup.

A six-inch Ordnance Survey map of the area around the Blackman Estate had been little more enlightening, showing vague similarities to the swirls of the necklace in places, but more often utter disparity. None of them had been able to relate the idol to the necklace or map in any way whatever.

'There is a theory,' Anderson went on after a pause, 'worked out by some mathematician or other, that no one person on the planet is more than five relationships removed from any other. If so, I imagine that no more than two relationships separate Persephone Chealingham and myself.'

'Another seduction, sir?' Creech asked.

'Why not?' he responded. 'She must be twenty or so, an ideal age, and her mother is said to have been beautiful. Failing that, I can always work on this Baronet. According to his listing in the peerage, he is very much the countryman: hunts, shoots, breeds cattle, pigs and even goats. With luck he'll be getting a shooting party together in the New Year.'

'Very likely, sir. Indeed, I would advise that as a safer course of action than the seduction of Miss Chealingham.'

'Safer, Creech, perhaps, but not nearly as much fun. In most matters, Creech, I am prepared to give way to your considerable wisdom and experience, but when it comes to my relationships with women, I must ask you not to interfere.'

'As you please, sir, but I advise caution.'

'Very well, I won't spank her behind for her until I've secured the cache. How's that?'

Creech had gone faintly pink, but responded with a nod. Vicky entered as Anderson went back to studying the idol. She was in a thick jumper and jeans, her hair washed and brushed, her make-up restrained, giving no hint of what she had allowed herself to be put through the night before.

'Getting anywhere?' she asked as Anderson patted one blue-clad buttock as she passed.

'Not really, no,' Anderson admitted. 'I think we need to be on the ground, in Leicestershire.'

'OK, but this time, I want to come. I'm fed up with being left here.'

'I thought you rather enjoyed it?'

'That's not the point.'

Anderson considered for a moment, weighing the possibilities offered by Persephone against Vicky's very obvious, and available, qualities. The ideal choice was obvious.

'You can come, then,' he stated. 'Assuming I manage to secure the invitation, but on the understanding that you do as you are told, and pretend to be my maid.'

Nich sat cross-legged on the floor of Ysabel's flat, surrounded by a sea of paper and studying a sheaf of half a dozen sheets covered in his own angular, spidery script. Outside, the day had already faded to dusk, and an anglepoise lamp illuminated the room in addition to the main light and several candles. On the bed, Ysabel lay in her favourite face-down position, her legs kicked up and her shoes hanging from her toes as she too scanned a sheaf of notes.

'This is fascinating stuff,' she remarked after a while, 'but all a bit out of date. I don't suppose there's anything much left on the estate that was there in Blackman's day. Other than the buildings, of course, and I don't suppose students of occult architecture are going to be any more welcome than pagans and such. Whose interview are you reading?'

'Frea Baum's,' Nich replied. 'It's the most recent description of the estate, from when she last visited Hecate, to whom she was something of a mother figure. It's mostly just outrage at what Gerard Chealingham had done with the place. Temples used as pig sties; the great altar moved outside and made into a fountain; the Hall of Many Gods made into a stable, with the statues stuck up on the roof and the shrines used to show off the horse-show prizes; the great pentacle used as stock fields with the sacrificial goats in the middle. Dreadful, I know, but not much use to us.'

'So they kept the goats?' Ysabel asked.

'Looks like it. Remember that Blackman was pretty well self-sufficient. I think he got most of the herds when he bought the place and, from what Frea says, they're still there.'

'Could we pretend to be stock buyers?' Ysabel asked. 'That would give us an excuse for visiting.'

'I'm not sure I really look like a stock buyer,' Nich demurred. 'You certainly don't.'

'No, maybe not,' Ysabel admitted. 'What about being biologists, or agriculturalists rather, goat experts?'

'A possibility,' Nich admitted. 'The goats were Blackman's own breed. Black Sacrifice, he called them. Apparently he brought stock back from lower Egypt and crossed them with pure black British longhairs to produce what he considered the ideal sacrificial goat. Such dedication to the art! How could anybody think him a fake?'

'The idea's ridiculous,' Ysabel agreed. 'Maybe if we wrote to this Chealingham bloke, saying we were PhD students perhaps, and asked if we could study the goats, I reckon we'd be in with a chance. The student bit would account for our looks. OK, it's slow, but we might be able to get there in a few weeks. I doubt if Croom can finish the job by then.'

'It's worth a try,' Nich agreed.

Vicky lay face down on the bed. Her jeans and panties had been taken down and her hands had been tied behind her back. Anderson was lazily caressing her naked bottom, stroking her cheeks and occasionally running a finger up the soft groove between them.

'You'll make a good maid,' he said. 'Do you think I should put you in frilly knickers and one of those little flounced skirts that lifts up when you bend over?'

'Don't be silly!' she chided.

'You're right,' he answered. 'It would only risk giving old man Chealingham a heart attack, which would be sure to bring our stay to an end. Still, I might make you offer him sex, if it will help in any way.'

'Not that again! Why are you so determined to make me have sex with other people?'

'Not any other people, Vicky, just dirty old men, and other girls.'

'Other girls, maybe. Dirty old men, no thanks. It doesn't do anything for me.'

'So you say, but you'll be down on old Creech's cock soon enough, and you'll love it.'

'I will not!'

'Enjoy it? Or suck him off?'

'Either!'

He slapped her bottom, just hard enough to make her cheeks wobble and draw a slight squeak from her lips.

'Ideally,' he went on, 'you'd do as you were told, whether you liked it or not. In fact, I think I'd rather you didn't like it, but did it anyway, simply because I told you to.'

'Pervert.'

'Yes, I know,' he admitted.

'Isn't it enough to be able to do as you like with me?'

'Yes, but if you really want me to be in control of you sexually, you'll have to learn to do as I say, without reference to your own will.'

Vicky responded with a doubtful grunt.

'You're going to have to do it sooner or later,' Anderson stated firmly. 'Suck Creech, that is.'

'No, I won't!'

'Oh, yes, you will. It's in your nature. One day, you'll be turned on enough and your resistance will break.'

'It won't.'

'Know thyself, young lady.'

'I do.'

Anderson chuckled, and very gently began to spank her, just patting her bottom with his fingertips, until she had begun to purr and push it up. Slowly, her knees began to part, stretching her lowered panties and jeans, until she had made her sex available from the rear. He ignored the offer, continuing to play with her bottom as he went on.

'Creech is loyal to me, but not in the way he was to my father. Do you know, I suspect my mother used to have to pleasure Creech. Once a week, I think, on a Sunday afternoon.'

'More likely its just figment of your dirty imagination,' Vicky answered.

'I don't think so. She always used to seem agitated at lunch on Sundays. We'd have a roast, invariably, game in season, but more usually beef, lamb, pork or chicken, in rotation. It would be served at two o'clock precisely, a ritual you would have thought sufficiently comforting to set anyone at ease. Afterwards, my father would retire for a nap, I would be chivvied out of the house and left to my own devices. My mother . . . who knows? I suspect she went to the pantry or up to his room.'

'You didn't peep? I'm amazed!'

'There are no windows in the pantry, are there? Otherwise I would have.'

'Total pervert. Why would your father make her do that?'

'Who knows? Simple sadism? To ensure Creech's loyalty? I suspect it was really for her satisfaction. Women often like to feel they're being made to do things when they want to but it is socially unacceptable.'

'Men too.'

'Sometimes, perhaps. Women more, I think. Women are more susceptible to social pressure. It's a herd thing, I imagine, like baboons.'

'Baboons?'

'Yes. I was watching a programme about it. The female baboons stick together, with a rigid hierarchy under a matriarch, and woe betide any lesser females who don't toe the line. The mature males are largely solitary, and do as they please. Very telling, I thought.'

'Very convenient, more like. So . . . what do you think your mother had to do?'

'Hard to say. Probably just masturbate him, maybe use her mouth. I doubt Creech would have fucked her. My father would have considered that to be "getting above his station", always a favourite phrase of his.'

'Your father sounds positively Victorian!'

'Oh, yes, a regular feudalist. I suspect it was largely an act, but he certainly lived the part. I've always rather admired his attitude.'

'So I notice. Are you going to do anything with me, or just stroke my bottom?'

'I'm not sure what I should do with you. Let me see. What day is it?'

'Sunday, of course . . . oh, no, not on your life!'

'No? What if I were to give you a choice, go down to

105

the pantry, right now and ask Creech politely if you can suck his cock, or I'll bugger you.'

'Bugger me.'

His fingers immediately delved between her cheeks, to tickle her anus with a fingernail. She sighed and pushed her bottom up, expecting penetration. He went on.

'How about if I was to bugger you, but instead of coming up your bottom, I'd pull out and stick my dirty cock in your mouth? How would that be, Vicky, bumhole to mouth, maybe several times before I come?'

'Do it,' Vicky sighed. 'And put your finger in ... please?'

He continued to tickle, teasing the mouth of her anus, until the little muscle had begun to twitch. She pushed her bottom higher. Still he tickled, then abruptly he had grabbed her, sliding his hand under her tummy to grip her by her sex, even as his finger forced the tight hole he had been exploring. She gasped as her bumhole popped, again as two more fingers were thrust quickly into her wet sex. Immediately she was in heaven, masturbated anally and vaginally as she squirmed her bound hands and thought what he had threatened to do to her. He began to rub his cock on her leg, stiffening quickly.

Her fantasy grew with her pleasure as she was masturbated, her mind fixed on the thought of having his cock thrust up her bottom hole, then being made to suck it. The phrase he'd used stuck in her mind, bumhole to mouth, so dirty, so utterly indecent, bumhole to mouth ... bumhole to mouth ...

'Do it,' she gasped. 'Bugger me, Anderson, bugger me well ... then make me suck your lovely cock. Up my bum, then in my mouth ... please ... now ...'

'No,' he answered, and stopped rubbing.

'No more goats, please!' Nich begged. 'How do these people do it?'

'Different things interest different people,' Ysabel retorted.

'Fair enough,' Nich answered, 'but for all of me these goat fanciers can keep it to themselves.'

'I thought you liked goats?'

'Only so far as they play a part in religious symbolism. Short of a stag, a goat serves as the best possible representation for the Horned God, and with a goat at least there's a vague chance of making it do what it's supposed to.'

'Yes, do you suppose Blackman's mother was really put to a goat by Crowley?'

'I doubt it. As I understand it, the ritual was designed for Leah Hirsig, Crowley's mistress, but it is doubtful whether she went through with it, and I can find no reference at all of Gaea Blackman being asked to substitute. The idea was to slit the goat's throat at the moment of orgasm.'

'That would have been quite some ritual! I do feel a bit sorry for the goat, though.'

'Yes, it does seem a bit hard on the goat, but at least it would have died happy. Besides, I expect they'd have eaten it.'

'That wouldn't have made the goat feel any better, would it? Poor thing . . . I mean, it's humping away merrily, wondering why the nanny goat it's up has been shaved, some vicious bugger slits its throat, and then they eat it! Talk about adding insult to injury!'

'I disagree. Better to be eaten than simply discarded. Anyway, it wouldn't have known.'

'Maybe. I'd let the goat live.'

'I agree, and it would come terribly expensive on goats if you performed the ritual on a regular basis.'

Ysabel didn't answer, but put her chin in her hands as her face set in a thoughtful expression. Nich went on.

'You're like Crowley in a way, in that your rejection of a strict Catholic upbringing set you on the path. His family were Plymouth Brethren.'

'Yes,' she answered. 'I know, and I've been thinking about what you said about drawing from Christian rituals. I think I'd rather pervert them.'

'That's the Satanic path, Ysabel, but if it pleases you . . .'

'It does. I don't think you should ask, either, not any more,' she answered. 'Do it when you think I need it, sure, but I rather like the idea of just being taken and thrashed, without warning.'

'Very Satanic.'

'Or a ritual might be better,' she went on dreamily, 'to know in advance what was going to happen to me, exactly, down to the last details, and that nothing would be spared. There would have to be some people to watch, and candlelight, and plenty of incense . . . It's a shame my group are too soppy to do it.'

'That's wiccans for you,' Nich said.

Ysabel made a face and shifted on the bed. When she spoke again, it was suddenly, and with urgency.

'Cane me, Nich, only this time, stick a candle up my bum first and do me as it burns.'

'That certainly sounds Catholic,' Nich remarked.

'Never mind the theology behind it, just do it. You can use one of those purple ones. Stick it well in.'

She had lifted her bottom, and reached back to tug up her long black skirt, exposing her thighs, then the plump swell of her cheeks within big black panties. Nich rose, grinning, and walked to the triple candlestick in which the purple candles burned. They were thick, if perhaps not quite as thick as his cock, and long. He blew out the central one, pulled it from the holder and put the base to another flame, twisting it to melt the wax into a smooth, round head.

'Lube me up,' Ysabel sighed, 'and we'd better put something under my tummy.'

Nich nodded thoughtfully. On the bed, Ysabel knelt up to make a pile of pillows where her hips would go.

Nich took a towel from the back of a chair and laid it over the pillows. Taking hold of her panties, he peeled them down and tugged the gusset free from between her thighs, leaving a puff of dark-gold hair and a hint of chubby pussy on show. He turned to her chest of drawers. The top surface was cluttered with make-up, bottles of perfume, a bewildering variety of jars, tubes and boxes of less obvious function. He chose a tube of a jelly-like substance he hoped was suitable for lubricating girls' bottom holes and applied it to the base of the candle.

As he turned back, he found Ysabel draped over the pillows, her bare bottom now high and wide, with the big, firm cheeks a little apart. Crossing to her, he spread her cheeks with his fingers, stretching her anus wide. She sighed, then gasped as he squeezed the cream onto her hole.

'That's cold!' she complained.

'Not for long,' Nich responded and pressed the base of the candle to her anus.

She gave a low moan as her ring pushed in to the pressure. Nich watched as the glistening flesh moved, in, then apart as her hole took the candle base. She moaned again as the candle began to slide up her bottom, a good half its length disappearing inside her before Nich stopped and let her cheeks close. She wiggled, making the candle move, and made a little purring sound in her throat.

'That feels nice,' she sighed. 'Go on, light it.'

Nich nodded and reached for the lighter on her bedside table. She looked back, her eyes big with apprehension as he flicked the lighter into life and applied the flame to the wick. It took immediately, and Nich stepped back as the flame rose up, to fetch her cane from where they had left it in the living room.

When he got back the wax had already begun to melt, and Ysabel's trembling had grown stronger still. He peered close, and as he watched a drip ran slowly down, but stopped before it reached her skin. A second followed, bigger, rising on the bump of hard wax made by the first. It hung poised for an instant, then dropped. Ysabel's flesh twitched and she let out a whimper as it splashed on her skin. Nich nodded in satisfaction.

'Pull your breasts out,' he ordered.

She obeyed immediately, the candle wobbling in her bottom as she tugged the dress high up around her neck. Her bra came up, flopping her fat white boobs out beneath her, the nipples already stiff. Nich felt his cock start to harden, and more as she sank down again and the abundant breast flesh squashed out on the bed. Her bottom lifted, presenting a target for the cane.

'Beat me, Nich,' she sighed, 'hard.'

He nodded and stood back to tap the cane across her bottom. Her soft flesh wobbled to the touch, and immediately the pool of wax at the top of the candle spilled over. Ysabel squealed as it poured down into the cleft of her bottom, and her cheeks went tight. She was clutching the bedclothes and whimpering as the trickle solidified in the tight groove between her cheeks, but she stayed down and said nothing. Once more Nich took aim, lifted, and cut down across her bottom.

Ysabel screamed and jerked in her pain as the cane struck. Hot wax flicked from the candle, drops only, but catching her in her crease and on the small of her back, to leave her shaking her head in pained reaction and clutching harder still at the duvet beneath her. She began to mumble, the words of a prayer or mantra, and to curl her toes.

'Six?' Nich asked.

'Six, yes,' she managed. 'Very hard . . . punish me, Nich . . . hurt me.'

Nich tapped the cane to her bottom, lifted and held still, watching the molten wax slowly pool on the trembling candle top. Ysabel was shaking hard, and he knew the wax would spill before much had built up, but he waited until what he was sure was the last possible moment before striking.

The cane hit. Ysabel screamed, and screamed again as hot wax splattered across her bottom, full on one of the raw, fresh cane welts. Nich allowed himself a satisfied nod and once more lifted the cane, holding it high over her bottom as he freed his cock into his hand.

'You're going to fuck me, aren't you?' Ysabel gasped.

'Of course,' Nich answered. 'It is my privilege to do as I wish with your body when you are punished, is it not?'

'Yes,' Ysabel answered, 'whatever you want ... whatever ...'

Nich felt an abrupt rush of blood to his cock at her words, immediately realising the implication. Smiling quietly, he brought the cane down again, hard across Ysabel's buttocks, to splash hot wax across her skin one more time and again wring a double scream from her mouth. For a moment she was whimpering in pain, before the noises once more turned to a broken, wordless babbling.

'There is certainly something religious in the quality of your ecstasy,' he remarked.

'Shh!' she urged. 'Just cane me, Nich ... really punish me ...'

'So be it. Lift your bottom'

She obeyed, her bottom coming up slowly to let her cheeks open. Nich waited as he watched new wax melt, then reached out the cane to tap the base of the candle. Wax spilled down the side, to fill the shallow, fleshy groove around her penetrated anus. She screamed and went tight, even as he struck, the cane whipping down across her bottom with the full force of his arm.

'Four,' he announced.

Ysabel's answer was a fresh whimper, and she began to sob in hard, choking gasps, but once more her bottom lifted and opened. Her big cheeks were twitching, to make the candle shake and the light flicker. Nich leaned close, to admire the way the wax had set in her anus, creating a tight seal around the candle shaft. Again he tapped, lifted and struck, wax splashing out over Ysabel's bum cheeks, to send her briefly into a wild, agonised dance before she once more managed to take control of herself.

Nich waited until she had stuck her bottom up again, now so high that the candle protruded vertically from her anus, as if decorating a fat, fleshy cake. Five rich-red welts showed on her cheeks, all above the candle, and criss-crossed. In her new position, enough cheek showed below the candle and above her thighs to make a good target of unmarked flesh. He tapped the cane to it. Ysabel flinched.

'Last one,' he said, and struck.

The cane lashed down full across the fat of Ysabel's bottom, catching the candle as her soft meat deformed. The shaft broke, spraying hot wax up into her bottom cleft and over her back, to set her screaming and writhing, her fists thumbing at the duvet, her feet kicking behind her. Nich stroked his cock as he waited for her to get over her pain, then mounted the bed. The candle had gone out, but the wick held the broken shaft in place, with the upper half lying in the cleft of her buttocks, wax congealing around the tip to glue it to her skin.

Her bottom was a mess, decorated with six angry red welts and spotted purple with wax and hot red spots where the cane blows had knocked the hardened pats free. More wax had splashed her sex, clogging her hair and blocking the hole. He made an abrupt decision. If her cunt was sealed it was clearly significant, so his cock was going up her bottom. He reached out, to ease the candle free, her skin pulling out on the hardened wax. She winced and gasped as it peeled free, then sighed as the thick candle shaft left her bottom. Her anus stayed open, a gaping hole into her body, glistening with lubricant.

'I'm going to bugger you,' he said, taking hold of the big black panties.

Ysabel was shivering as her panties were removed, and her fingers were locked hard in the cotton of the duvet cover. Nich spread her legs and climbed between them, cock in hand. Her bumhole had shut, but was still loose, and pulsing, to squeeze out a little worm of lubricant as he got ready to penetrate her.

He put a hand down, to spread his target. Ysabel stuck it up, offering herself for buggery. His cock pressed to her hole, the soft, sore flesh spreading to his helmet as he pushed, and he was in, sighing as warm rectal flesh engulfed him.

Ysabel accepted the penetration of her anus with a whimper, and began to pant as Nich crammed his erection slowly into her back passage. He pushed harder, moving back and forth in the hot, slimy tube around his cock. She was gasping and squirming her bottom on him by the time he had his full length inside her. He stayed kneeling, entranced by the lewd sight of her anal ring stretched taut around his intruding cock and the way her flesh moved to her buggery.

She moved, lifting her body, and Nich saw that her hand had come back, to allow her to masturbate as she was buggered. He kept moving, and began to spank her, slapping at her already severely welted bottom cheeks as she rubbed herself. Just the sight of her big, hurt cheeks quivering to his slaps was enough to bring to urge to come up her bottom to the point where he knew he could no longer hold back. His self-control gone, he mounted her, jamming his cock hard up her bottom hole, over and over as his orgasm rose up. Buggered fast and hard, Ysabel went into her own orgasm, screaming out her ecstasy as his hard belly slapped on her hot, welted buttocks. He felt her anus lock on his cock shaft as she went into orgasm, and simultaneously filled her rectum with spunk, spurt after spurt as her hole went into spasm on his straining erection.

'Last chance,' Anderson gasped as he felt the start of his orgasm.

Vicky gave her head a violent shake, sending her black hair tumbling around her. Anderson tightened his grip on her bound wrists and on his cock, pushing it down to the sloppy entrance to her arsehole.

'Downstairs!' he grunted.

'No! Just put it in, will you?'

'No,' he answered and came in her bottom hole.

His teeth were gritted in ecstasy as he watched the thick white sperm erupt from his cock into the fleshy cavity of her well-fingered anus. She was wriggling as her bottom hole filled with spunk, but he held her tight, her legs pinned beneath his and her bound wrists pulled back cruelly hard. Only at the very peak did he lose control of himself and push his helmet into the sperm-soiled mouth of her bumhole, to enjoy the feel of her hot anal flesh as he finished himself off.

'You bastard . . . you utter shit!' she gasped as he pulled back.

Anderson said nothing, but chuckled as he watched her hole close, the sperm squashing out to run down over the bar of flesh between anus and vagina and into the lower hole. Again her bumhole opened, slowly, to make a slippery pink pit, only to close again and leave a sperm bubble glistening in the bedroom light. Croom popped it with a finger.

'OK,' Vicky sighed, 'you've had your fun with me . . . now make me come, please?'

'No,' he answered. 'Not until you've been downstairs and come back to show me the sperm in your mouth. If you take your time I'll be ready for you again when you're done.'

Vicky's response was a long, exhausted sigh.

Six

'Well, that was remarkably easy,' Anderson Croom
stated as he held up the gold-edged card he had pulled
from an envelope. 'I am invited to dine with a Miss
Annabella Cappaldi and a Mr Tod van Riemon, a
couple well known in the upper echelons of London's
dinner party set, or so I'm told. I think I must have got
in on the strength of that dreadful article in ... in ...
what was the name of that rag, Creech?'

'*London Girl*, sir.'

'Oh, yes, *London Girl*, of course. Anyway, Persephone
Chealingham will be there, I believe on the strength of
being an old schoolfriend of Annabella's and a handsome catch for wealthy City types who want the
obligatory country house without having to pay for it,
thieving hoi polloi that they are. Now, where's that tart
of mine? We'll be needing to buy her a uniform.'

'I believe Miss Victoria has not yet come down, sir,'
Creech answered.

'Ah, no, she wouldn't have, would she? I'll forget my
own head next!'

'Very droll, sir.'

Anderson cast Creech a doubtful glance, but if there
had been any sarcasm in the remark, then none showed
in the elderly butler's face, merely a calm attentiveness.
Dismissing the thought, he made his way upstairs, to the
bedroom, where Vicky lay on the bed, naked and

trussed up into a foetal position. A feather duster protruded from her anus, while her hair and face were decorated with blobs and streamers of come. One eye was stuck shut. She had been gagged, a stocking held taut over her mouth, with a section of orange just visible where the satsuma he had made her take in her mouth forced her lips apart.

'Ready?' he asked.

She gave an urgent nod. He chuckled and crossed to a wardrobe, to open the drawer in its base and extract a thick vibrator of a pink, jelly-like substance. It was roughly cock-shaped, but with a small jelly bear straddling the shaft so that the animals lips could be made to kiss the user's clitoris.

Vicky's position left her sex on full show, her pussy lips stretched out lengthways, with just a little fluid showing at the mouth of her hole. Anderson came close, to ease the thick vibrator up into her sex, fucking her for a bit, before positioning it with the bear's lips to Vicky's clitoris. A quick adjustment of one of the ropes binding her legs to her body held it in place, and he turned it on. Vicky gasped as a muffled buzzing began.

Anderson went to sit on a chair, to watch as Vicky began to respond. He was enjoying both her helplessness and the intimacy of watching her body, with her vagina penetrated and her muscles twitching in an erotic reaction over which she had no control whatever. It was quick too, her buttocks starting to tighten and her back starting to arch as she struggled to control the contact of the bear's mouth on her clitoris. Then there was a sudden flurry of contractions by the muscles of her sex and anus and she was coming. Powerful shudders started to run through her body as she squirmed in her ecstasy, the duster waving wildly behind her adding a comic touch, and he found his cock growing stiff in his pants despite the recent orgasm taken over her face. When she had at least come down, he pulled the vibrator out, gave her a brief, perfunctory fucking and came over her bottom.

'It looks like we will be going up to Leicestershire,' he remarked casually as he wiped his cock on the pair of panties she had been trying to put on when he had caught her and tied her up. 'I've got my invitation, so all I need to do is exert a little charm on Persephone.'

Vicky turned to glare at him out of her clear eye.

'Don't worry,' he said. 'I won't fuck her unless I have to. Maybe she'll be game for a threesome, who knows? You'd like that, wouldn't you?'

Vicky gave a sulky nod. He laughed and smacked her bottom, then cursed as he realised that he'd put his hand in his spunk. He wiped it off on her hip as he went on.

'She probably won't, of course. Why do women always get so jealous? I mean, clearly they all want me to themselves, but you would have thought they'd realise that a little playful depravity would make me more keen on them, and not less. That's what I love about you, of course, you're such a slut.'

Vicky wriggled slightly, pushing out her bound wrists.

'Not comfortable?' he asked. 'Did I twist your arms too far back? Hmm, maybe I should have bound them around your legs instead, but I do like a tied woman's hands behind her back – it sets off her vulnerability, I feel.'

She managed a muffled noise in her throat and once more wriggled her bound wrists.

'Patience,' he said thoughtfully. 'Hmm, there is one thing we could do, one of your favourites. Once we've got Blackman's cache, we won't need to worry about the Chealinghams any more, and in the circumstances an acquaintance might even prove embarrassing. As you'll be my maid, perhaps I should spank you in front of them. That should get us thrown out, I imagine.'

Vicky nodded, then shook her wrists again.

'OK, time I untied you, I suppose,' he said, 'or, at least, once you've promised to do your duty by Creech.'

117

She shook her head. He went on.

'Uh, uh, I'll have none of that. It's Sunday tomorrow, so as soon as you've had a civilised pause to allow your food to go down after lunch, into the pantry with you and down you go.'

Again she shook her head, more vigorously than before. He smiled and began to undo her bonds, still speaking.

'You'll do it in the end, I know you. The idea's in your head, isn't it? I bet you masturbate over it, no?'

Vicky shook her head with renewed vigour. Anderson laughed.

Persephone Chealingham accepted a glass of Champagne and paused to study her fellow guests. Of the other people in the room, several were known to her but the only one she counted a worthwhile friend was the hostess herself, her old schoolfriend Annabella Cappaldi. Inevitably there was Annabella's boyfriend, the unctuous Tod van Riemon, whose sole virtue from Persephone's viewpoint, and, she suspected, Annabella's as well, lay in his being the heir to a sizeable manufacturing firm. Talking to Tod was a man she didn't know, a city man by the look of his suit, and full of his recent success in some hideously boring business deal in Frankfurt. The third man was a city friend of Tod's: suited, slim, intense, with a high income and a proportionately high self-opinion.

The two other women were an accountant from the firm that handled Tod's father's company and an accountant from Percy's firm, both thoroughly cosmopolitan and with lives revolving around their firms, their cars, their flats and, of course, men. Persephone found herself wishing for the wide, gentle countryside of Leicestershire, where at least everyone she met didn't immediately want to talk about the specifications of their BMW or Porsche.

Both the single men had struck up conversations with her. Neither appealed. The fourth was still to come, and she found herself hoping he would be more interesting. Even as she took her first sip of the Champagne the doorbell chimed.

Persephone watched in faint hope as Annabella went to answer the door, returning moments later with a bunch of tiger lilies, a box of handmade chocolates and a bottle of Champagne of a marque she did not recognise. Following Annabella was a tall man, strikingly handsome, with thick black hair thrown artlessly across his forehead. He was dressed in immaculate black tie, immediately putting the grey and blue suits of the other men to shame, as did his physique.

The newcomer glanced around, smiled and nodded to Persephone, passed a carefully judged compliment on Annabella's gown, acknowledged the other and took up a glass of Champagne from the sideboard. Persephone's first impression of the man was that, while undoubtedly handsome, he was extraordinarily affected. The combination of black tie and tiger lilies suggested a character of considerable flamboyance and old-fashioned courtesy; sadly, she reflected he was almost certain to have neither but simply turn out to be a more pretentious City type. Yet he was an improvement on any of the other men. When Annabella asked the company to sit down, Persephone engineered the seating arrangements so that she had the relatively harmless Tod van Riemon on her right and the stranger on her left.

Vicky sat on the bed, her chin in her hands, feeling bored and frustrated. A slim, tooled steel vibrator lay on the bed beside her. With Anderson in London attempting to seduce Persephone Chealingham, she had intended to soothe her ruffled feelings by masturbating over something, or someone, of whom he would disapprove. She knew it was a petty revenge, but that was not the reason she had abandoned the idea after getting no further than lifting her nightie and pulling aside the frilly panties he liked her to wear in bed.

There was no fantasy that would have met with his disapproval yet satisfy her. Thinking of other men would only amuse him, even the celebrity icons he so despised. Women were worse, while with any abstract scenario of bondage, spanking or erotic torture, she knew that her mind would inevitably come to focus on him at the moment of orgasm. Then there was the constant pressure to provide sexual favours for the butler, which was beginning to intrude into her head despite her best efforts to keep it out.

An idea occurred to her, something irrelevant to Anderson, yet delightfully rude. Peeling her frillies down her legs, she bared herself, then lay back, thighs spread as she reached for the vibrator.

Anderson Croom lowered himself into his chair with a delicious feeling of anticipation. Persephone Chealingham, now seated within a foot of him, was everything he had imagined her to be and more. Of medium height and compact build, the contours of her body were well enhanced by her clinging dress of deep-red velvet. Firm, high breasts and a smooth curve to her hips suggested the kind of muscularity derived from a vigorous outdoor life. Her complexion, also, had none of the slightly artificial look so typical of London, but was clear and as smooth as cream. Her unusually fine, dense hair was so dark as to have a bluish sheen and was pulled into a rather severe French plait. Regular, intelligent features with just a touch of sensuality to the lower lip completed her beauty.

True, she lacked the opulent curves of Tabitha and Elizabeth Ferndale, or the svelte lines and refined sweetness of Felicity Chatfield, but nobody could have everything, and variety was, after all, what counted.

When all was said and done, Persephone was certainly appealing physically and the circumstance of their meeting had already built up a mystique around her.

Holding a conversation with her proved harder than he had anticipated. The first course was spent persuading the young man sitting opposite him that he had no interest whatsoever in something called Client Risk Maximum Return Pensions, which sounded more larcenous than any of his own schemes. Tod van Riemon, to whom Croom took an immediate dislike, monopolised her throughout the fish course. With the main course he finally managed to find a break in the conversation long enough to turn to her, finding her large, bright eyes studying him with pleasure and more than a touch of good humour.

'Anderson Croom,' he introduced himself.

'Persephone Chealingham,' she replied. 'A bit of a mouthful, I'm afraid. You must call me Sephany – everyone does. So what do you do?'

'Nothing, if I can possibly help it,' Croom answered.

'Nothing?'

'Well, not nothing, strictly speaking, but I know when people ask me that question they mean work. I don't work.'

'Not at all?'

'No. You see, I don't really believe in the Protestant work ethic, whereby everyone has to spend the best part of their life in drudgery. The way I see it, those of us with enough money to get by should stand back and give the other fellows a chance. You see, if I worked, I'd just be depriving some worthy chap of a career as a . . . a barrister, or a wine merchant, you know, what it is people do.'

'Oh . . . er . . . right. So, what do you do with your time?'

'This and that. I've a decent spot of land down in Surrey, mostly oak wood, and I have a fellow rear me pheasants, partridge, that sort of thing. I ride a lot too.'

'You ride? So do I! Now that I'm eighteen Daddy says I can ride his hunter, Beelzebub. He's sixteen hands, pure black, the most beautiful horse you could ever imagine. With any luck I'll be able to take him out when the Cottesthorne meet next ... You do ... do, er ...'

She leaned close, so close that a stray strand of hair tickled his ear, sending a shiver through him. For a moment her lips touch his ear, as if she was going to kiss, or nibble. When she spoke it was in a whisper, a single word.

'Hunt.'

'Absolutely,' Anderson answered, at full volume, 'at every opportunity. I don't give a damn for these abolitionists and their sentimental claptrap, and I don't care who knows. Jealousy, that's all it boils down to.'

Persephone's eyes were glowing.

Vicky threw the vibrator down in disgust. It was sticky with her juice, her sex was sore, and so was her bottom hole, where in her rising desperation for a good orgasm she had pushed the vibrator into her ring rather more firmly than was sensible.

The fantasy had failed, despite an hour's worth of attempting to focus. The start had worked, with her imagination running on taking Anderson's hunter, Charlemagne, out for a ride, and needing to adjust the girth strap on one of the lonely woodland paths near the house. The sheer size of the beast's cock had always brought her a twinge of very sexual embarrassment, but she never before allowed herself to explore the possibilities it offered. Now she had, thinking of how the enormous pink and brown penis would sometimes extend from its sheath, and imagining that happening as she adjusted the strap.

Her idea had been to picture herself being overcome by her own dirty mind, daring herself to touch the huge cock, then to rub it, lick it and suck it, as she gradually grew more wanton. She had intended to come as she imagined attempting to take it in her vagina.

It hadn't worked. Every time her excitement had started to rise, Anderson had somehow intruded into her mind, egging her on, to strip, to rub her breasts on the horse's cock, to make it come over her head or in her face. Deciding that the problem lay in Charlemagne being his horse, she had tried something different. In turn she had imagined indulging herself with a different horse. In every case Anderson had entered the fantasy, and in every case Creech had been behind his master, cock ready for sucking once she'd been thoroughly dealt with.

Anderson Croom lay back with an indulgent smile. Persephone was mounted across his body, her glorious bottom towards him, pushed out to show the full moon of her cheeks, her tight, brown anus and the junction of cock and cunt. She was nude, her bum and boobs bouncing as she rode his cock, in high delight as she fucked herself. He had folded his hands behind his head, happy to admire the view and let her do the work.

Her bottom was a delight, round and full, yet decidedly muscular, as was the rest of her body. The temptation to spank her had been close to overwhelming, and his resistance had come to the very edge of breaking point when she had been undressing. She had deliberately pushed out her bottom to let him watch as she slid her lacy black knickers down, and only by closing his eyes had he held back.

From Annabella Cappaldi's they had taken a brief cab ride to the Notting Hill flat her father owned, just two streets away from Brady and Gordon's auction house. Memories of Felicity Chatfield kicking and squealing as he set about her bottom had brought his temptation up, and Persephone's deliberately rude strip-tease had taken it to breaking point.

123

He had held back, and contented himself with making her suck his balls as well as his cock as she brought him to erection. She had done it with no more than a trace of reluctance, then asked to mount him in return. He had obliged, and been treated to several repeats of 'This is the Way the Lady Rides', delivered in a breathless contralto. When he had swivelled her around to admire her bottom she had barely paused in her singing, and only stopped when her hand had gone down between her thighs to take herself to orgasm.

Anderson reached out as she began to masturbate. He took hold of her bottom, squeezing a cheek in each hand as he began to thrust himself up into her body. She arched her back, throwing her head up in ecstasy. Her anus was showing, and he slipped his thumb onto the little hole, tickling even as it began to contract in orgasm. She wiggled herself onto him, pushing her bottom back. He pushed the top joint of his thumb into her squirming hole, knowing that it was that or slap her quivering bum cheeks. With his spare hand he grabbed her hair, tugging her head back. Persephone gave a crow of delight and went wild, her flesh jiggling more crazily than ever as she thrashed in orgasm. His resistance went, but he was there, his cock jerking inside her, the sperm exploding out over his balls and into his pubic hair even as he released her hair to slap her bottom.

'Shit!' she swore, betraying an earthiness she had kept hidden even during sex. 'Anderson, you've spunked up my pussy!'

Vicky bit her lower lip, struggling with her emotions as she stood in the empty corridor. She was barefoot, in a silk robe with her nightie and the ridiculous frilly panties underneath, nothing more. The old house seemed unnaturally quiet, as it always did when Anderson was away, as if his very presence brought it to life. She knew it was ridiculous, a fancy, but she could not shake the feeling that he and it were linked. He had lived there his entire life, as had his parents and grandparents before him, maybe others. So had Creech, almost, living in the little upstairs flat since before she herself had been born, seemingly as timeless and stable as the house itself.

She shivered as she looked up. She shook her head, telling herself that she didn't need to be standing in the corridor, that she should be asleep in bed, that she should be doing anything other than dwelling on the utterly humiliating act which Anderson had forced into her head. Yet she was, and for all that she knew she was being manipulated, her nipples were uncomfortably stiff beneath her nightie and her sex so wet that her inner thighs were slippery with her own juice.

Still she hesitated, telling herself that she should go back into her room, that she hated Anderson, that to obey would be the final step in her submission to him. The last was true, and for all that the very thought of taking the old man's cock in her mouth made her retch, she found herself walking slowly down the passage.

Her emotions grew stronger with every step, mixed feelings, awful and exquisite. Excuses forced themselves to the front of her mind: that he would prove too old to get an erection, that he would be asleep, that he would reject her. She knew that she could still suck on his limp cock, that to wake him would make the agonising humiliation of what she had to ask worse still, that to be rejected would be the final insult, and leave her wallowing in an ecstasy of self-abasement as she masturbated in the corridor.

She reached the end of the passage, to stand for one long moment, staring out at the moonlit garden. She turned to climb the narrow, uncarpeted stair that led to his flat. She lifted her hand, and brought it down on his door with a gentle tap. There was no response, and a great flood of relief washed over her, to be followed by regret stronger still. Then she caught the faint creak of old wood and her heart was in her mouth. His voice sounded from beyond the door, cracking slightly with age.

'Miss Victoria?'

'Yes,' she answered, her own voice hoarse and faint.

'May . . . may I come in . . . please?'

'Please do,' he answered.

She turned the door handle, her palm so wet with sweat that the polished brass slipped a little in her grip. It twisted, came open, and she stepped inside, her nose wrinkling at the smell: polish, mothballs, and simple age. Creech appeared in the door to his living room, not in pyjamas, as she had expected, but in his black work suit, his tie still fastened. In his hands he had a silver spoon and a cloth. Suddenly the idea of asking to suck his cock seemed not only impossibly rude, but absurd. She managed a weak smile, lost for what to say, or how to explain her presence.

'May I offer you a glass of port?' he enquired.

'Please, yes,' she answered, and followed him into the tiny living room he occupied, built in beneath the eaves of the house.

The smell of polish had grown stronger, and she saw that he had silverware spread out on a newspaper, along with the polish and several clothes. There was an ancient radio, no television, but bookshelves against either wall, crammed with leather- or cloth-bound volumes and only the occasional shiny dust jacket of a newer publication. Everything was as spotless as it was Spartan, the only real luxury the decanter of deep-ruby liquid set on a plain sideboard.

'A sixty-three,' he remarked, pouring a glass. 'Possibly the finest vintage of the last century. Quinta do Noval.'

'That's nearly twice my age,' she answered. 'Does Anderson . . . I mean . . . sorry.'

She trailed off, suddenly feeling awful for the question she had been about to ask.

'Mr Croom allows me a free selection from the cellar,' Creech answered, 'ostensibly on the grounds that I would have drunk myself to death long before I made any serious impression on it.'

He gave a dry chuckle, which Vicky found herself echoing, then went on.

'This, however, is from my own stock. Mr Croom is a generous employer, as was his father before him, and his grandfather before that. My personal expenses are minimal, and so I have tended to buy a few cases in the better vintages.'

'You were employed by Anderson's grandfather?' Vicky queried.

'As boots, in 1938,' he answered. 'At the age of fourteen.'

'Nineteen thirty-eight,' Vicky echoed. 'You must have seen some changes.'

'A few,' Creech admitted, and settled himself into a worn leather armchair with his glass.

Vicky sat down on a straight-backed chair, which somehow seemed appropriate. She sipped her port, which proved as rich and mellow as any Anderson had served her. As she swallowed it seemed to trace a velvet path down her throat, and left her mouth full of the taste of ripe black cherries, plums and an almost meaty savour. For a while they sat in silence, both savouring the port, Vicky also hiding her embarrassment behind the glass. At last Creech placed his glass to one side and folded his liver-spotted hands across his waistcoat.

'To what do I owe the pleasure of this visit?' he asked, his voice low and kindly.

'I . . . I was bored . . . lonely,' Vicky answered, then, before she could hold back, the words had come tumbling out. 'I . . . I have to ask to . . . to . . . fellate you, to suck your cock.'

Instantly her cheeks were burning and, as she buried her face in her hands in tormented shame, she knew her

127

cheeks would be just about as red as the ancient port. Nothing happened, no angry or shocked words, no harsh accusation of playing a cruel joke, or tormenting him, which she had expected. Finally she plucked up the courage to peep out from between her fingers.

Creech sat as before, his face impassive, save perhaps for the faintest hint of a smile. His fingers were at his crotch, slowly undoing the buttons of his fly. Vicky's mouth fell open, and she continued to stare from between her fingers as one by one the buttons came loose, as he burrowed his hand into his fly and the woollen underwear beneath, as he pulled out a thick, pale penis and a heavily wrinkled scrotum in a nest of pure white hair.

'Must I?' she sobbed, at last taking her hands from her face.

A voice was screaming at her in the back of her head, telling her that what she was about to do was utterly unacceptable, worse than taking spankings, worse than grovelling nude at men's feet, worse even than taking pleasure in wetting and soiling her panties.

'Only if you wish to,' Creech answered.

'You ... you know?' she asked. 'That Anderson wants me to?'

'I did not,' he answered. 'I confess that I thought your motive might be pity. You have always struck me as an exceptionally compassionate young lady.'

Vicky shook her head.

'Not pity, no. I ... I've been told to.'

'And do you wish to?'

She found herself nodding, her true emotions simply too complex to express. Standing, she swallowed the rest of her port, her fingers shaking so badly she nearly dropped the glass. Warmth flooded through her as the port went down. Her fingers went to the cord of her robe, automatically.

'Shall I?' she asked.

'Strip?' he asked. 'I think so. Perhaps in your pants if you are shy.'

She nodded as sudden gratitude for his calm, understanding behaviour and the offer of keeping her panties up washed over her. Tugging the cord loose, she let the robe fall to the chair behind her and took hold of the hem of her nightie, never once taking her eyes from the big, flaccid penis she knew she was going to be taking in her mouth.

The nightie came up, her panties were showing, her belly, her breasts and she was topless, only her frillies guarding her sex. As she tried to place the discarded garment over her chair, she dropped it, bending automatically to pick it up, and only then realising the way in which the posture flaunted her bottom.

'You are very beautiful, if I may say so,' he remarked.

'Thank you,' she answered, her voice barely audible.

Her sex felt warm, urgent, in need of cock, to be fucked by Anderson as she deliberately humiliated herself by sucking the butler's penis. When he got back, he was sure to ask her, and when she admitted she had done it he would make her tell the whole story, in detail, probably while she was fucked on her knees, buggered even. Immediately she realised that she had to be nude.

'I . . . I'm going to take my panties off,' she croaked, even as her thumbs pushed into the waistband. 'F . . . front or back?'

'Back, please,' he answered.

Vicky turned, her head swimming with humiliation as she stuck out her bottom and began to ease the frilly panties down. She was imagining every detail of what she was exposing as it came bare, the swell of her buttocks, the crease between, the tight brown pucker of her anus, her shaved sex lips.

Her panties down, everything showing, she held still for a moment, then let them drop and stepped clear, nude. Placing her hands on her head, she made a slow turn, showing her body the way her first ever boyfriend had made her do it the night she lost her virginity. Creech, she realised, would already have been in his seventies.

'Beautiful, thank you,' Creech said.

Vicky managed a wan smile. He moved a little forwards in his chair, making his cock more easily available for her mouth. She went down to her knees, mechanically, a big part of her mind still struggling to accept what she was doing. He lifted his port glass as she shuffled forward on the ancient carpet, to between his open knees. She swallowed hard, unable to meet his gaze, her eyes still fixed to his cock. He took it, holding it out, the bulbous head already starting to emerge from within the unpleasantly meaty foreskin. Slowly, she leaned forwards, her mouth came open, and in went the cock.

An image of herself came to her as she began to suck, nude on her knees to a man nearly four times her age, cock-sucking. She closed her eyes, unable to cope with the sheer emotion of what she was doing as her tears started. Still she sucked, working her lips gently up and down the barrel of his penis as it grew slowly harder and the helmet began to poke out from the foreskin into her throat. He tasted slightly of polish, but mostly of man, old man.

He let go of his cock and began to stroke her hair, perhaps because she was crying, perhaps simply because he was stiff enough. The gesture gave her a new touch of the odd gratitude she had felt before, only to provoke fresh humiliation at the idea that it should be her, and not him who was privileged. As he had offered her the chance to keep her panties up and she had taken them down, so at his gesture of sympathy she began to put more effort into sucking him.

Taking his balls in one hand, she began to stroke them, using the other to masturbate him into her

130

mouth. He gave a low sigh, the first sign of pleasure, and the pressure of his stroking hand grew ever so slightly. She made a slide of her lips, to peel back his foreskin and take the salty, pungent cock head into her mouth, then deeper, as her mouth filled, right into her throat until she felt herself start to gag.

Abruptly she pulled back, and began to tug harder, tossing him into her mouth in the hope that he would come before the urges of her body grew too strong. She needed to masturbate, far more strongly than she had earlier, and she knew that this time there would be no difficulty in coming. If she gave in, she knew it would represent a submission deeper even than that already given, yet with every push of his now hard cock into her mouth she could feel her resistance melting.

'Easy,' Creech soothed. 'Please do not rush.'

Vicky gave a despairing sob on his cock, but slowed, letting herself enjoy the sensation of cock sucking as she always had. Already Creech's age seemed less important, but only that he was a man, with a cock to pleasure her, a cock she had in her mouth, which she was obliged to suck until he spunked. Many had done it, boys and men, enough to have given her a reputation as a thorough slut at college. Most had made her swallow, or spit the come out in front of them. Some had done it in her face or over her breasts, even in her eyes, deliberately. Only Anderson had ever made her lick what she spilled off the floor.

She gave in, the last of her always fragile inhibition snapping as her hand went to her sex. Creech gave a dry cluck as she began to masturbate, maybe of approval, maybe knowing, and took another sip of port. Vicky rubbed harder, now revelling in her humiliation, thinking of all the men she had sucked, of how bad her reputation had been, of how much it had hurt, and how much her shame had excited her. Anderson alone had understood, and now she was down on his butler's cock, sucking eagerly on his erection, nude and grovelling at his feet, stripped bare, her stupid frillies peeled down in a childishly indecent display of her bottom. He had been right, as always. It was where she belonged, cock-sucking on her knees as she masturbated, nude and uninhibited, his slut to do with as he pleased, to order as he pleased, to degrade as he pleased . . .

Her orgasm hit her, and she was sucking in desperation on Creech's cock, hard enough to make him gasp. Wave after wave of the most exquisite pleasure went through her, not only of physical sensation, but of complete mental surrender. Even at the very peak she kept sucking, and wanking at his shaft, praying for a mouthful of thick, slimy sperm to complete her utter debasement.

It never came, Creech holding his poise as her orgasm tore through her, and not even putting his port glass down. Only when she was fully done did he speak, his voice low and soothing as he continued to stroke her hair.

'I apologise for even thinking you pitied me, Victoria. Now, if you could perhaps perform that wonderful trick where you purse your lips once more?'

Vicky nodded around her mouthful of cock. All her shame and uncertainty had begun to flood back as her orgasm faded, and if it seemed ungrateful not to finish what she had begun, she wanted it to be over quickly. Once more she made a slide of her mouth and began to bob her head up and down, allowing his cock to push into the back of her throat each time. He gave a moan of pleasure, and finally put the glass down as his fingers locked in her hair.

Each time the fat cock head pushed into Vicky's throat she was gagging, but she forced herself to keep on, sure that he would soon come, and that she could cope with whatever spunk he managed to produce. Her lips were growing sore, and her sense of degradation

132

returning ever more forcefully, yet still she sucked, faster and harder, until at last his cock jerked.

Instantly her mouth filled with spunk, not the weak dribble she had expected, but a great gush, ejaculated right down her throat. She was choking at once, but he had her by the head, too lost in the pleasure of orgasm to realise. Her throat went into violent contractions, sperm exploded from her nose, she farted loudly as her whole body went into a single, hard contraction, and then she had been released.

She rocked back, panting, mixed mucus and sperm running from both nostrils, a long strand of it still joining her lower lip and his engorged cock head. It broke as she hung her head down in utter defeat, now overwhelmingly ashamed of herself for what she had done, and the pleasure she had taken in it. Yet there was no denying that pleasure. She said nothing, but let her mouth open as she hung her head. Slowly, the wad of sperm and saliva in her mouth rolled out over her lower lip, to fall onto her breasts with a wet plop.

'Thank you,' Creech sighed. 'Most enjoyable. I think you might need a cloth.'

Vicky nodded in meek acceptance as he passed her one of the cloths he had been using to clean the silver, the cleanest. She knew that if it had been Anderson she had sucked, he would have given her the dirtiest, and she managed a weak smile as she took it.

Anderson Croom rested his chin in his hand, and for perhaps the seventh or eighth time tried to take an interest in the large and lurid poster advising on the practice of safe sex. He felt distinctly uncomfortable, with his dinner jacket and black bow tie only partially concealed beneath his coat, and that in itself plainly expensive beside the clothes of the other people in the late-night clinic.

Persephone had gone in to see the nurse, leaving him feeling still more out of place, but he still found himself speculating as to whether she was having to undergo any intimate and embarrassing physical examinations. The thought of her in stirrups appealed immensely, with her evening dress pushed up around her waist, her lacy French knickers off and a speculum pushed well up her sperm-moist vagina. Possibly, he reflected, the nurse might douche her, or make her take a pessary, perhaps anally. It was an amusing thought, and he wondered if he would be able to persuade her to let him insert it, or at least watch.

He felt a stab of disappointment as she came out with nothing, and more when they had left and he told her she had simply been given a pill, and not even inspected vaginally. Refraining from making any potentially upsetting jokes, he took her arm and began to steer her back towards her flat.

Nich Mordaunt felt his eyelids begin to droop, the picture of the goat before his face shimmering slightly in the light of the desk lamp.

'I'm getting tired,' he admitted to Ysabel, who was lying face down on the bed in her favourite position.

She was naked, with her fleshy bottom decorated by six well-placed cane welts. The cane still lay on the floor, along with two plates, both stained orange from spaghetti sauce, pushed to the side to clear space. Wine bottles, one empty and another half full, stood on the desk. At one side of the room, two thick black candles had burned down to the rim of the black iron holder in which they stood. The third protruded from between Ysabel's buttocks.

'A few more questions,' Ysabel replied, 'and then we may as well call it a night.'

'OK,' Nich agreed, closing the book on goats and passing it to her. 'Fire away.'

She took the book, wriggling herself into a more comfortable position and making the candle in her bottom hole wobble.

'What,' Ysabel asked, 'is the principal distinguishing characteristic that separates goats from sheep?'

'Goats' tails go up, sheep's tails go down,' Nich answered.

'Very good. Now, which three continents are goats native to?'

'Europe, Africa and Asia,' Nich answered. 'Try something harder.'

'OK. Name the winner of the green rosette for best in show, Llanelli, July 1904.'

'Search me. Do you think he would know that?'

'Maybe; never underestimate a fanatic. After all, can you tell me where England's longest stone row is, or which symbols are associated with the god Grimm?'

'Certainly,' Nich replied, sounding slightly affronted. 'The longest row is on Dartmoor and runs from the top of Green Hill, south for some two and a half miles, to a stone circle on the Erme Plains. Grimm's stones are . . .'

'Exactly,' Ysabel interrupted. 'The answer's Valley Maid, by the way, a short-haired black nanny. Try naming me a town that produces goat's cheese.'

'Valençay in the Loire valley,' Nich replied. 'They're shaped like square volcanoes.'

'Fair enough. To what order of mammals do goats belong?'

'Artiodactyls,' Nich yawned.

'Correct.' Ysabel sighed. 'All right, I suppose that's the best we can do. Let's do the letter, then crash.'

'That was a bit close,' Persephone said as she climbed into the bed. 'I should have said, really, I know – but, well, you were such fun.'

'So were you,' Anderson answered enthusiastically. 'Wonderful, and please don't blame yourself. I had condoms in my coat pocket but, like you, I simply got carried away. You have the most beautiful b . . . body.'

She giggled as she reached out for the bedside lamp, to turn it off and leave them in darkness spared only by a dull gleam where the curtains were a trifle open. Anderson stifled a yawn, and Persephone gave a satisfied purr as she cuddled into the crook of his arm. He hugged her close and kissed her hair.

'What if it doesn't work?' she asked sleepily.

'You get pregnant,' he answered.

'You'll have to come up to Leicestershire anyway,' she said happily.

'Absolutely,' he agreed, struggling to keep a sigh from his voice.

Seven

Nich drew the Triumph to a halt at the gates of Brooke House. Their plan to secure an invitation to the estate had worked faster and more efficiently than he could have dared hope for. A letter had come back, almost by return of post, and from Sir Gerard Chealingham himself. It had been long, and mostly about goats and other livestock, but had included the crucial invitation, asking both him and Ysabel not only to come up as soon as they liked, but to stay at the house itself. They had packed what they needed, including the spider and as many books on goats as they could conveniently carry, and left the next day.

Looking up at the gates, he felt an awe more profound even than that which affected him at Stonehenge or the Grey Wethers. The columns that flanked the high gate were a history lesson in themselves. Now topped with stone pineapples standing in great urns, he knew that this typically eighteenth-century feature was in fact a new addition. In Blackman's day, a statue of the Horned God had stood on one side, that of the Earth Mother on the other; while the columns themselves had been inscribed with potent symbols, picked out in brass and polished daily. Prior to that, when the Brooke family themselves had owned the manor, the columns had been unadorned and topped with globes of stone instead of pineapples.

While the inscriptions had been removed from the columns, the gates themselves stood much as they must have done in Blackman's day. The twin faces, matching the statues, remained as the central bosses of each gate, intact except that the unfortunate Horned God had been shorn of his horns and had his beard restyled into a more acceptable shape, with no fork. Nich, who had thought the face intact as they approached down the long stretch of road that ran towards the gate, stopped to stare in horror at this sacrilegious alteration. His only comfort lay in the face of the Earth Mother, her apple-cheeked serenity having apparently been considered acceptable.

A neat brass plaque on each column now proclaimed the address as Brooke House, another notice dissuading casual visitors. NO HAWKERS OR CIRCULARS it had originally read, but the words OR CULTISTS EITHER had been added beneath in neat, black letters. A third sign stated that trespassers would be prosecuted. Nich, reasoning that he had been invited, even if it was under false pretences, allowed the bike to roll a little way forwards, and gave the gates a firm push. They swung wide, and his sense of awe grew stronger still as they entered the grounds. The drive was a ribbon of gravel running between imposing limes and curving gently to the right, with the roof of the house just visible above a screen of yew. To either side, the grounds were thick with trees, some old and largely deciduous, some part of the screening conifer wood Blackman had planted to confound visitors of prurient interest.

Visible here and there through the trees were numerous small, stone buildings. These, Nich was aware, were not the classical follies they at first appeared, but each a temple devoted to a specific merging of deities. Ignoring the urge to explore, he continued down the drive, passing through a second set of pineapple-topped columns to stand in front of the house itself. The front was instantly recognisable from photographs and pictures, a classic mid-eighteenth-century façade, unaltered since its commission by the Brooke family. The only thing out of keeping with his mental image of the place was the fountain that stood in the centre of the carriage sweep, a great basalt cup that had once been Blackman's high altar. Originally it had stood in the main hall of the house.

Nich reflected that Blackman's occupancy must certainly have left a strong resonance of magic, creating a site of power that would be permanent, regardless of what use the house was put to. It accounted for the strength of his feelings, and so strong was the haunted ambience that as he parked the bike he was half expecting Blackman himself to come through the door, white hibernal robes fluttering behind him.

The crunch of a foot on gravel shattered his reverie and Nich turned to see a handsome middle-aged woman rounding the corner of the house. Dark haired, tweed clad and buxom, with a ruddy, countryside complexion, she was as far from the spectral image of Julian Blackman as it was possible to imagine. Nonetheless, he realised, if it was not Julian Blackman himself, then it was sure to be his daughter.

'Good afternoon,' she queried, slightly defensively as she came towards them. 'Can I help you at all?'

'I'm Nich Mordaunt,' Nich supplied, quickly pulling his helmet off. 'This is my friend Ysabel. We were invited to study your goats.'

'Oh, the goat students; of course,' the woman replied, with a single sidelong glance at Ysabel's green hair. 'I do beg your pardon, only we get more than our share of uninvited visitors. Anybody would think the house was a museum. I'm Hecate Chealingham, how do you do?'

'Pleased to meet you,' Nich replied, bowing stiffly from the waist.

'Very,' Ysabel added uncertainly.

'Do come in,' Hecate continued, now openly friendly. 'If Gerard finds you he'll whisk you straight down to the goats and I'm sure you'd like to freshen up first. Did you have a good journey?'

'Yes, thank you.'

'I always think motorcycles must be dreadfully uncomfortable. I know I'd be exhausted. We've put you in the Garden Room, Nich, on the first floor at the end of the west wing, it has a bay with a quite wonderful view. Ysabel, you're in the Blue Room, next door, which looks down across the fields. We have one of the finest prospects in England, I always think.'

'I'm sure of it,' Nich replied as he was ushered into a spacious hall in which he could just recognise the contours of what had been the principal altar room. Nich paused to look around, finding no evidence of the room's past purpose. Clearly the Chealinghams had gone to considerable lengths to eradicate the physical evidence of the cult's occupancy, leaving only those things of relatively normal appearance.

'Would you care for a glass of beer?' Hecate asked as she steered them through the double doors at the far side of the hall and into a long drawing room that looked out over the fields.

Both accepted, and Nich was left for a moment to gaze out across the Leicestershire countryside. Hecate Chealingham had not been wrong in describing the view as exceptional. Brooke House stood on a ridge overlooking a shallow valley and another, lower ridge that formed the lip of a broad vale. Behind the house an area of ornamental garden sloped gently down to end abruptly at a ha-ha. Beyond was the great pentacle of thick hedges planted by Blackman, at such a low angle to Nich's vision that only the sides of the hedges and the sixteen rowan trees placed at the hedge junctures could be made out. The valley bottom was shrouded in trees,

140

the land then rising again, with a square field set directly opposite the house. In the centre of the field rose a little knoll, covered in sycamore trees and sheltering a small folly which Nich knew to be the Temple of Pan-Vaunus. Moving slowly up the field was a ponderous black animal that Nich took to be a bull of unusual bulk.

'Here's your beer,' Hecate's voice sounded from behind him. 'Beautiful, isn't it? I always feel so privileged looking out across that view. The nearest group of fields are what we call the Pentacle, although you can't really see it properly from this angle. Gerard's down there somewhere, moving the Cynosure. That's our prize bull, look, you can see him walking up the field – oh, yes, and there's Gerard, by the gate.'

Anderson Croom stood back, smiling broadly as he rubbed his chin. Vicky stood before him, looking somewhat sulky in her smart and demure maid's uniform, blue, discreetly decorated with cotton lace in cream, and about fifty years out of date. Underneath she wore seamed stockings, a thick girdle, a full bra and a pair of baggy bloomers, which he knew as he had made her dress in front of him. A lace cap and square-toed shoes completed the ensemble, while having her luxurious black hair curled up into a tight bun had added a subtle extra touch of servility.

'Excellent!' he declared. 'I can barely wait to spank you in it. In fact . . .'

'Not now!' Vicky protested. 'You'll spoil my hair, and probably my make-up . . .'

'Indeed, sir,' Creech agreed, 'we really should be on our way if we are to arrive in proper time for dinner.'

'Oh, I don't know,' he said. 'Five minutes to spank her bottom for her, another five for her to suck –'

'And half an hour for me to tidy up and redo my make-up,' Vicky cut in. 'You men don't realise how much effort girls put into our appearance for you. Well, you should, Anderson, because you're easily as vain as any women I ever met.'

'True,' Croom admitted, 'although I'd make a bet Mad Nich takes longer over his make-up. I wonder what's become of him? Sulking in his lair, no doubt!'

'Possibly, sir,' Creech answered, 'or he may have decided to bypass the riddle altogether and go to Leicestershire himself, hoping you will lead him to Mr Blackman's treasure.'

'Nonsense, Creech,' Anderson answered. 'How would a fellow like that get himself invited to a respectable country house? And from what Sephany says about her father's obsession with poachers, God help him if he's caught lurking about the grounds.'

Nich and Ysabel walked across the Brooke House formal gardens and descended the stile to the side of the ha-ha, crossing a narrow strip of turf to a gate in the outer circle of the Pentacle. Now that he was close to it, he could see that the hedges had been planted in what had originally been a single field of exceptional size and now enclosed the Pentacle as rough pasture. Reaching the gate, he was glad to note that the field he was about to cross contained nothing more threatening than a small flock of diminutive dark-brown sheep, presumably some rare breed. At the point where the two hedges ahead of him converged was a gate, beyond which the central clump of six rowan trees could be seen.

A warm front was pushing in from the west; the great, grey bank of clouds bringing the threat of rain and a breeze that was making the rowan branches shiver. The sun disappeared behind the cloudbank as they made their way across the field. A cluster of goats had formed around the gate in the hope of food. They scattered when he approached, forming a defensive group in the little grove with the Billies at the fringe.

Nich paused at the gate, amused by the goats'

reaction. Taking a notebook from his coat pocket, he flicked through the pages until he came to the description of the Pentacle as given by Frea Baum. As he had thought, the grove in the centre was dedicated to the goddess Fauna, diametrically opposed to the Temple of Pan-Vaunus on the opposite hillside and sacrilege for any man to enter. Nich wondered if the proscription included male goats, a doctrinal point on which no authority he knew of gave an opinion. Possibly, he reflected, the grove could be used to test whether Croom was or was not an initiate.

'Who the Devil are you?' a stern voice demanded.

Nich looked up from his notebook with a start, finding a solidly built man standing at the next gate along and levelling a shotgun in his direction.

'Nich Mordaunt, Ysabel O'Donnel,' he called out hastily. 'The goat students. You must be Sir Gerard Chealingham?'

The man's expression immediately relaxed, becoming a genial grin although his skin colour lost none of its redness. Nich waited as Sir Gerard came through the gate and walked across the goat field, and took his hand when it was offered.

'Sorry about that, my boy,' Sir Gerard boomed heartily. 'Thought you might be poachers. Now that I've had a closer look at you I can see you're not. Never met a poacher yet who wore black nail varnish, or one with green hair. You're students, you say?'

'Yes, sir,' Nich assured him.

'What university?' Sir Gerard demanded.

'Parkway,' Nich informed him.

'One of these newfangled jobs, eh? Polytechnics, really. Mark you, there are really only two universities, Oxford and Cambridge. Not that I could get into either of them, so that makes us even. More importantly, you're goat people, and if you want my opinion that says a lot about a fellow's character. What do you think of these beauties, then, eh?'

'Very fine indeed, Sir Gerard,' Nich replied. 'We've been reading up about the flock, as it goes. They were originally a cross between Theban blacks from the lower Nile and British black longhairs, weren't they, including I believe Valley Maid, the winner of the prize for best in show at Llanelli in 1904?'

'Good heavens, you certainly know your stuff!' Sir Gerard exclaimed. 'Good show! Well, you're very welcome to stay for a while. In fact, we're going to have something of a house party. Sephany, that's my daughter, is down in London at the moment, but she's coming up, along with her new man, a fellow by the name of Croom.'

Creech swung the Bentley around a fountain carved of basalt and shaped like an enormous cup. With dusk already falling, several of the windows of Brooke House glowed with yellow light, creating a welcoming image. The tyres crunched on the gravel as the great car came to a stop, Croom alighting immediately and extending his hand to the red-faced and white-whiskered man who stood on the lower step of the house's Grecian portico.

'Anderson Croom,' Croom introduced himself. 'You must be Sir Gerard Chealingham.'

'Humph, yes, that's me,' the man admitted. 'So you're Sephany's young man. You'll make yourself at home, of course. Be our guest, what?'

'I'd be honoured,' Croom replied as Creech began to unload the cases from the boot of the Bentley. 'This is Creech, my butler, and my maid.'

Vicky had also left the car, her expression of sulky resentment quickly changing to a smile as she curtsied to Gerard Chealingham.

'Butler, eh? Don't get many of them these days, not in private employ. Creech, eh? And a maid too. Pretty girl . . . Humph, right, fine. We've put you in the Green Room, Croom. Second floor, smack above the master bedroom. Best view of the grounds. You can see right into the Cynosure's field – he's my prize bull, a splendid animal I'm sure you'll want to see. Not now, of course, getting dark. I'll get Hecate to make a couple of rooms up for your people presently. Any preference, Creech?'

'I am not particular, sir. Anywhere on the top floor would be quite suitable.'

'Top floor, eh? I'll see what we can do. Anyway, do come in. Meet everybody. You know Sephany, of course. Hecate's down in the village, then there's a couple doing some work on the goats. Fine pedigree flock we've got, you know.'

Sir Gerard led the way into the house, passing through the front door into a hall the ceiling of which reached the level of the second floor. Opposite them splendid twin staircases rose on either side of a broad double door, curving up and back to a wide gallery at the level of the first floor. Polished wood, marble and granite created an atmosphere enhanced by two immense landscapes in gilt frames and numerous smaller portraits. Croom stopped to admire the hall as Creech melted silently upstairs, Vicky following him with a last backward glance.

'You must meet the goat people,' Sir Gerard went on. 'They're doing some work on the pedigree. It's an odd flock, you know, built up by Hecate's father. He started with two pairs of Black Thebans, apparently, brought them back from Egypt after the war. Only useful thing the fellow ever did – aside from sire Hecate. Father her, that is; or should it be beget her? You know what I mean, anyway. Barking mad, he was, old Blackman, one of these religious sorts, d'you know, not C of E; sacrifices and so forth. Anyhow, he mixed the Thebans in with some black Welsh longhairs, so I've got a unique breed; pure black, very fine. Strange, d'you know, all that mumbo-jumbo, and in the middle of it he's doing some sterling work breeding goats. Plenty of 'em, too, I've put 'em in the middle of the Pentacle.'

'The Pentacle?' Anderson asked.

'Yes, group of fields shaped like a magician's pentacle, you know, five-sided star in a circle. Some of old Blackman's nonsense, but they make fine enclosures for the beasts. Eleven little fields there are, with sixteen trees at the junctures and a little grove in the middle. Apparently the trees are a demonstration of some mathematical business called Dudeney's Conundrum, or so Hecate tells me. D'you know, most of the stock here has been pretty well pure-bred for over two hundred years?'

'No, I didn't,' Croom admitted.

'Yes, 1764, old Sir Bartholomew Brooke started his stockbooks. I'd have 'em today if the idiot I bought the house from had had the common sense to keep 'em. Anyway, the goat chap. Funny-looking fellow, but knows his goats. Strange, you know, they always shy away when he goes to look at them.'

'Really?' Croom asked as a sudden suspicion entered his mind.

'Yes, not normal for the goats, you know, they're not usually at all timid.'

'Oh,' Croom answered. 'I don't suppose he's red-haired, not quite my height, wears a lot of black?'

'That's the fellow,' Sir Gerard answered. 'D'you know each other?'

'We've met,' Croom sighed, even as Sir Gerard opened the great double doors to reveal Nich standing talking to Persephone.

Anderson Croom pulled his tie into a faultless black butterfly at his throat. The Green Room was every bit as fine as Sir Gerard had implied, making him feel thoroughly relaxed and at home. Having got over the initial shock of discovering that Nich had also managed to secure an invitation to the house, he had come to realise that it would in fact be an advantage. It was beyond doubt that Nich would have the spider concealed in his room, and if he couldn't steal it, then he was losing his touch. Careful questioning had revealed that Nich and Ysabel had been placed in rooms at the end of the west wing on the first floor.

'Tonight,' he remarked to Creech, who was setting out a selection of cufflinks on top of a chest of drawers, 'we obtain the spider, and by tomorrow we will know the location of Blackman's hoard. Then, just as soon as I've had my fill of young Persephone, we bag it, and off we go. Who knows, Hecate's a handsome woman, and she might well prove game for a warm bum and a stiff cock, maybe Nich's girlfriend as well.'

'Is that wise, sir?' Creech cautioned him. 'You will recall events at Ferndale Manor.'

'That was just bad luck, Creech. Besides, I suspect both Hecate and Ysabel of having pretty liberal morals. Persephone's hot stuff, too. None of your prissy city girl about her, good dirty country, through and through. By God, though, mother and daughter together, wouldn't that be something?'

'True, sir, but still . . .'

'Oh, don't fuss so, Creech, you're like an old mother hen sometimes. I mean to say, how can I go wrong with Sir Gerard spending most of his time with that damn bull? I imagine Hecate gets bored rigid. And besides, what did I tell you about offering advice on my sex life?'

'Very well, sir. If I might suggest the black onyx cufflinks with the crests?'

'Fair enough,' Croom replied holding out his cuffs for the links to be inserted. 'Fearsome animal though, that bull. Oh, and if you could get my new emerald-green cummerbund out. I want to cut the best possible figure tonight.'

'I have already laid out the black cummerbund, sir,' Creech said. 'Sir Gerard is something of a stickler for formalities.'

147

'Come, come, Creech, a dash of colour never hurt.'

'The black cummerbund, sir,' Creech insisted.

Creech had judged correctly. Dinner was conducted with a formality belonging to an era a hundred years past. Croom, who had been hoping that Nich would look seriously out of place, was annoyed to find him dressed in conventional evening dress. It was a less than perfect fit, and he suspected it was hired, yet he could not deny the stylish and faintly eighteenth-century air given by his red pigtail being brushed out and tied with a wide black ribbon. Black nail varnish and red enamelled cufflinks shaped like barbed, eight-pointed stars provided the sole element of eccentricity.

Sir Gerard, his own dress orthodox to the point of obsession, greeted them both with equal gruff courtesy, becoming more genial as the meal proceeded, with Creech serving. The women added colour to the table, Hecate dressed in pearl-grey, Persephone in a rich red and Ysabel in green.

It quickly occurred to Anderson that, while he dared not denounce Nich openly, he might be able to draw him into revealing his religious background and so hopefully wreck his cover as a goat expert. By the time they had reached the game course he had successfully steered the conversation onto the topic of astrology.

'Absolute nonsense, the horoscope stuff in the newspapers,' Sir Gerard was saying in challenge to Nich's cautious acceptance that the future might be predictable to an extent. 'I mean to say, if one-twelfth of the population shared the same experiences every day, you'd think we'd notice, eh?'

'Actually,' Nich replied, unable to resist the bait, 'to assess the craft of divination by astrophysical conditions at birth in terms of popular horoscopy is hardly fair. A valid comparison might be for someone to dismiss Christian art on the basis of a child's scribbled drawing

148

of God. When shown the glories of Michelangelo's Sistine Chapel, I imagine they would be forced to reconsider.'

'I take it you feel you could do better, then?' Croom tempted.

'I would like to think so,' Nich replied. 'For instance, I can say without hesitation that Sephany is a Sagittarian.'

'You're right!' Sephany exclaimed. 'Hang on, though, you must have seen my birthday cards in the stable.'

'Perhaps, or perhaps it is because you have all the principal traits of the Sagittarian. You are warm, practical, athletic, a lover of the outdoors and of animals . . .'

'Thank you Nich,' Persephone responded warmly. 'Is that really true?'

'It's certainly true of your character,' Anderson cut in quickly. 'But it proves only that Nich has had an opportunity to study you; and, of course, your birthday cards. Serious science requires a more rigorous approach. Any theory must be fitted to the observed facts. The acid test of a theory under the scientific method is whether it can be used to make predictions in an unfamiliar situation. I hardly think Nich's ideas are capable of such precision. Try, for instance, to predict my star sign.'

Nich steepled his fingers.

'Let me see. You are flamboyant, generous, rather arrogant . . . Yes, the egotist, Leo.'

'It so happens you're right,' Croom admitted. 'But that proves nothing.'

'It is also a sign that is notoriously incompatible with Sagittarius,' Nich remarked.

'You're making that up!' Anderson objected.

'What are you, Nich?' Persephone asked.

'Scorpio; very, very compatible with Sagittarius.'

'I'm not at all sure that works,' Hecate remarked. 'I also happen to be a Leo, and Sephany and I have always got along, haven't we dear?'

Persephone nodded and smiled around a mouthful of pheasant and peas.

'Yes, but it's rather different between a mother and her daughter,' Nich replied. 'There is a strong element of the divine in the relationship, transcending normal astrological considerations. Take Gaea and Demeter, for instance. In one aspect mother and daughter, in another the same goddess.'

'D'you believe in this pagan business, then?' Sir Gerard enquired.

Anderson caught the note of hostility in their host's voice and hoped that Nich would not have the sense to back down.

'Yes,' Nich answered stoutly. 'In a sense, anyway. It's not unusual these days, you know.'

'You don't go around camping on people's land without permission, do you?' Sir Gerard asked hotly. 'There's nothing worse than disrespect for another man's property.'

'Not at all,' Nich answered. 'I –'

'Humph, that's all right then,' Sir Gerard interrupted. 'We had some of those New Age Johnnies down on the big meadow a few years back. Moved in as if they owned the place. I let the Cynosure out and they soon cleared off. Touchy fellow, the Cynosure, gored a man once.'

'In general I disapprove of New Age practices,' Nich continued tactfully. 'My principal tenet is that all beliefs are inherently true, by definition. I am what is called a pantheist.'

'What a remarkable coincidence!' Hecate said brightly. 'My father was one too.'

'I'm C of E myself,' Sir Gerard declared. 'Just the one God. Much simpler, don't you know. A fellow knows where he stands, what?'

'I hardly think the Christian faith can be considered monotheistic,' Nich objected. 'I mean, the senior deity is threefold for starters, then there are various grades of angel, saints and, of course, Satan and the nether hordes. What's more, it recognises the deities of other faiths. It is in fact one of the most comprehensively polytheistic religions of all.'

'No, no, that's Catholics you're thinking of,' Sir Gerard objected as Creech filled his glass. 'Different Johnnies altogether, Catholics. No, what I really can't abide are these people who won't leave you in peace. You wouldn't believe the sorts who turn up here. We've had people coming onto the land, calling Hecate all sorts of names, just because she wouldn't follow on with her father's tommyrot. Everyone's entitled to their own opinion. Live and let live, that's what I say, so long as they don't try to force it down other people's throats.'

Croom cursed quietly to himself. Sir Gerard was proving considerably more liberal than his crusty exterior had at first suggested.

Vicky paused as she reached the bottom of the stairs from what had once been the servants' quarters of Brooke House. From downstairs she could hear the tinkle of light conversation, cutlery and glassware. The sounds put a new edge to her general feeling of resentment at being made to act as a servant, as did the scent of roast meat to her hunger.

Anderson thought it was immensely funny, both having her as maid and making her go without her dinner until she had an opportunity to dine from the scraps the others had left. Anderson had also given her the spanking he had been threatening all day, across his knee with her maid's uniform turned up onto her back and her big bloomers pulled well down. It had been done as a punishment, not for anything specific, but, as he said, to help her appreciate her role. Afterwards she had been made to suck his cock but told not to touch herself, adding sexual frustration to her woes. The final insult had been to criticise her for struggling too much while held down over his knee, and so spoiling the crease of his dress trousers.

Now she was expected to steal the spider from Nich's room, a prospect that set her stomach fluttering despite the knowledge that she was alone in the upper storeys of the house. For one thing, Nich could hardly fail to notice that it was gone. Anderson's assurances that Nich would not dare denounce them had done little to calm her nerves.

As she padded softly down the corridor she was desperately trying to find an excuse for what she was doing if caught. If it was by one of the Chealinghams, they were going to think she was a thief and the police would be called. Nich's reaction she could only speculate on, or Ysabel's. Also, she was certain that they would have anticipated her move and hidden the spider.

Sure enough, as she searched first Nich's rucksack, then Ysabel's, it was to find only clothes, books and the necessities of a visit at a strange house. She was left with her heart hammering and her fingers trembling, listening for noises and trying to think what she would have done in Nich's place.

To simply give the spider to Ysabel was too obvious, while to hide it elsewhere in the house was to risk it being found by one of the Chealinghams, or the women from the village who did the cleaning. Outside would be better, yet it would need to be accessible. With sudden determination she walked back to Nich's room and across to the bay window. The central part was a door, and there was a balcony outside, with thick ivy on the walls at either side, an ideal hiding place.

Five minutes later she was in the kitchen, eating steak and kidney pie as Creech admired Blackman's spider.

Anderson Croom swallowed the last of his port with a feeling of elation bubbling up inside him. A subtle signal from Creech at the sideboard had told him that they had secured the spider. They would now discover how the idol fitted into the puzzle, and that would be that, save for the delicious erotic prospects offered by the situation.

Most openly, there was Persephone. She had made it clear that, while her father would have disapproved of them actually sleeping together, a blind eye would be turned to discreet visits to her room at night. She was also in the east wing, well away from her parents, which would allow him to dish out the spanking he so desperately wanted to apply to her well-rounded bottom without having to worry too much about noise.

Better still, if he wasn't expected to be in her room all night, it would give him free rein to indulge himself with Vicky. There also seemed to be every possibility that Ysabel and even Hecate might prove susceptible to his charms. Certainly both had been flirting, not openly, and each in her own way, but definitely flirting. To leave the house with Blackman's cache and all four girls well fucked seemed an excellent ambition.

The only fly in the ointment was that if Ysabel clearly found him interesting, then the same was true for Persephone and Nich. She clearly found his eccentric views appealing, while he had been doing his best to ingratiate himself with her all evening, to the point where Ysabel's jealousy had begun to show.

As Creech refilled his glass he found himself considering whether it was worth giving Nich a chance with Persephone in order to improve his access to Ysabel. It stung his pride a little, but the answer was clearly yes, just as soon as Persephone had been spanked, and perhaps sodomised.

Eight

Anderson Croom slipped a dressing gown of deep blue silk over his shoulders. A gap in the curtains showed the Leicestershire countryside bathed in shadows from the irregular light of a gibbous moon coming through scattered clouds. Standing, he made his way to the door on silent feet, inched it open and peered into the corridor. Persephone had to be first, both because it made sense and because he knew he was expected. The warmth of her good-night kiss still lingered on his lips.

The windows of the main staircase opposite his room provided a faint light. Somewhere on the edge of awareness he could make out the faint noises of water in the pipes and radiators and the fainter hum of the boiler. Otherwise there was no sound at all. The far end of the corridor was sunk in absolute blackness, the end staircase leading down to the floor below invisible.

He moved quickly, his bare feet noiseless on the carpet, one arm extended to keep track of where he was in the corridor. He found the stairwell and descended quickly to the lower corridor, also dark, but with a line of pale light showing beneath the door at the end – Persephone's door. Grinning, he eased it open and slipped inside.

She was at her dressing table, sat on a low stool as she dabbed the make-up from her face. She had let her hair down, and it fell around her shoulders in a soft black cloud. Her sole garment was a simple cotton nightie, pulled tight to her buttocks in a way that made it quite clear she was bare underneath. His cock twitched beneath his robe at the sight, and he stepped quickly forwards, gathering her into his arms as she rose. She responded, full of passion as their mouths met. He slid a hand down, to cup one round, muscular bottom cheek, and with the touch he knew it would be impossible to hold back. The desire was too much. Persephone had to be spanked. As she melted into him, he was already inching her nightie up over her bottom.

Vicky shook her head in annoyance. She was sat on the bed in her tiny top-floor room. In front of her, the spider sat on the necklace, seven of the legs slotted into seven grooves, the eighth extending over one side, as if pointing. It worked exactly as they had anticipated it would, but it had brought them no nearer to their goal. The idol still didn't fit in.

Finally she had retired to her room on the top floor, taking Blackman's notebooks and the sacaralia with her for safekeeping. All now stood on the bare utility drawers in her room. Their failure to complete the puzzle was not her only reason for feeling irritable. Anderson had promised to come up to her, but told her he would be late. She was sure that meant he intended to visit Persephone first, which hurt.

A gentle tap on the door signalled the return of Creech, who had gone downstairs to retrieve what remained in the port decanter.

'Come in,' she said, and managed a wan smile as the elderly butler favoured her with a conspiratorial wink.

'The perks of service,' he said quietly, placing a half-full wine bottle and two glasses beside the idol. 'Although I fear Sir Gerard's taste in port leaves something to be desired.'

'Thank you, anyway,' she answered. 'I need a drink, I'm fed up.'

Creech poured deep-red fluid into one glass and passed it to her. Wanting to talk, Vicky let her feelings spill over as she took it.

'I mean, I'm not the possessive sort, and I try not to mind, but I really think he might at least have come to me first!'

'Mr Croom can be somewhat cavalier, it is true,' Creech responded, 'but, to be fair, there is at least no hypocrisy in his attitude.'

'True,' Vicky sighed.

He didn't answer, concentrating on the port he had poured himself. Vicky took a swallow of her own, trying not to think of Persephone in Anderson's arms. It didn't work, but after a moment the picture changed to Persephone over Anderson's knee, struggling in the full pain and shock of a hard and unexpected spanking. When they had met briefly, Persephone had treated her as if she didn't exist. She smiled.

'A penny for your thoughts,' Creech remarked as he lowered himself into the ancient wooden rocking chair that was the room's only seat.

'I was imagining that bitch Persephone getting her big arse smacked,' Vicky replied. 'She blanked me completely! How do you put up with it all the time? I mean, you're what, seventy-nine, and you said yourself you've managed to put a fair bit aside. Why don't you retire? Then you wouldn't have to be spoken down to all the time, and ordered around.'

'I think you will find that the same would be true in most walks of life,' he answered, 'certainly those that were open to me as a young man. As to why I haven't retired, I enjoy working for Mr Croom enormously, and there are certain perks.'

'Yes, there are, aren't there?' Vicky answered, blushing as she remembered how it had felt to strip and take his cock into her mouth, both the first time and the Sunday following.

The second time she had held back from masturbating, and the long sex session with Anderson that had followed had been one of the best, culminating in an exquisite mutual orgasm as he buggered her well-smacked bottom. Now he was with Persephone.

'Do you suppose she'll squeal much?' she asked.

'Like a pig, I would imagine,' Creech answered, and smiled.

Vicky laughed, began to speak, hesitated, then said what had come into her mind.

'Come on, get out your cock and I'll give you a nice slow suck.'

Persephone allowed herself to the steered gently towards the bed. She was ready for sex, her body responding to the slow build-up of her anticipation. Her nipples were hard, her skin sensitive, her pussy urgent. All evening she had revelled in the attention of Anderson, and of Nich too, until her head was full of romantic fantasies of them duelling over her, and rather less romantic ones of them sharing her between them.

Anderson held her easily, so strong she was sure she would not have been able to break free if she wanted to. It was perfect, his unashamed masculinity and refinement an ideal balance, allowing her to feel completely feminine yet also to retain her self-respect.

He had her close, her nightie held up over her bottom, allowing the cool air to touch her cheeks and brining her a delicious feeling of naughtiness. One hand was stroking the small of her back, the other the nape of her neck, to send thrills up and down her spine. His cock was pressed to her belly, a hard, hot lump. They reached the bed, his kisses grew more urgent still, then broke. He sat, pulling her after him, only not onto his lap, but over it.

Persephone squealed as she went bum up, taken totally unawares. He had her by the neck, and forced her head low, even as one knee kicked up, to lift her bottom. A leg, lean and powerful, twisted around her own and she was splayed open, the cool air now on the naked rear of her sex and her anus rather than simply her bottom cheeks. She giggled in shock and puzzlement, then shut up abruptly as her face was pushed firmly into the bedclothes. A very large and very hard hand pressed to the crest of her bum cheeks, and she realised that she was about to be spanked. She tried to protest, a muffled squeak, half nervous humour, half real. Croom simply chuckled and gave her bottom a squeeze, then spoke.

'This, my dear, is the way the lady rides!'

She gave an indignant grunt, but she had already decided to let him do it. It felt good to be in his grip, for all the humiliation of having her sex and bottom hole on such blatant display. She knew that she had no escape anyway, and was wondering how it felt to be spanked by a man.. Then his hand had cracked down across her naked bottom and she realised just what a stupid decision it was.

It hurt crazily, a great, bruising wallop, hard enough to knock the breath from her lungs and make her legs jerk in his grip. He laughed at her response, and curiosity and her very sexual shame were replaced by shock and a furious indignation. The instant she was over the initial pain she lurched to the side, only to have his leg tighten on hers and her face forced so hard into the bed she could no longer breathe.

'Splendid!' he crowed. 'I knew you'd be a fighter!'

He didn't even pause. The second slap caught her bottom, up under her cheeks as they wobbled to her frantic struggles, a third, and the spanking had begun in earnest. She began to writhe, her whole body jerking to the stinging smacks, her free thigh kicking spasmodically, her arms snatching at him and at the bedclothes. He merely laughed, and louder as her struggles grew more frantic, bringing her humiliation and her horrible sense of helplessness up with her pain. She tried to lift her head, to scream for her mother, to shout him down, anything, but again and again her face was pushed into the covers. Finally it stopped, and he spoke.

'No squealing, darling, or your panties go in your mouth, and I'll just hold your nose if you try to keep them out. Got that?'

She gave a miserable nod, but as the spanking began again her face had been pushed into the covers anyway. As the last shred of her reserve broke, she burst into tears. For one instant she was allowed to catch her breath, her head lifted by the neck, then her face was back in the covers.

'There, there,' Anderson said happily, still spanking away, 'don't take on so. Your cunt will soon be as warm as your bum, and you'll see it's for the best.'

Persephone fought harder still at his words, her thighs and arms pumping. Anderson merely tightened his grip. The spanking never stopped, the slaps of hand on bum flesh ringing out around the room with his laughter. The dreadful stinging grew hotter, hotter still, and, just as he had predicted, her sex began to grow warm and urgent.

New, raging humiliation hit her, stronger by far than what she had felt before, at the realisation that his appalling behaviour was turning her on. It was impossible, the very idea that such a hideously undignified thing could be done to her and it would make her excited. Yet it was happening, the need for a stiff cock in her vagina soaring as she was punished, and not just any cock, but his, the man who had given her the spanking.

Still she fought, determined not to give in, determined to hold back her feelings no matter how strong. Still Croom spanked, now singing This is the Way the Ladies Ride in a soft baritone as her bottom danced and jiggled to the smacks. Her pain began to fade, replaced by a warm, urgent feeling, making her smacked bum the centre of everything. It felt hot and big, her anus sensitive, her sex yet more so. She began to shake her head, now fighting not to escape, but to hold her feelings down. It made no difference. She gave one last, desperate lurch, but he held her easily, and she realised it was going to happen, and she was going to let it.

As if reading her mind, he stopped. Persephone's head was released. She came up snivelling, blind with tears, her mouth full of spittle and mucus. Her bottom was a huge, glowing ball behind her, and as he changed his grip, all she could do was let out a broken sob.

She was turned, turned over onto the bed, her thighs rolled up and open. With her sex spread, he mounted her. His cock found her vagina. In it went, filling her with shameful ease, her passage as creamy and open as it had ever been. Taking her firmly under her shoulders, he began to fuck her.

Vicky mouthed eagerly on Creech's cock. She was on her knees, her dress off, her bra up, her bloomers down, boobs and bum pulled out in a rude show which had helped him come to erection with a speed that belied his years. He was still dressed, his suit immaculate save for the unbuttoned fly, bringing the exposure of his cock and balls into sharp, and extremely rude, contrast.

She had taken her time, letting her own feelings build so that she could cope with what she had decided to do. He had been patient, watching her striptease as he stroked his cock and sipped port. She had little idea of what to do, but had played peek-a-boo with her boobs and bum before baring them properly, from a memory of some ancient documentary on striptease.

It had worked, and by the time she had gone down on his cock, he had already been hard. There had still been a jolt of shame as she took him in her mouth, but less than before. She had realised that the idea of being on her knees to suck an old man's cock was becoming familiar, and with that she had abandoned the last of her self-respect and begun to put all her skill into the task.

Now he was getting near to orgasm, and her own need was rising. She let her hand slip down between her thighs, to find the warm, urgent crease of her sex. She began to fiddle with herself, teasing and trying not to think about Anderson. It didn't work. For all the pleasure she was taking in sucking on the butler's cock, the nagging certainty that it was exactly what he would have expected of her would not go away. Soon he would have come in her mouth, she would have swallowed and rubbed herself off. When she told Anderson, he would laugh. Still she masturbated, only to stop at the memory of something he had said. She pulled back from his cock.

'You ... I mean,' she managed. 'That is ... Mrs Croom, Anderson's mum, she used to do this, didn't she?'

'And his grandmother before,' he replied. 'I will never forget the way she blushed as she told me to get ready for her.'

'Just sucking, yes?'

'Yes, more would not have been suitable.'

'Is that what you think, or what they said?'

'It is what was implied. Personally, I have always been happy to accept whatever the family's ... shall we say "tastes"? What the family's taste's allow.'

'Perversions would be better. Do ... do you want to fuck me?'

'That would be very generous, Victoria.'

'No, it would be nice. You've got a lovely cock, big and smooth. I want it in me.'

'Be my guest.'

'I will. Shall I go on your lap?'

'That would seem sensible.'

She was giggling as she rose, and blushing. It didn't stop her turning to present him with her bare bottom, or from taking his cock in hand and guiding it to the mouth of her sex as she settled into his lap. His hands found her breasts even as she was entered, and she quickly sat down, easing herself onto his erection. She moaned as her vagina filled with cock, a response compounded of ecstasy and a little shame.

Creech had begun to caress her breasts as she started to fuck herself, bouncing in his lap to make the chair rock and move his penis inside her. Soon she was wriggling her bottom and pushing back to take his cock as deep as she could and to rub her buttocks against the coarse weave of his suit. It felt glorious, and she became ruder as her inhibitions fled and her pleasure rose up. First she clutched her hands to his, over her breasts, encouraging him to feel them. Then she reached back, to spread her bottom cheeks and let the cool air to her anus. Lastly, she put her hands to her sex and began to masturbate as they fucked.

The instant she touched her clitoris she knew she would be there in moments. It felt so rude, so improper, to be mounted on the butler's cock, his hands on her boobs, her bumhole showing behind. He was going to come too, his cock jerking inside her, his fingers tight on her nipples. It happened, and as her sex filled with sperm she began to come herself, wriggling her bottom on the hard shaft inside her and rubbing hard at her clit.

As she came, she was thinking of Anderson, and how outraged he would be at her behaviour, her deliberate disobedience, when he had sought to humiliate her and she had gone far beyond his expectations. As she rode her orgasm she was smiling, and as she came down she determined to tell him when he had his own cock deep in the same hole now full of Creech's.

Finished, she settled back with a sigh, leaning her weight into his body, to make the chair rock backwards.

A sudden crash brought her quickly to her senses. Twisting around, she found that the top of the rocking chair had knocked the jade idol off the chest of drawers. It lay on the ground, apparently undamaged, except for the base, which had split in two, revealing a hollow interior and a piece of folded cloth.

Anderson slipped quietly from Persephone's room. His mouth was set in a manic grin he was having considerable trouble controlling, while it took a conscious effort not to laugh. Within the room, she gave a low groan and he had shut the door.

Following her spanking, there had been no resistance at all. He had fucked her, on her back and on her knees, and only his inability to hold himself back from orgasm had prevented him from buggering her, a treat he intended to indulge himself in anyway. She had taken it panting and grunting, her resentment dissolving as soon as she was well filled with cock, only to return after she had come, masturbating in the sperm he had ejected over her belly and pubic bush. Yet for all her tears, she had clung onto him when he said he ought to leave.

A few swift steps took him to the base of the staircase that connected the floors of the east wing when there was a faint burst of light at the far end of the corridor. He pulled himself quickly into the dark mouth of the stairwell. The light had been extinguished an instant later but a soft orange glow that sent shadows leaping on the walls at the end of the passage remained, the light of a torch muffled in cloth. Then it had vanished up the symmetrical staircase of the west wing.

Frowning, he moved quickly up the stairs, reaching the top in time to peer out and find the light moving slowly down the long corridor of the second floor, towards him, or rather, he suspected, towards his room. Sure enough, the light stopped outside his door and swung round, revealing a faint silhouette, black on black shadow. Even in the near total darkness it was apparent that the figure was shorter than he had expected, and possessed more curves. It was not Nich Mordaunt, but Ysabel O'Donnel. His frown changed back to a smile.

Vicky smoothed the folded sheet they had found in the base of the idol out on the top of the chest of drawers. It was leather, a whole skin, small, perhaps from a new-born goat, deep-grey in colour, and marked with silver lines and symbols. The lines marked the boundaries of the estate, the symbols the various temples in the grounds and the house itself. Further symbols showed around the edges, in the same transposition cipher Anderson had worked out from Blackman's notebooks.

'A map, clearly,' Creech remarked.

'Not a map, the map,' Vicky answered, and reached for the spider. 'Now I realise what Blackman meant by placing the thorax over the cup. There is no cup on the necklace. He meant that huge bowl-shaped thing at the front of the house.'

She took the necklace, placing it on the map. A hole beneath the spider's raised thorax allowed detail to show through, and she carefully positioned it over the blank rectangle that marked the carriage sweep in front of the house. She made a face. None of the swirling patterns of the necklace fitted the map, although in places they looked as if they should, as before.

'I suggest you turn the spider, Miss Victoria,' Creech suggested.

Vicky complied, watching the eighth leg as it described an arc, which quickly reached the edge of the map.

'Note,' Creech went on, 'how the circle runs. A large arc to the north of the house lies outside the grounds, with a little bit not even on the map. Then to the east and west the arcs are either in woodland or open fields, and again not always on the estate. The map is not accurate enough to pinpoint an exact spot in a field or wood. To the south, however, the arc crosses the hillside opposite the house, all of which is estate land. Here, where the arc crosses an imaginary line running due south we find a symbol.'

'A temple,' Vicky agreed. Creech reached for the notebooks.

Standing pensively in the corridor, Croom wondered what he should do.

Ysabel had gone into his room, and she had not come back out. Possibly she was there in the hope of an erotic encounter. Possibly she had come to try and steal Blackman's sacaralia. In either case, there had been an unexpected grace about her movements, which combined with his memory of her voluptuous curves to set up a familiar ache in his groin.

It was hard to judge how she would react, but he felt confident that if she was burgling his room, he would be able to dish out a spanking to put all other spankings to shame. He would get away with it, he was sure, the threat of calling the police surely enough to buy her silence despite her hot bottom. There would be shock, and outrage, maybe tears, all the things that made unexpected spankings the most satisfying. On the other hand, she might be hoping for sex, in which case he could afford to spank her and fuck her too, as he had Persephone.

He found his lips suddenly dry. The memory of her the way Ysabel's big breasts had quivered beneath the green velvet of her dress at dinner had risen up, and his cock with it. A dozen paces took him to the door; a deft twist of the handle and he was through, ready to show anger, or delight, as the occasion demanded.

Ysabel stood at her window, watching the moon, her back to him, with her green hair falling to the hollow of her back, a thin nightie hinting at the plump hemi-spheres of her bottom

'Anderson Croom,' she said softly as she half turned, neither evincing surprise nor making any attempt to conceal her breasts.

She gave her shoulders a supple shrug. Her nightie fell away, the neck catching for one instant on a long and very erect nipple, then down, to leave her nude. Croom gulped, unable to find words but knowing that rejection was the last thing on her mind. She came towards him, to take his hand and kiss him gently on the forehead.

'You'd like to make love to me, wouldn't you?' she asked in a voice of silk on silk.

'Yes,' Anderson managed.

'That's so sweet, and I'd like it too, but there's just one thing . . .'

'Anything.'

'Nich tells me you like to dish out spankings, whether the girl likes it or not?'

'What a thing to say! As if . . .'

'Uh, uh, I know you do, Anderson, and believe me, there is nothing I would like better, really hard . . . so I cry . . .'

Croom swallowed hard.

'My pleasure,' he growled, and made a grab for her.

She danced back, giggling.

'Not here, silly! Sir Gerard is directly beneath us! I want you to hurt me, Anderson, I want you to take me far beyond the point where I can keep quiet . . .'

'I'll gag you,' he offered, 'now come here, you little tart!'

'No! Come downstairs with me. I'm right at the end of the west wing, we can do it there.'

'What about Nich? He'll be next door, and it's not that far down to the master bedroom. I had to shut P . . . I mean, I'll have to gag you anyway.'

'Fine, but don't worry about Nich. We're friends, and lovers, sometimes, but we pagans don't think the way

166

you do, or at least, not Nich, any more than you do. Anyway, I want you. You're not scared of him, are you?'

'No, not at all.'

'Good, then come with me. Oh, one other thing – let me see your ring.'

Croom held up his signet ring. Ysabel inspected it carefully in the moonlight and then turned on her torch. He waited, puzzled.

'Nich was right, your ward sign is a green man. It's perfect, the corn and the wild wood. Mine is for Demeter.'

'Sorry?' Anderson asked.

'Come on, Anderson, you needn't pretend to be innocent with me. You know full well what a green man is.'

'Of course I do,' Anderson replied. 'It's my family crest, and has been for centuries. That doesn't make it a ward sign, whatever that is.'

'Please don't play me for an idiot, Anderson,' Ysabel asked, genuinely pleading. 'Not if you want to punish me.'

'I might just punish you anyway,' he answered, reaching out to take her firmly by the wrist.

'Just say you believe,' she answered.

Anderson hesitated, but she had come close, and he could feel the heat of her breasts against his chest and smelled the scent of her skin. Under the hand on her waist he could feel her too, warm and smooth, the curve from tiny waist to broad hip intensely female.

'I do now,' he said.

'I'll kill him!' Vicky snapped, glancing at her watch.

'Possibly he has fallen asleep?' Creech suggested. 'He was somewhat intoxicated.'

'He'd better not have! Still, at least that means he hasn't fucked Persephone ... I'm going down. I can show him the map too.'

'As you please. I intend to retire, so perhaps you should take everything down?'

'Sure.'

She quickly began to push the artefacts into their leather holdall, until she got to the map. For a moment she hesitated, then, deciding to torment Anderson, she tucked it well down into the bodice of her uniform.

Nich grinned as he peered into the near blackness of the corridor. Anderson Croom had led Ysabel into her room, shutting the door behind them. It had worked, giving him a free run at Croom's room. Moving quickly, he ascended the connecting stair, only to stop dead as he reached the corridor. A slender figure was walking down the passage toward him, female, fully dressed. Too tall to be either Persephone or Hecate, and obviously not Ysabel, it could only be Anderson Croom's maid. Clearly Croom's definition of service extended beyond mere housework.

Standing stock still, Nich watched as the girl came to Croom's door and pushed it open. For a moment she was in moonlight, and he realised that she was carrying a case of some sort, also something that glinted a waxy green as she turned – the idol.

'Strip,' Croom ordered as he sat down on Ysabel's bed.

Ysabel hurried to turn the bedside light on, then went to the middle of the floor. She was trembling as she took her nightie in her hands and lifted it, exposing her plump thighs, the yet plumper bulge of her pubic mound, her broad hips, her tiny waist and lastly the fat globes of her breasts.

'Delightful,' he remarked, casually pulling his cock from the gap in his robe. 'A right little butterball, aren't you? Fat, but firm. Do you have any stockings? Tights, perhaps?

'Tights, yes.'

'Fetch. Three pairs.'

'Three?'

His answer was a powerful slap to her bare bottom. She squeaked and jumped, clutching at her cheek against the sudden pain. With her arousal sky-rocketing at the way he was treating her, she scampered to her rucksack. There was a three-pack of thick blue tights at the bottom, and she passed it to him.

'And your dirty ones,' he demanded. 'Do you wear knickers under them?'

'Yes, of course . . .'

'Then your dirty knickers too.'

'My dirty knickers?'

'Do as you are told.'

'Anderson?' Vicky queried as the door opened. 'Where have . . . Nich! What do you think you're doing here?'

'I had come in the hope or retrieving my property,' Nich answered coldly. 'A large iron spider, which I believe you took from the ivy outside my room during dinner.'

'I did not . . .' Vicky began indignantly, and stopped as she realised that the spider was visible inside large the leather wallet she had borrowed from Creech. Nich raised his eyebrows.

'OK, I did,' she admitted. 'I . . . I don't know. Oh, bollocks, it's just a joke, isn't it?'

'Don't worry. It would be entirely against my principles to report the theft. So what brings you here? You are Croom's lover, as well as his maid?'

'Yes . . . no,' she answered. 'I'm not his maid at all. I'm his girlfriend.'

'His girlfriend? An open relationship, I take it?'

'No! Yes, sort of. Not that it has anything to do with you!'

'Perhaps not, yet considering he is currently in bed with my own girlfriend . . .'

'In bed with Ysabel? I thought he was with Persephone?'

'No, Ysabel. May I suggest we follow their example?'

'You cheeky little shit!'

Ysabel shut her eyes as she was hauled roughly across Croom's lap. She was stark-naked, and helpless. Her wrists were bound with one pair of tights, her ankles with another. Both had been clean pairs. The dirty ones were in her mouth, stuffed in once she was securely tied, with Croom holding her nose until she was forced to gape. Her dirty panties had then been pulled down over her head, adding the scent of her sex to the taste, along with a hint of stale sweat.

Her whole body was shaking in response to the firm, casual way he had handled her, bringing out all her deepest fantasies of punishment and atonement. She was scared, yet she had never felt more ready, both for spanking and the fucking that would inevitably follow.

'My, but you've no shortage of meat,' Croom remarked as he began top stroke her bottom. 'I do adore fat-bottomed girls!'

He laid in, not hard, but really enjoying himself with her bottom, spanking her with a playful intimacy that made her feel more helpless than ever. He had her, bound and gagged, and could use her as his sex toy, to spank, hard or soft, to grope, to explore, to fuck, as he pleased. Immediately she was sticking her bottom up for more, and to make her big cheeks pull apart for a show of her anus.

'Eager, eh?' he chuckled. 'Well, how about that dirty little hole of yours? Both of them, maybe.'

The spanking stopped. Fingers moved down between her bottom cheeks, to her vagina and anus. He began to tickle her, and to laugh as she began to wriggle in helpless reaction. Two fingers slid up into her sex. He spat, the warm gobbet of saliva catching her anus, where it was rubbed in and her hole quickly penetrated.

A second finger forced her bottom hole, his smallest, and together they slid up, until she was being gripped between her cunt and anus.

'So,' he said, 'what would a Satanist do with a fat little thing like you? Roast her and eat her? Perhaps, but it's really too soon after dinner for that. Whip her? Undoubtedly, and I'll see to that soon. Fuck her and leave her pregnant? Maybe, but no. One just can't afford to go leave brats all over the country nowadays. Hmm, what would you remember . . . what would stick in your mind?'

Nich eased his cock into Vicky's sex. With the warmth of her flesh surrounding his penis, he was feeling thoroughly pleased with himself, not merely because his cock was hilt-deep in such a beautiful girl, but because she was Anderson Croom's girlfriend.

She took it well, holding her legs up for him by her lowered bloomers and sighing gently as he moved inside her, clearly in no more of a rush than he was. Possibly, he considered, she actually wanted Croom to catch them. It was an amusing idea, but not one in which he could afford to indulge.

Pulling out, he took her by the hips, turning her. She responded, going with the pressure, to turn up her bottom, a pert ball beneath the uniform skirt. She wiggled as he turned her skirt up to expose her, and pulled her back in tight to make her cheeks spread and leave both the pouted purse of her sex and her tightly dimpled anus available. Grinning more broadly than ever, he slid his cock back into her. She purred as he began to fuck once more, now faster, with the full intention of taking himself within a moment of orgasm and then coming over her lovely bottom.

Ysabel's body jerked in pain as the stick lashed down on her unprotected bottom. Anderson had taken it from the large Swiss cheese plant that grew in a pot in one corner, as the only thing suitable to beat her with.

The thrashing had been everything thing she had imagined in her darkest fantasies, and more. Her whole bottom was a mass of ridges and welts, many laid across one another, to a total of which she had long lost count. It stung crazily, but she was past caring, simply twitching in her bonds to each cut as he laid into her. He was laughing maniacally as he thrashed her. Her sex ached, in desperate need of cock, with the bed beneath her soggy with her juice and the sweat now trickling freely from her whipped bottom.

Anderson had begun to masturbate, tugging at his cock as he beat her, until now it was fully erect, jutting from his hand. She had watched it grow through one tear-stained eye, the other covered by her dirty panties, all the while thinking of how it would feel in her when the whipping was over, a thought intruding between each agonising cut of the bamboo. Now he was ready, and as he finally hurled the bamboo down she knew the big cock was going into her body.

He wasted no time, climbing onto the bed and straddling her body. His hands took her hips, lifting her, and sending stinging pain from her cane cuts as displaced sweat trickled into them. His cock settled between her cheeks as her bottom came up, then pushed between them to the mouth of her sex, a little way in, out, and to her anus.

'One up the bum, no harm done, eh?' he chortled.

Consternation flared in her head as she realised she was to be buggered. She squeaked and wriggled, trying to get her sex to his cock head, and clamp her anus shut at the same time. He pushed, grunting with effort. Her teeth gritted against the stabbing pain as her anus pushed in.

'Damn, but you're tight!' he swore. 'Doesn't Nich ever bugger you? He must be a bigger fool than I thought, if not, with that arse to play with!'

He dismounted, leaving Ysabel panting and sobbing on the bed. Her anus hurt, bruised from the attempted buggery, but deep down a need was rising, for sodomy as the final degradation of the punishment she had wanted. It was right for her, she knew, ideal that the man who had beaten her so hard should take his pleasure up her bottom. She gave in, her hips lifting even as he mounted her again, sitting himself across her bound legs. Her cheeks were hauled apart, something hard pressed to her anus, and in. A cold, squashy sensation hit her as whatever he had was squeezed up her hole and around the mouth, and then it had begun to burn.

'Your toothpaste,' he explained, as her eyes went wide in shock and pain. 'Damn painful on the old cock too, so no whining.'

He finished with a sigh of pure satisfaction, wiped his hand on her bottom and pressed his cock to her anus once more. This time she had no choice, the burning pain in her anus making it impossible to clench had she wanted to. His cock head pushed in, her fiery ring spreading to it even as the toothpaste he had wiped on her cane welts began to burn, and he was up, his helmet wedged firmly in her bottom.

With grunts and exclamations of pain, he buggered her, forcing his cock inch by inch up into her rectum, until she felt bloated and out of control. With the full fat length of his penis up her back passage, he began to thrust, his belly rubbing on her whipped bottom, and every push squashing her bulging bladder until she was sure she would wet herself. She could do nothing, only lie there with her muscles giving little involuntary jerks as she was sodomised, her pain and degradation boiling in her head.

For a long while he buggered her, Ysabel on the edge of consciousness, not knowing if she would faint, or come from the way her sex was being rubbed on the bed

173

covers. Again and again she thought he would spunk in her as his pushes became urgent, but always he stopped, sighing deeply as he brought himself back under control. Again and again she came within an ace of wetting herself, only holding back at the last second. Several times he drew out, only to penetrate her burning anus once more, or to squirt fresh toothpaste into the gaping hole. Her bowels felt bloated, and it had begun to ooze out over her sex, adding to her woes. Twice he stuffed his cock briefly up her cunt, bringing her pain higher still, and her reaction that much closer to orgasm. Once more and she would come, she was sure of it, but when his cock left her anus one more time, he climbed off her bottom.

His weight moved on the bed. The panties were peeled up over her face, to reveal his cock, still half stiff, just inches away.

'Suck it,' he ordered, fumbling the soggy tights from her mouth.

For a moment her eyes locked in horror on the mess of toothpaste and slime on his penis, then they had shut, her mouth had come open and his cock had gone in. The mingled tastes of mint and her own bottom filled her head. He took his shaft, wanking furiously into her mouth as she sucked, and then he had come. The first eruption went down her throat, the second full in her face as he pulled free. The third was in her mouth again as he pushed his erection back between her sperm-stained lips, and deep in. She sucked, lost in a haze of pain and humiliation as she cleaned him. He kept his cock in until she had made a thorough job of it, then pulled back.

'Not bad at all,' he remarked. 'Eager little slut, aren't you?'

'Yes,' she gasped. 'Now make me come, use me . . . hurt me . . . whip me while you frig me . . .'

'Sorry, old thing,' he answered. 'My girlfriend will be waiting for me.'

He rose, pulling his robe across his body.

'No!' Ysabel squealed. 'I need to come! Please!'

'Sorry.'

'Don't be such a bastard! At least untie me, so I can do it.'

'I dare say Nich will see to your cunt,' he answered, 'once he's got bored of trying to burgle me.'

'I need to pee too!' she wailed.

He merely chuckled and made for the door, only to stop as his hand found the knob.

'Oh, the gag,' he remarked. 'Mustn't forget that, must we?'

He moved back, to pick up her dirty panties and tights.

'Open wide,' he instructed, 'or do I have to hold your nose?'

'I'll take it,' she gasped, 'but I need to come!'

'Fair enough,' he said. 'Gag in, and I'll rub your cunt for you, I promise.'

Ysabel opened her mouth, realising he had only been teasing as her panties were pushed in and her tights wrapped around her head. As the knot was tied off he spoke again.

'Sorry, but that last remark was a lie. Nightie-night.'

Vicky gasped in ecstasy as Nich's tongue found her clitoris. She lay on her back, her sperm-smeared bottom wriggling into Anderson's bed, her thighs high and wide. Nich had come all over her bottom, leaving her high but unsatisfied.

He had obliged her before she had a chance to ask, flipping her back over and burying his face in her sex. Now her orgasm was approaching, and she was caressing her breasts through her uniform as she was licked, lost to everything but the pleasure of her body. She moaned aloud as it started, clutching at her breasts. Her back arched, her sex went tight and she was there, purring and squirming herself into his face in a long, delicious orgasm, her eyes shut and her mouth wide in sheer bliss.

It stopped, suddenly.

'More!' she demanded, pushing her sex up.

The only answer was a thump as Nich rolled from the bed. She opened her eyes, to find him already at the door, the leather satchel in which she had the idol, necklace, spider and notebooks in his hand.

Anderson slipped quietly from Ysabel's room, ignoring both her desperate squirming and the mewling noises she was making through her gag. Nich, he was sure, would still be searching his room, given that there was nothing there and plenty of hiding places.

For a moment he considered a confrontation, only to abandon the idea. It served no purpose, it seemed unlikely that Nich would take anything other than Blackman's sacaralia and the books, while Creech had everything of real value. It was clearly a better idea to go upstairs to Vicky, and while his cock was somewhat sore and his balls ached, he felt confident of doing justice to her in due time.

Striding rapidly back down the corridor, he paid a brief visit to the loo, then ran light-footed up the main staircase. A smaller stair led to the top floor, and he quickly reached her room, pushing inside to find the interior bathed in dim moonlight, and empty.

Assuming she had also needed the loo, he sat down on the bed to wait, wondering how best to make use of her. Time passed, somewhere in the house a clock struck a quarter-hour, then one o'clock. Puzzled, he got up once more.

Ysabel squirmed in her bonds. Her bottom hole felt loose and sore, and she was sure that if she didn't get free, or Nich didn't come in to her soon, she was going to have a nasty accident. There was also an alarmingly full sensation in her bladder, and it was rapidly getting worse as the evening's wine worked through her body.

In utter desperation, she squirmed around until her bottom was over the edge of the bed, sticking it out so that she would only pee on the floor. Just the thought filled her with agonising shame, which grew worse with the pain in her bladder, with her hope of Nich's return the only thing that kept her holding it.

At last she heard stealthy footsteps in the corridor outside. Relief surged through her, only to die as they passed. What could only be Nich's door shut with a click. The pain in her bladder grew suddenly worse, her eyes popped wide and it had happened, urine spurting from her quim, backwards, to patter into the floor as her eyes shut in unbearable shame.

She didn't even try to stop, but let it come, despite the hot pain where it was running down over her lower bottom cheek and the cane welts Croom had given her. The smell was thick in the air, adding to her misery, but as the tears began to roll down her face she knew only too well that the moment she was released her fingers would be at her sex. When she came her mind would be focused on one man – Anderson Croom.

As the last of the pee trickled down over her bottom cheek, the door opened. Nich spoke.

'I've got it!' he declared. 'Not just the notebooks, either, the . . . What happened to you?'

'She went to look for you, sir,' Creech stated, his lined face moving in the effort of hiding a yawn. 'We had . . .'

'There you are!' Vicky spoke as she entered the passage behind them.

'Where have you been?' Anderson demanded.

'Having sex with Mad Nich, if you must know,' she answered hotly, 'and before you have a go at me, remember that you've just fucked Ysabel as well as that stuck-up bitch, Persephone.'

177

'You mean you fucked Mad Nich?'

'You say I can do as I like!' she retorted.

'Yes, but Mad Nich!'

'He was rather good, actually, but he took the idol and stuff . . .'

'You're joking!'

'No, but –'

'Hell!' Croom swore. 'What did you think you were doing, Vicky? I suppose you let him tie you up or something? Honestly, of all . . .'

'No, he made me come, then pinched the stuff while I was still high. I said he was good.'

'I don't care if he was Adonis and Rudolf Valentino and the Marquis de Sade all rolled into one, now he's got Blackman's stuff! You stupid slut!'

'It doesn't matter, anyway,' Vicky answered bitterly. 'Creech and I worked it out. The cache is hidden in something called the Temple of Pan-Vaunus.'

'It is? Excellent! Why didn't you say so?'

'Unfortunately, sir, the temple is located at the exact centre of the bull's field,' Creech added.

Nine

Ysabel yawned behind her hand as she helped herself to bacon from a silver-lidded platter. Only Sir Gerard and Hecate were at table, and both had greeted her with cheerful smiles, to her relief after the events of the night. She added eggs and toast to her plate, poured herself a black coffee and went to sit down, lowering herself carefully onto her tender bottom.

'How are you two doing with the goats?' Sir Gerard addressed Ysabel as he handed the butter to her.

'Very well, thank you,' she answered, trying desperately to remember the details of the story she and Nich had agreed on. 'We're getting there. Of course, we'll have to get over to Egypt before we can get anything worthwhile on the comparative anatomy front.'

'My father was in Egypt during the war,' Hecate replied. 'With Monty in the desert, but, of course, you'd know that because of the goats.'

'You, father seems to have had some unusual beliefs,' Ysabel said carefully, judging it a safe question given the all too obvious plethora of temples and other relics of the cult that littered the grounds, also a good way to get off the subject of goats.

'He was an extraordinary man,' Hecate answered her, 'but very private in his way. I was only nineteen when he died, you know, and I spent a lot of my time away at school. I never really feel that I knew him.'

'Oh?' Ysabel prompted.

'Yes, I suppose it's sad, really,' Hecate continued. 'And when I was home the house was so full of people that there was never a moment's peace. He had nearly two hundred people living here at one time, you know, and then there were the rituals.'

'Rituals?'

'Oh, yes, and I had to attend them all. There was the ritual of the dawn and the ritual of dusk; the rituals of noon and midnight; moonrise ritual and moonset ritual; and those were just on a normal day. I really got frightfully bored by it all.'

'Load of nonsense,' Sir Gerard put in around a mouthful of kipper.

'When Daddy died the estate turned out to have been left to me,' Hecate continued, 'and I closed the whole thing down. I did feel a bit bad about it, but it really was too much. We've changed things around a bit since then, of course, but actually, it was only earlier this month that we auctioned all Daddy's stuff off. It's odd, because in itself it never meant that much to me, but in a way I felt it was letting go of my childhood. Silly, I know, but that's why I kept it so long.'

'Fetched a tidy sum. God alone knows why,' Sir Gerard said. 'There were one or two fine carvings, but mostly it was a load of mouldy old rubbish. Combined deities, forsooth!'

'So you didn't share any of your father's beliefs?' Ysabel asked Hecate, ignoring Sir Gerard.

'Well, it wasn't really like that, you see,' Hecate answered. 'It's rather hard to explain . . . Did you have to attend compulsory chapel at school?'

'Yes,' Ysabel admitted. 'I was at a convent, in Cork.'

'And have you grown up a Christian?'

There was a brief pause as Ysabel struggled not to choke.

'Sorry,' she managed when she'd got her breath back. 'No, I didn't, I've never been in a church since.'

'Well, exactly, you see,' Hecate continued. 'People who find religion are always terribly keen, but those born into it tend to rebel against it, and that's how it was with me. Now I'm inoculated against it, you might say.'

'Same here,' Sir Gerard added. 'School chapel was a frightful bore. Weddings and funerals, that's about my limit, that and the loan of the meadow for the odd function. Have to keep the vicar happy, of course.'

'But you went to public school too, Hecate?' Ysabel asked.

'Oh, yes, I got a double dose. Christianity during term and pantheism in the hols.'

'I have heard people speak of your father as something of a visionary,' Ysabel hazarded. 'When researching the goats.'

'He could be very convincing,' Hecate replied, 'and he had some remarkable ideas.'

'The fellow made it up as he went along,' Sir Gerard commented, wiping his lips with a napkin. 'Still, the temples and stuff come in handy for the livestock. Well, I think I'll stroll down as far as the Cynosure's field, see how the old boy is this morning. See you down there, perhaps, Ysabel?'

'Er . . . yes, we'll be out shortly,' she answered.

'I should go, too,' Hecate added. 'Sephany and I are going into Melton Mowbray for a few bits and pieces. Is there anything I can get you?'

'No, thank you,' Ysabel answered, and returned thoughtfully to her breakfast.

A moment later she heard Hecate calling to Persephone to hurry up, then the clatter of boots on the stairs. As Sir Gerard left, Nich appeared, looking thoroughly pleased with himself.

'Feeling better?' he asked as he began to investigate the tureens. 'Good grief, do people still serve breakfast this way?'

'I'm a bit sore, thanks,' Ysabel answered him, 'otherwise all right. Thanks for staying in with me.'

'What else could I do? So Croom is a Satanist, then. I knew it all along. He actually admitted it, did he?'

'Yes, he told me, shortly before beating me black and blue, buggering me and leaving me tied up to wet myself. He's a Satanist, take it from me.'

'Well, yes, it certainly goes with his behaviour.'

'I found out something else. Hecate has no idea whatsoever about her father's legacy to her, and she's agnostic.'

'Yes? You're certain?'

'She told me, or as good as. She feels much the same way about the Blackman Cult as I do about Catholicism, but she'd been hanging onto the stuff because it reminded her of her childhood. It is safe, isn't it, the sacaralia?'

Nich glanced to the door before speaking.

'I've hidden it under a loose floorboard in a different room. I shan't tell you which, in case Croom gets at you.'

Ysabel responded with a shudder that was entirely genuine but echoed by a sudden tickling sensation in her sex. Nich went on.

'That resolves my last doubt, then. Blackman's legacy will be ours, just as soon as we work out his riddle.'

Standing at the window of the Green Room, Anderson Croom looked out across the frost-covered Leicestershire fields. The sky was a clear, cold blue, the air absolutely still, leaving every detail in sharp perspective. The Temple of Pan-Vaunus was clearly visible, and the Cynosure of Chealingham had just emerged from it. From a distance, the bull looked impressive enough. Close up, he knew, it looked positively alarming, an impression made stronger by Sir Gerard's enthusiastic description of how it had once gored a New Age traveller.

'How do you advocate going about the theft, sir?' Creech enquired.

'During the day, impossible,' Anderson Croom remarked. 'At night, easy enough, just so long as we can get the bull out of the field, or at least distract it. That's where you come in, Vicky.'

'Me?' Vicky demanded. 'I don't know anything about bulls.'

'You don't have to. I just need you to be a little friendly with it, intimate, if that's what it takes.'

'You have to be joking! It must weigh a ton, and if you ask me, it looks mental.'

'More like a ton and a half, if I'm any judge, but you don't have to let it fuck you, Vicky, or even get on the same side of the gate. You just need to tease a little. It's just an animal and, more importantly, a male. Just keep it distracted long enough for me to rob the temple. Tickle it behind the ears, stroke its balls, whatever it takes ... damn it, you're a girl, you should know how to tease.'

'Men, yes, not bulls!'

'I'm sure the essential principles are the same, just keep him thinking he's going to get more, toss him up a little if you want to, but don't let him go all the way.'

'Dead right!'

'Meanwhile, I should be able to get to the temple and find Blackman's cache. According to the notes it's under an eight-sided slab, which shouldn't be too hard to spot.'

'What if more than one visit should be required, sir?' Creech asked.

'Then I make more than one visit,' Anderson responded. 'We can stash the gold or whatever it is in the boot of the Bentley.

Vicky gave a doubtful snort, then promptly bent to the task of making the bed as a knock sounded at the door.

'Come in,' Anderson called, turning to find Persephone already in the room.

'Good morning, Anderson,' she greeted him, with a sweet and unfamiliar shyness that went straight to his cock. 'Mummy and I are going into Melton. You'll come, won't you?'

'Yes, of course, good idea,' Croom said quickly. 'Just let me get a spot of breakfast down myself, and I'll be with you.'

He grinned as the door closed behind her.

'See what I mean?' he addressed Creech. 'Spank 'em hard and they'll eat out of your hand.'

'It clearly isn't a map in the conventional sense,' Nich stated, frowning down at the three artefacts. 'No, it will be symbolic, yet ultimately it must relate to the physical reality of the estate. Once we crack his code . . .'

'Well, it's beyond me,' Ysabel admitted, peering at the lines of neatly inscribed symbols in Blackman's smallest notebook. 'Both astrological symbols and alchemical symbols mixed with hieroglyphs . . .'

'That's typical of Blackman's way of thinking,' Nich broke in. 'Croom thinks the spider's leg points to something, but I'm not so sure. Could the extended leg be allegorical? Blackman being Blackman, it might relate to anything within any theological macrocosm. Who had a spider god?'

'Search me.'

'Search me too,' Nich admitted. 'But we'd better work on it. Croom hasn't even bothered to ask for the stuff back, and that can only mean one thing.'

'He knows where Blackman's hiding place is,' Ysabel agreed.

Dropping the bags in the hallway, Anderson stood to stretch. His arms ached, as did his legs, his feet and his back. He was certain that they must have visited very shop in Melton Mowbray, several of them twice. He had also purchased both Persephone and Hecate several expensive gifts, on the pretext of providing roofers for their hospitality.

It had been worth it, he was sure. Persephone's mix of adoration with a degree of wariness had softened until he was sure that she would be ripe for sodomy, perhaps while a little drunk. Hecate had also responded to his cautious flirting, and if it seemed unlikely that he would be able to bed the two of them at the same time, it could not be dismissed as impossible.

Persephone came in from the car, bright-eyed and slightly flushed. They had eaten in Melton Mowbray, leaving the bulk of the afternoon free for whatever entertainment he might devise. The only problem was how to get her alone, which she herself solved as she spoke.

'You'll come riding with me, won't you Anderson?' she said cheerfully. 'Daddy said I could take Beelzebub for a run.'

'I'd be delighted,' he replied instantly, an image of her in jodhpurs and tight-waisted pinks flashing into his mind.

'You can ride Wellington. He's the only one who can keep up with Bee over any distance. I just need to change, so give me a minute.'

She disappeared up the stairs, taking them two at a time. He followed at a more leisurely pace, admiring the way her muscular bottom moved in her jeans and thinking of how it looked bare. In his room, he changed quickly into the riding gear Creech had left set out ready as if by telepathy. Only when he came back downstairs did his mood of good-humoured anticipation drop. Persephone was in the hall, just as pretty as he had imagined, but in a riding jacket of deep bottle-green rather than red. Unfortunately she was not alone. Nich had just come in from outdoors.

'Anderson and I are going riding,' he heard Persephone say. 'Would you like to come along too?'

'I was rather hoping for a decent gallop, actually,' Anderson cut in. 'I'm not sure Nich could keep up.'

'Well, I . . .' Nich began.

'Fancy yourself, do you?' Persephone laughed.

'I,' said Anderson Croom, 'was practically born on horseback.'

'So was I,' Persephone warned, 'and I've yet to meet the man who can beat me!'

'We'll see, shall we?' Anderson replied. 'Just show me the course and I'll leave you standing.'

'Ha! You think so!' Persephone said, feigning indignation but clearly delighted at the prospect of the race. 'Come on, then, grab a hat and we'll go! Nich can watch.'

Anderson threw Nich a superior look as they made for the door.

Nich hurried to find Ysabel. He was certain that Croom's true intention was to lose Persephone, then locate and loot Blackman's books, and he was determined to follow. Riding was out of the question, his experienced limited to a single trip on a donkey at a fair.

Ysabel was in her room, face down on the bed to spare her bottom, a pencil in her mouth as she studied one of the notebooks with a frown of concentration.

'I think Croom's about to make his move,' he announced. 'He's on horseback, but it's sure to be somewhere in the grounds, so we can follow him.'

'Sure,' she answered, rolling herself quickly off the bed. 'But what about Vicky, and the butler?'

'Hell,' he responded. 'Where are they?'

'Upstairs,' she answered. 'They have been all day.'

'Maybe that's where it's hidden?'

'If so, they haven't found it. They'd have come down to tell Croom.'

'True. Curse the lot of them! Look, I'll follow Croom as best I can, you keep an eye on the others. Hell!'

Anderson Croom reined Wellington in on the carriage sweep. The horse was a fine bay hunter, but a hand shorter and clearly lighter than the magnificent Beelzebub. He nodded as he studied the map she had given him, then passed it down to Nich. It showed Persephone's favourite gallop, across the valley to what appeared to be an old workings of some sort. Doubtless, he reflected, it would be both overgrown and lonely.

'How much start would you like?' Persephone asked as she trotted Bee out of the stable yard.

'None,' Anderson replied coolly. 'How about you?'

'Hey!' Persephone chided. 'Don't get too big for your boots. The last time somebody beat me I was twelve! That was Daddy, before his gout started to play him up.'

'Well, then, it's about time someone else did.'

He brought Wellington around, so that he could whisper to her.

'And I shall, too. Six of the crop to the loser, bare. How's that for a bet?'

Persephone had gone pink, and didn't answer, only to nod suddenly. Anderson gave her an evil grin and was about to tap her coat-tails with his crop when he saw Sir Gerard and Hecate coming out of the house.

'Hello, Daddy, Mummy,' Persephone called. 'Anderson and I are going to race, over to the old mine.'

'Splendid idea, my dear,' Sir Gerard replied. 'Fine sport, a good cross-country.'

'Sephany was telling me how you haven't beaten her since she was twelve,' Anderson said. 'I intend to put that right.'

'We'll see about that, shall we?' Persephone answered him, her face now bright pink. 'First to reach the old mine sheds wins.'

'First to tie up,' Anderson added.

'Fine,' Persephone answered him. 'Come on, then!'

Anderson Croom urged Wellington into motion, wielding crop and reins as he yelled for speed. Persephone followed suit, Beelzebub matching Wellington pace for pace so that the two horses were soon tearing down the ride at a full gallop. They took the ha-ha together, angling along the side of the Pentacle and down towards the stream.

Persephone turned Beelzebub down the length of the stream, aiming for the ford and the half-collapsed gate at the bottom corner of Pellow's Wood. Even as she turned she saw that Anderson was aiming plum for the stream. Wellington crossed it in a shower of glistening water droplets and took off across the slope.

She saw immediately what Croom was doing. His path would take him up to the gate by the top right-hand corner of Pellow's Wood, gaining time on the field. What he couldn't know was that the gamble would bring him down into the worst of the mine tailings, a mistake that more than one of her previous adversaries had made. As Bee crossed the stream she reined him in a little, keen not to wear him out too early. Croom, she knew, had won himself perhaps a minute's lead, but it would be lost when he reached the top of the tailings dump and a slope that nobody in their right mind would try to take a horse down. If he imagined he was taking a riding crop to her bottom, he had another thought coming.

Urging Beelzebub past the bull's field, she fought down an unwelcome but instinctive stab of disappointment. It was not right that she should have her bottom beaten, however it made her feel, and it was time Anderson Croom paid for his arrogance if he was to be her boyfriend. At the top of the field she took the gate with ease, urging Beelzebub into a full gallop along the lane. Her determination grew as she fought against her mounting arousal at the prospect of taking down her jodhpurs and panties for the crop.

Above the mine the lane opened over a high slope. There was no sign of Anderson, and she forced a laugh even as a second, sharper pang of disappointment hit her. Urging Beelzebub sideways, they scrambled down the steep scree slope that had been the undoing of so many of her suitors. His hooves slithered on the dry, crumbling earth and shale, Persephone calling encouragement to him even as she jerked her head back to look for Anderson above. There was no sign of him, and she found herself wondering if he had had an accident. The route he had taken would mean threading his way through a maze of eroding spoil heaps, any one of which might give way beneath him. Then, at the base of the slope, she caught sight of something that made her heart skip a beat – a hard hat, lying forlorn in a puddle at the base of the last tip. He was ahead. Hoof marks and a tumble of black spoil showed where Wellington must have faltered. She reined in, her mouth falling open as she followed the tracks back to a slope of tailings that was to all intents and purposes a cliff. Scuff marks showed in a broad line, suggesting that Anderson had made Wellington slide sideways down the slope.

'The idiot!' she exclaimed.

'Hardly the tone to be taking with a man who is about to apply a riding crop to your backside, I think,' Croom's voice sounded from behind her.

She wheeled Beelzebub around, to find him walking nonchalantly towards him, bare headed, his beautiful pink coat filthy and torn at one shoulder.

'You could have killed yourself!' she snapped. 'Or poor Wellington.'

'A risk worth the game, I think,' he replied.

An angry retort rose to her lips, only to be swamped beneath a great tide of embarrassment. She didn't answer, but felt her face set into a sulky pout. Anderson

189

had taken her reins, and was leading her towards the mine sheds, a cluster of concrete and corrugated iron structures among scrubby elder and silver birch. A tight knot had formed in her stomach, of anger and shame at the prospect of having to take her panties down for a beating, also at having been out-ridden. She knew she couldn't refuse, and half of her wanted the punishment, yet as she dismounted she found excuses tumbling from her lips.

'Not here, Anderson. We'll be seen!'

'Nonsense,' he answered casually. 'This is you father's land, isn't it?'

'Yes, but . . .'

'Well, then, what better place for the daughter to be whipped. You're not trying to back out, are you? I never took you for a bad sport!'

'No! I'm not, but . . . but . . . it's a bit cold. Couldn't you just spank me tonight or something? I don't mind that, so much, in the bedroom.'

Anderson Croom merely laughed.

Nich peered cautiously over the edge of a tailings dump. The central part of the mine was well below him, the building's clearly visible, also the two horses. Anderson Croom and Persephone had gone into one, he leading her by the hand. He shook his head and glanced back to the wood he had just come through, getting scratched and dirty in the process.

Anderson rubbed his hands in pure glee. Persephone stood in front of him in the old mine building, her face still set in the expression of sulky resentment she had worn since losing the race. She was plainly going to go through with it though, he was sure, and once he'd whipped her, he fully intended to bugger her, just so long as he could manage an erection in the cold autumnal air.

'Bend over,' he ordered, 'out of that window. That way, there'll be no chance whatever of us getting caught.'

She nodded nervously, and took her hard hat off, then turned to lean her upper body out of the low window he had indicated. Bent down low, she was forced to go knock-kneed, with her bottom stuck up and out to make a straining globe of chubby girl-flesh within her jodhpurs. A harp-shaped sweat stain showed the outline of her sex lips, plump and inviting.

He stepped close, to tug at the ancient window and drag it down to the level of her back, trapping her. A piece of wood wedged into the gap between window and frame ensured that she had absolutely no way of escape.

'Hey!' she protested. 'You didn't have to do that!'

'I just wanted to be sure you keep your promise,' he answered.

'I will!' she snapped. 'I keep my bets, you bastard!'

'Temper, temper,' he said, and patted her bottom.

'Six, you said, remember,' she pouted.

'Absolutely,' he assured her. 'Six, on the bare.'

Her response was a sob. Both horses were visible, tethered to the wire supports on the shed opposite. Both were regarding their mistress quizzically, perhaps sensing her distress. Croom chuckled as he noticed that Beelzebub's monstrous black cock was protruding a good foot from its sheath.

'Always good to have an audience for a girl's spanking,' he remarked. 'Especially one so plainly appreciative. Maybe you should give them both a nice suck afterwards? I bet it wouldn't be anything new.'

'Shut up!' Persephone squeaked. 'What a thing to say!'

Anderson laughed and stepped back to admire her rear view. She stayed still, waiting in bitter silence. Only the slight twitching of one calf betrayed her emotion. He reached his crop out, to trace the sweaty outline of her

191

sex through her jodhpurs, then the curve of one full
bottom cheek.

'Beautiful,' he remarked, making no effort to keep the
gloating tone from his voice. 'And mine to do with as I
please. Time to pop those jodhpurs down, I think.'

Persephone gave a little whimper as he pushed his
thumbs firmly into the waistband.

'One, two, three and up pop the dumplings!'

He tugged, and she gasped as the jodhpurs were
jerked down to expose the full width of her bottom, now
covered only in the straining cotton of her panty seat.

'That one works best when you pop a girl's tits out
unexpectedly,' Anderson remarked, 'but with a bum like
yours, dumplings is pretty apt.'

He gave her a resounding slap, up under the bulge of
her bottom cheeks, to draw out an indignant squeak
and briefly set her panting and dancing on her toes.

'Do you have to be so rude?' she demanded as she got
her breathing back under control. 'It's not very romantic.'

'Romantic?' he queried. 'Being cropped on the bare in
a filthy old shed is romantic?'

'Yes, in a way,' she answered, more sulky than ever.
'You know, it's always happening in books and films,
when the hero punishes the heroine . . . and then she
falls in love with him.'

He chuckled and took a firm hold of her panties,
speaking as he began to ease them slowly down.

'I know the sort you mean, but they never have
enough detail for me. I like to get the full works. Saving
actual porn, films never give more than a peep of bum
slit. I want a proper moon as the girl's knickers come
down, arsehole and all, and a proper view of her cunt.
You see, that's what makes a man's cock hard. Hmm,
you are pretty behind, aren't you? Such a pouty little
cunt, and I just adore the way that little brown arsehole
of yours twitches. And you smell right, rich, very
feminine indeed, and just a little sweaty.'

Persephone had begun to sob, and to slump down. Anderson adjusted her panties, everting them around her thighs, far enough down to leave everything showing, but still allow her legs to spread easily.

'Bottoms up!' he said jovially, catching her another hard smack across her now naked seat. 'Come on, there, girl, stick it up! Let's see where Willy goes to be sick.'

'Anderson! You are disgusting!'

'I know,' he admitted. 'Now come on, make a proper show for me and I'll go easy on you.'

Slowly, reluctantly, Persephone raised her bottom, her knees coming together, her back down, her cheeks spreading to expose her ready sex and the brown dimple of her anus.

'Glorious!' he chuckled as his eyes locked on her bottom hole, a dark spot at the centre of a star of tiny lines, slightly sweaty, very rude, and an irresistible target.

'I always wonder,' he remarked casually, 'how it must feel to have your bottom nude to a man, knowing he's going to beat you and fuck you afterwards. You crave it, yes, but how do you square that with the humiliation you must feel?'

'Bastard!' she hissed. 'Just do it, will you?'

She had turned to look back through the broken window, her face red in her embarrassment, more, he suspected, for his comments than for the show she was making of her rear view. Anderson lifted the riding crop and gave it a meaningful waggle.

'Go on then,' she sighed. 'Do it, and you can fuck me if you must, but don't come inside me!'

'I won't, you have my word,' he answered. 'Your pussy is as safe as if you were wearing a spiked chastity belt.'

As he spoke he had tapped the thick leather snap of the crop against her bottom. She turned quickly away, but not before he saw that she was biting her lip. Again he tapped, making her bottom flesh quiver, and as he lifted the crop the muscles of both her thighs began to twitch, along with her anal ring. Once more he licked his lips, adjusted his cock in his jodhpurs, and brought the riding crop down hard across Persephone's bottom.

She gave a scream of pain as it hit, her whole bottom bouncing as her flesh was struck, and one leg going into an involuntary spasm, to set the toe of her riding boot briefly drumming on the concrete floor. Wellington gave a nervous snicker and moved sideways. Beelzebub moved closer, pulling on his rein as one huge eye rolled around to observe his mistress's pain. Beneath him, his now erect cock quivered.

'He's certainly fond of you,' Anderson remarked. 'I could probably get him in here, if you like, but there's not a lot of room for him to mount you.

'Shut up, Anderson!' she gasped. 'Just beat me, if you're going to!'

'Absolutely,' he assured her, and slashed the riding crop hard across her buttocks.

She hadn't expected the blow, and screamed in pain and shock, then went into a wild, uncontrolled dance, her whole bottom wobbling up and down as she bounced on her toes. Anderson burst out laughing.

'You utter bastard!' she swore, finally recovering her breath. 'That was too hard! And you said you'd go easy if I showed properly!'

'Sorry,' Anderson chortled. 'You're just too good to resist. If you don't want men to abuse you, you shouldn't be so beautiful!'

'I suppose that's supposed to be a compliment,' she sighed. 'That's two.'

'Two it is,' he confirmed, 'I can count, you know, and besides, all I need to do is read the lines off your bum.'

He moved across her body, tapped her bottom again, this time on the less-bruised cheek, lifted and gave her a firm, exact cut. She winced and one leg kicked up, but no more. Nor did she speak, but hung her head in acceptance of what he had done.

Again he took aim, applying several gentle pats to one cheek, until her muscles had begun to twitch in anticipation. He gave the cut, a little harder, and again she jumped and gasped, but no more. A moment later she began to shake her head.

'Warm?' he asked.

She nodded and her bottom twitched. He paused, admiring her sex, and way her juice had splashed onto the insides of her bottom cheeks and thighs with the impacts of his crop. Her sweat was coming too, making her bottom glossy and slick and gathering at the top of her crease and in the hole of her anus. His cock was near hard, and as he gave himself a much needed squeeze he reflected that, as long as he got into her body quickly, the cold would not be a problem.

'That makes four,' he said. 'Two to go.'

Persephone nodded and pushed out her bottom out a little more to keep her promise of making a good display. Croom chuckled, thoroughly enjoying her obedience and making her be deliberately rude.

'Five then,' he said, and brought the crop down across her bottom with a healthy thwack.

She gave a yelp of pain, then a whimper of shame and self-disgust as she lost control of her bottom hole to release a long, sonorous fart. Anderson Croom dissolved in laughter so strong it hurt, to leave him doubled up and clutching himself.

'You utter bastard!' Persephone swore.

'I'm sorry,' he managed after a moment. 'But you are simply adorable! God, I love girls who get in a state over their bodily functions, and as if you could possibly help it, when you're being whipped!'

She gave a hiss of frustration, but kept her bottom up. Her sex was open and receptive, her hole showing

195

as a tiny black cavity into her body, while her anus was twitching rhythmically.

'Ready for fucking, I see,' he remarked. 'Just one more, then.'

Even as he finished speaking he brought the riding crop down, as hard as ever, full across her bottom. She screamed and went into her wild, uncontrolled dance, bucking and kicking, swearing and tossing her head. He moved quickly, freeing his cock and jamming it between her thighs as he took her firmly by the hips. He missed, his cock head sliding up along the wet groove between her sex lips instead of into her. She gasped in pleasure, and an instant later had stuck her bottom up to meet his body. This time his cock found her hole and he entered her.

'Wonderful what a combination of horse-riding and a good beating does to a girl,' he remarked, and began to fuck her.

She was loose, her sex as open and well lubricated as any he had felt on first penetration. He was quickly fucking merrily away, holding her by the hips and admiring the six angry red welts he had put across her bottom. She took it gasping and panting, shaking her head until her hair flew loose of the net, her gaze directed down, then suddenly up, towards the huge black cock that hung quivering beneath Beelzebub's body.

'So that's what's on your mind, is it?' Croom chuckled. 'That would make your eyes pop, wouldn't it? Well, sorry I don't quite make the grade, but I do have my little tricks, such as this.'

He spat, landing the gobbet of mucus exactly on her anus.

'Bull's-eye!' he declared happily.

Persephone gave a gasp of disgust, but moaned in pleasure as he put his thumb to her bottom hole. He began to open her, fucking her gentle as he eased her passage to the sound of her whimpering, gasping response. Only when she was nicely open, with her anus a wet, gaping cavity around his thumb, did he pull his cock free of her sex.

'Not yet!' she wailed. 'Fuck me, Anderson!'

'With pleasure,' he answered, easing his thumb from her anus.

Her hole closed with a hiss of air, and then his cock was touching, her wet flesh pushing in.

'No!' she squealed. 'Not that . . . Not up my bum! Not with your cock! That's gross . . . that's . . .'

He pushed harder, gritting his teeth as she struggled to hold her sphincter tight and keep him out of her rectum. She began to wriggle, her body jerking and shaking in the trap of the window, her bottom cheeks wobbling frantically, but unable to break free. Again he pushed, only to give in as his cock bent painfully back.

'Let me in, damn you!' he swore. 'Come on, girl, where's the harm in a cock up the bum?'

Her answer was a muffled, wordless squeak. Taking it for assent, her pushed again, only to find her as tight as ever. Still he pushed, determined to break her will, until once again it began to hurt.

'There are some things,' he grunted, 'that every girl needs to learn. One of them is just how damn good it feels to have a cock up her bottom!'

'No!' she hissed. 'Come on, Anderson, not up my bum . . .'

She broke off with a pained grunt as he pushed harder still at her bottom hole, her ring pressing in to make a hot, tight bowl around his cock head, but not giving.

'Why not?' he whined.

'It's dirty!' she stormed.

'You didn't mind my thumb?'

'That's not the same . . . Ow! Anderson, you're hurting . . . It's . . . it's . . . oh, for God's sake! I mean I'm dirty, Anderson, now . . . I'm ready . . . ready to . . . you know!'

'Oh, I don't mind that,' he assured her, 'and I promise I won't make you suck, OK?'

'Oh, how gross! How could you even ... Oh, my God ...'

She broke off to a long, miserable moan. He held her tight, waiting for her anus to go loose as he tried to coax her into surrender. She was shaking her head, but she had stopped struggling, and he was sure it was simply a matter of time.

'I don't mind, darling,' he insisted. 'I didn't think you would, either. You're a country girl, aren't you, not one of these obsessively clean city types? Come on, let me in ...'

'OK,' she sobbed, 'if you must, but you're not to tell, anyone ... promise?'

'I swear,' he puffed, and pushed even as her ring relaxed.

He gasped as the head of his cock pushed in past the tight constriction of her anal ring. So did she, a sound of ecstasy, but also of despair and disgust. He closed his eyes in pure bliss as the meat of his foreskin squeezed slowly up into her bumhole, an ecstasy almost too great to endure. Only when it was in did he look again, to watch the remaining few inches of his erection go up, bit by bit, her anus pulling in and out with each shove. Persephone gave a series of low, disgusted moans as more and more cock was packed into her rectum, but she was no longer trying to stop it.

Her insides felt hot and delightfully slimy on his penis, encouraging him to push deeper, and harder, until he was right in. With his taut ball sack pushed to her empty cunt, he paused, sighing in pleasure at the wonderful sensation of being fully immersed in her delightful bottom.

'By God, that feels good,' he gasped.

Persephone's response was a shamed whimper, but she had her bottom thrust well out. As he began to move his cock in her well-filled rectum, she was soon grunting with passion and pushing herself back to meet his thrusts. He got faster, his belly slapping on her whipped bum cheeks, his teeth gritted, struggling to control himself, and failing, as, totally unexpectedly, her anus went into the frantic, spasmodic contractions of orgasm. Persephone screamed, the note filled with as much shame as ecstasy as she climaxed on his cock, and they were coming together. Even as he squirted sperm into her bowels he realised that her anal orgasm had probably been as unexpected for her as it had for him.

She was sobbing deeply as her body went slowly limp. For a moment he let her alone with her emotion, as his orgasm faded slowly away. Only when a sudden jolt of cramp in one calf hit him did he begin to pull back, and give her a hearty slap on her bottom to jolt her out of sudden misery.

'Cheer up!' he said. 'That was damned good. I never knew a girl could do that!'

She didn't reply, but winced as his cock popped free of her bottom hole. Looking down at his penis, he regretted his promise not to make her suck him clean afterwards, but decided to keep it. Shaking his head at his own softness, he pulled a handkerchief from the pocket of his pinks. Still smiling, he stood back, to wipe himself and to watch her anus close, with the dirty sperm emerging from the still twitching hole in a series of little, bubbling farts. Finally Persephone found her voice.

'Could you let me out now, please? If you've finished.'

'He is such a bastard!' Ysabel breathed as Nich settled into a chair with an exhausted sigh. 'How did he trap her?'

'Under a window,' Nich explained. 'I think he wedged it to keep her in place. Then he used a riding crop on her, six strokes. How she screamed!'

'Was it done ritually?'

'No, just for the fun of it, I think. He is utterly devoid of morals. Beating her like that, and I'm sure he was in her bottom at the end, but I don't think she agreed to buggery. Still, she seemed happy enough afterwards.'

'Yes,' Ysabel agreed with a wistful sigh. 'I bet she was.'

'Yes,' Nich agreed, ignoring the implication of her response, 'but he didn't try and lose her. If he knows the location, he's pretty confident we don't. I'm sure he does, or he'd have been after Blackman's sacaralia, so that means he's deciphered the code but knows we won't be able to. The depth of his knowledge must be extraordinary, curse him!'

Anderson Croom settled into a sofa with a contented sigh. His entire body now ached, but the memory of buggering Persephone was not one that would pass quickly. Few girls had put up quite such a spirited resistance, let alone taken so much pleasure in the act once he was up. None had come on his cock without having their pussies frigged, ever.

Outside, the day was beginning to fade to dusk, and he had begun to wonder if the suggestion of a beer or a glass of sherry would be well received. He had just decided that it would and to seek out Sir Gerard when Hecate came into the room. She shut the door carefully behind her.

'May we have a quite word, Mr Croom?' she asked.

'Anderson, please,' he responded. 'And yes, of course.'

'Perhaps upstairs?' she suggested.

'Naturally, yes,' he answered, rallying quickly and hoping that the implication of her words was what he suspected, for all his sore cock.

'Gerard has gone over to our neighbour, Mr Woolmer,' she went on, moving quickly towards the opposite door. 'Mr Woolmer farms geese, and Gerard is hoping to get one for this evening.'

'Splendid,' he answered, following her across the dining room to the door into the servants' quarters. 'Is Sephany not, er . . . coming down yet?'

'No,' Hecate answered firmly. 'She is resting on her bed, face down. I have just spent half an hour rubbing cream into her bottom.'

Anderson hastily closed his mouth, which had dropped open in surprise.

'I do think you were a little rough with her,' Hecate went on. 'She is only eighteen.'

'Oh . . . er . . . well,' Anderson stammered. 'A little, maybe . . . er . . . but . . . er . . . she seemed to cope well enough. I mean to say, she's a big girl, and . . . er . . . we all have to learn, after all . . . cruel to be kind, that sort of thing.'

'Oh, I understand, Anderson, but she is a little young, and maybe not really mature enough . . .'

'Whereas you?' he queried, hoping that he had caught the implications of her statement correctly.

'Oh, I understand very well, Anderson, very well indeed.'

He responded with a grin, letting his eyes move down across her body, to admire the swell of her breasts and hips, mature, yet still firm and shapely. The thought of her rubbing cream into her daughter's smacked bottom had sent the blood rushing to his cock, which already felt uncomfortable in his trousers, and more so for over use.

They had reached the bottom of the servants' staircase, which was too narrow for them to walk abreast. He struggled to cope with what she had said as he followed her up, all the while with his eyes locked to the roundness of her bottom and the way her cheeks moved beneath her tweed skirt. By the time they had reached the second floor, he had recovered his composure enough to take her arm.

'So,' he said, 'do you get disciplined, or is it just good hearty fun?'

'It goes rather deeper than that,' she answered, 'but yes, Gerard beats me, now and again.'

'That's what I like to hear.' He chuckled. 'The best sound in the English countryside, the thwack of leather on female flesh. Better than damn cricket any day.'

'Not really often enough, nowadays,' she said wistfully.

'A shame,' he answered, 'and a surprise. If you were my wife, you'd be in permanent need of a cushion. Now, in here with you, and let's get that magnificent bottom out of your knickers, shall we?'

'Bare?' she queried as he steered her into his room. 'I'm not really sure . . .'

He took no notice, kicking the door shut and pulling her across to the bed. One swift movement and her arm had been twisted into the small of her back, another and she was over his lap, her gasp of shock at the sudden rough treatment still dying on her lips. She hung her head, and he chuckled as he realised that she was shaking.

'Still gets to you, eh?' he chuckled as he began to tug her skirt up. 'Funny thing about spankings, that. The thrill never fades.'

'It still hurts,' she sobbed.

He nodded sagely and completed the task of lifting her skirt, bringing the cotton slip she wore underneath up with it, to leave the full globe of her bottom showing but for tights and a pair of large white panties beneath. He cupped her bottom, feeling, then quickly pushed his hand down between her thighs to cup her sex. She felt warm, and damp.

'Ready little slut, aren't you?' he remarked. 'As bad as your daughter.'

She didn't answer him, but let out a low moan as began to rub at her sex. Her flesh felt wonderfully soft, and for all her age it was impossible to fault the shape of her bottom and thighs.

'You have the arse and legs of a twenty-year-old,' he remarked. 'Well, thirty maybe, but not an hour more. How old are you?'

'Is that a polite question?' she managed.

'A polite question?' he laughed. 'When you're over my knee with your bum stuck in the air? Hardly a polite situation, is it? Actually, I know how old you are, come to think of it . . . Yes, you must be forty-two, or forty-three?'

'How did you know that?' she asked.

'Never you mind,' he said quickly, realising that he had come close to giving his game away. 'Time you were spanked.'

She sobbed as he gave her sex a final rub. Adjusting his position slightly, he settled her body into a more comfortable position for spanking, then gave her a firm pat.

'No bruises,' she pleaded, her voice now breathless. 'Gerard would be sure to see.'

'Fair enough,' Croom answered. 'I'll cup my hand and keep it gentle, but by God your knickers are coming down!'

'But I thought . . .'

'No nonsense,' he answered, even as he peeled her tights down over her bottom. 'Tights down, knickers down, that's the way the ladies ride, as Sephany likes to say, generally while my cock's up her.'

'Anderson, please,' she said, 'could we not talk about my daughter while you're spanking me?'

'If you insist,' he agreed, settling her tights well down her legs, 'but it does make an interesting comparison. Ideally, of course, I should have you side by side, naked. Then I could make a proper comparison.'

'Anderson!'

He laughed and gave her a heavy swat across the seat of her panties, making her bottom wobble.

'Not another word,' he promised, 'not until you're safely spanked and fucked. Let's have these great big knickers down then!'

Her response was a weak moan as he caught the seat of her panties in his hand. He hauled, and down they came, revealing the full, pale moon of her bottom. She lifted it, allowing him to tug the panties out from beneath her and pull them well down, to the level of her knees.

As with Tabitha and Elizabeth Ferndale, Hecate was meatier than her daughter, and softer, but no less feminine. Intrigued, he hauled her bottom cheeks apart to reveal her anus, with the same puckered star shape and brown centre as her daughter's; lower, her sex showed the same plump, pouted lips. She gave a sob of humiliation.

'You have a pretty cunt,' he remarked, letting go.

Cupping one full bottom cheek, he began to fondle, wondering if he ought to hold back as she had asked, or give her a proper thrashing and then fuck her anyway. He wavered, tempted, then decided against it, sure that the loss was worth a chance at the greater prize, bedding mother and daughter together.

Using just his fingertips, he began to spank her, working patiently over her bottom, just hard enough to leave a delicate pink flush with every slap. She sighed in response, low and content, and had soon begun to push up her bottom. He began to spank a little harder, concentrating on his task, and letting his own arousal build slowly.

Hecate sighed with pleasure as her bottom began to bounce, her cheeks spreading as she pushed herself higher in her rising need. Anderson caught the scent of her sex, mixed with some heady perfume he didn't recognise. With his own excitement rising, he began to spank harder still, until she had begun to whimper and shake her head, responding to punishment with no more dignity than her daughter.

For him, there was a slight irritation at her willingness, but no more. His cock was responding in any case, hard against the softness of her body, and ready to be put into her. There was a dull ache in his balls, but he ignored the sensation, using her twisted arm to make her body rock against his cock and so stimulate himself.

Her bottom was flushed a rich pink, and stuck up so high that her cheeks were fully apart, her anus on show, and the wet hole of her sex made available, open and juicy. Growing bored with spanking her without the option of inflicting any real suffering, he stopped.

'Time you were fucked,' he announced, letting go of her arm. 'On your knees, so I can see that spanked arse while I do it.'

She nodded as she climbed up off his lap, and hastened to obey, kneeling on his bed with her bare bottom raised for entry. He came to her, and took a moment to free her breasts, undoing her jacket and blouse, then flipping her bra up to leave them hanging beneath her chest, round and heavy, her nipples stiff in erection.

He fondle her breasts as he freed his cock, and took her briefly by the hair so that he could feed it into her mouth, as much for the sake of having done it as his physical need. She sucked willingly, leaving him rock hard and ready for her sex.

Crawling around behind her, he wasted no time, but mounted her, slipping his hands under her chest to feel her heavy breasts as he pushed his cock into her body. She was gasping immediately as he began to fuck her, and had reached back to masturbate before he had even found his rhythm. He kept his pace, pumping into her and stroking her nipples as she rubbed at herself, waiting for the first contractions of orgasm.

They came, and he shut his eyes in bliss as her sex went into spasm on his cock, still pumping into her as she grunted and shivered her way through orgasm. As

205

she finished he decided it was time to come himself. He took a firm grip on her jacket, holding her in place as he pulled himself in deeper and harder.

'Not in . . .' she panted

'Oh . . . fair enough,' he answered, pulling his cock out and immediately pressing it to her anus.

'No, not . . .' she gasped, but broke off in a low moan as her sweaty anal ring gave way.

'Like mother, like daughter!' Croom laughed. 'Whoops, sorry! Mark you, she's a damn sight tighter up the bum than you are.'

'You . . .' Hecate hissed and broke off in a fresh gasp as he jammed the head of his cock up her bottom.

He held his grip on her, watching as her anal ring closed on the neck of his cock. She gave a little pained grunt as he began to masturbate, jerking furiously at his cock with just the head pressed into the warm cavity of her anus. It took moments, his shaft jerking in his hand, then erupting spunk up her bottom. He was still wanking as he withdrew, her anus closing slowly behind him, with the sperm oozing out of her bottom hole in just the same way it had from her daughter's just hours earlier.

'Thank you,' she sighed, 'but did you have to . . . up my bottom?'

'Yes,' Anderson replied frankly as he sat back on the bed.

'No harm done, I suppose,' she said, 'but really, you have very little respect for a woman's dignity.'

'None at all,' he responded casually. 'Clean my cock, would you?'

She gave him a look of pure exasperation, but then went straight to his crotch, without further protest, to take his rapidly shrinking penis into her mouth and suck up her own juices. He lay back with a contented sigh, reaching down to stroke her hair as her tongue and lips worked on his penis.

206

'It's not that, really,' he remarked, 'or at least, only so far as sex is concerned. One thing my father taught me – or rather, that I learned from my father's behaviour – is that women like to be dominated sexually. Even the most intellectual, even the most frightful viragos, they all appreciate a firm hand in bed, preferably applied to their bottoms. A lot of modern men simply don't realise that.'

She said nothing, still cleaning his cock, then kissing the tip as she drew back. He cradled her to his chest, still stroking her hair as he went on.

'We are, after all, animals at base, nothing more. Yes, we can rise above those base instincts but, as far as sex is concerned, why would we want to?'

'True, perhaps,' she replied.

'True, absolutely,' he said. 'Consider the baboon. Female baboons stick together, with a rigid hierarchy under a matriarch. Those lower in the hierarchy groom their superiors, and also provide cunnilingus –'

'Anderson, we are not baboons!'

'No, but there are parallels. Consider how much more comfortable women are together than men. If you were in, say, a restaurant, and a friend, or Sephany for that matter, goes to the ladies, I imagine you would go with her. If I was to follow Creech into the gents in the same way, you would think me peculiar in the extreme.'

'Well, yes . . .'

'You see, with women, that sort of intimacy, and sexual intimacy, is natural, something given to confirm membership of the troop, or in your case the social set, and status within that group.'

'What absolute nonsense! I don't have any sort of sexual intimacy with . . . with Mrs Woolmer, or the vicar's wife!'

'No, and that is the result of the unnatural restrictions we have placed on ourselves, largely as a result of repressive Christian teachings. Still, it is the natural order of things. You said yourself you creamed Sephany's bottom.'

'Naturally, I'm her mother.'

'Still, the two of you do seem exceptionally intimate.'

'No more so than most.'

'Rubbing cream into her spanked bottom?'

'Why, certainly. Call me old-fashioned, but I believe in physical discipline. I still spank her myself, occasionally.'

'You do?'

'Now and then.'

'By God! Over your knee?'

'Why, yes . . .'

'With her knickers down? Please tell me you take her knickers down?'

'I think you rather enjoy the thought, don't you, Mr Croom?'

'Enjoy it? Of course I do, I'm only human, damn it! I mean to say, the thought of a mother taking her grown-up daughter across her knee for a spanking? It's enough to give a man a stroke!'

'Some might consider that perverse.'

'Only complete fools. But you haven't answered my question. Do you take her knickers down?'

'Yes, of course. Why shouldn't I?'

'Dear God! You, er . . . you wouldn't do her in front of me, would you?'

'Certainly not!'

Vicky gave her bottom a satisfied wriggle. She was naked, and sat splay-legged in Creech's lap with his cock well up her vagina. Despite his politely made protests, she had managed to coax him to erection three times during the day, and each time taken her pleasure both in her mouth and her sex.

Each time she had gone through the same bittersweet cycle of humiliation, ecstasy and remorse. Always the

208

memory of how good her orgasms were with him brought her back for more. Between sessions, she had teased herself, and him. For much of the day she had been naked, or topless, and revelling in the slow but inevitable build-up of arousal the feeling of being exposed in front of him provided. Twice she had gone over his knee, once in her panties, once stark-naked, for gentle yet firmly applied spankings which had left her trembling with need. Both had led to sex.

The third time she had not been spanked. As she tidied his room in the nude, she had found an old-fashioned chamber pot, a discovery that had brought new possibilities for her self-inflicted humiliation. It had taken nearly an hour to pluck up the courage, and for her need to overcome her shame. She had then asked shyly if he would like to watch her pee, and done it, squatted over the pot with her sex lips held apart as the golden fluid sprayed out beneath her. By the time she was wiggling her bottom to shake the last few drops free of her pussy lips, his cock had been out and ready for sucking, then her hole.

Persephone lay back in the warm, scented bath water, her legs wide, toying with her sex as she struggled to come to terms with her own feelings. Her bottom smarted, and her anus was bruised, leaving her walking as if she had taken a twenty-mile ride bareback. She felt abused, yet the memory of how she had come when Anderson Croom's cock had been up her bottom was simply too good to be denied. It had been completely unexpected, an outrageously dirty physical response of which she could never have imagined herself capable. Yet it had happened, the culmination of all the contradictory feelings he brought her.

She had already masturbated herself to orgasm over the memory, twice. The first had been after a tearful confession to her mother, which had ended with her showing her welts and lying on her bed as her bottom was creamed. As soon as her mother had gone her hands had been busy between her legs, one attending to her clitoris, the other with a single finger wedged deep up her sore bottom hole. The second had been with him, a brief knee-trembler with her held up against the wall in his bedroom, but even as she was fucked she had been thinking of her anal orgasm. Once he had come over her belly she had masturbated in front of him, splay-legged on the floor.

She bit her lip as her fingers delved into the groove of her sex one more time. Her whole pussy stung, and even as she began to rub she was fighting down her shame at what she saw as a complete surrender of her self-respect, yet she knew she was going to do it, and would again.

Just one minute later she had come, and her finger was back up her bottom. As she pulled it out, she realised that she badly needed to talk to her mother.

Placing his glass of fine old Sauternes back on the table, Anderson Croom allowed his gaze to move around the company. Dinner had been as fine as the night before, and had lasted as long, with the excellent goose Sir Gerard had secured served as the highlight and accompanied by an Alsace of exceptional quality. There had been an air of mischief too, which he had particularly enjoyed, while the flirtatious conversation and coy or admiring glances from all three women had left him feeling thoroughly self-satisfied. Vicky, meanwhile, had demanded that she be given her due share of attention in the night. He hid his smile behind his glass as he wondered if he would be able to take care of all four.

Sir Gerard had captured the attention of Nich and Ysabel, and was explaining in detail his opinions on artificial insemination. Persephone, somewhat cut off from the conversation as she was between Nich and Sir Gerard, had turned her attention to the jam roly-poly.

Content to watch the others and let his thoughts drift, he sat back, only to feel Hecate's hand placed gently on his knee under the table. His attention caught, she leaned close, speaking in a soft voice at little more than a whisper.

'I have been thinking, Anderson, about what you said earlier.'

'Oh, yes,' he replied.

'Concerning Sephany and me,' she went on, quieter still. 'I have changed my mind. I think she is in need of exactly what you suggested.'

'A spanking? Properly? Bare?' Croom hissed as his cock instantly began to fill with blood.

Hecate gave the smallest of nods, then went on, speaking more normally.

'I really must speak to Sephany about encouraging you to take Wellington down among the mine tailings. You weren't to know, of course, but it was quite irresponsible of her.'

'Absolutely,' he agreed. 'Severely, I trust.'

Anderson cursed softly as he sat up in bed. It was pitch black, and Creech had awakened him from an unusually restful dream. Worse still, his balls ached and his cock felt tender, more so than at any time he could remember. After the two sessions with Persephone, one anal, and the session with Hecate he had felt tired yet enervated. Events after dinner had taken him to the edge of defeat. The brief conversation with Hecate had left his head swimming with erotic thoughts, of daughters being spanked by their mothers, and more.

First had been Vicky, caught in the scullery as she washed up, her bottom stripped, spanked and greased with goose fat before he buggered her. Persephone had come next, surprised as she undressed for bed and fucked across it with her clothes up and down so that she was showing both her breasts and her bottom. He had then intended to call it a day, but had met Hecate on her way to the loo. He had taken advantage of her, bent across the toilet bowl with her nightgown up and her big white panties down for rear entry. Ysabel, he was certain, had expected a visit, but it had been simply too much to cope with. In any case, there was the matter of Blackman's cache to see to. He shook his head, trying to clear away the cobwebs of sleep.

'Port, sir?' Creech offered from the darkness.

A torch flicked on, illuminating a glass of deep-red liquid on a tray and Creech's hand.

'Thank you,' Anderson answered. 'Is Vicky ready?'

'I'm here,' her voice answered him, deeply sulky.

'Well,' he said, 'this is it, then.'

Ysabel rolled onto her side, wincing as her tender bottom pressed to the bed. It had proved impossible to sleep, her bruises and the memories of the night before keeping her in a state of restless expectation. Nich had done his best, slapping her breasts until she was dizzy with pain and shaking, then pulling her onto his erection by the hair and making her swallow his come.

It hadn't worked, his natural concern and caution showing through despite his best efforts to act the sadist. She had thanked him as they kissed good night, but the orgasm she had taken under her fingers as his sperm flooded her mouth had been weak compared to the one taken over what Croom had done to her.

She had even hinted to Croom that he would be welcome to come to her again, and now she found herself starting at every tiny noise. The time, she knew, was well past midnight, perhaps as late as three o'clock. Croom, she was sure, would have been asleep for hours, probably after paying Persephone a visit – and yet for all her exhaustion sleep refused to come.

Sticking her thumb purposefully into her mouth, she began to count goats.

* * *

212

Anderson Croom, waiting in the darkened lane at the top gate of the bull's field, strained his eyes across to where Creech and Vicky were hidden at the bottom. Some minutes before a grunt had signalled the bull's presence, but despite the moonlight he had only been able to make it out as a dim bulk, now hidden beyond the Temple of Pan-Vaunus.

His heart jumped at a sudden metallic rattle, only to still as he realised that the bull must have reached the gate at the bottom of the field. A moment later a weak flash of red light came from the same rough direction, then two more – Creech's signal. His mouth curved up into a smile, as much at the thought of Vicky's reaction to the bull as at their success. She had been extremely apprehensive at the thought of touching the great beast, never mind its cock and balls. There was no doubt in his mind that the idea of masturbating the bull had touched an erotic cord in her, and as he climbed the gate he was already considering interesting ways to exploit her feelings.

He set off across the field at an easy jog. The sycamores growing around the temple shielded the house from view after only a dozen paces. Croom reached them quickly and ducked through the pillars of the temple. The inside was clearly a favourite resting place for the Cynosure and smelled both of dung and the rich odour of the bull itself. Ignoring the stench, he signalled Creech, then began to inspect the interior. The floor, where it was visible, was paved with strangely shaped slabs of stone, stained, but greyish white beneath. With considerable distaste, he began to use the edge of his shoe to clear the slabs.

The result came quickly. The central slab was octagonal and larger than the others, surely the cover of the hiding place. Also, while the smaller slabs were cemented firmly in place, the large one simply fitted snugly among its neighbours, without mortar. Even as he applied his crowbar to a crack, a warning flash of white light came from the bottom of the field. Turning, Croom found the massive black shape of the Cynosure lumbering towards the temple.

'My God, that was quick!' he muttered in alarm as he wrenched the crowbar clear.

The bull gave a snort and Anderson Croom took to his heels, the crowbar catching a pillar and dropping to the floor with a clang as he fled. With a slow, percussive drumming already in his ears, there was no time to pick it up. Behind him the Cynosure gave a bellow and changed his pace to a canter.

Croom was sprinting for his life back up the field. Suddenly the hedge and gate seemed tiny in the distance, the turf steep and uneven. He ran blindly, slipping on tufts of grass, the pounding of hooves growing louder, faster, changing tempo from canter to gallop. He imagined hot breath, the stab of horns in his back . . .

An outraged bellow sounded almost in his ear and then the top bar of the gate was in his hands, his body sailing over the top even as the bull slewed to a halt. It gave a single, frustrated snort.

Standing panting with his hands on his knees, he waited, shaking with fear. At length the crackle of footsteps on frosted grass signalled the approach of Creech and Vicky.

'God, that was close!' he panted. 'What happened?'

'Nothing,' Vicky answered.

'Nothing? What do you mean, nothing?'

'What I say. I couldn't . . .'

'Why not?' he demanded. 'Jesus, Vicky, what a time to get squeamish!'

'I wasn't being squeamish,' she answered. 'I couldn't reach! He wouldn't turn sideways.'

'Miss Victoria did her best, sir,' Creech confirmed.

'Damn him!' Croom swore. 'Ungrateful beast! I'd

have thought he'd be jolly eager after being shut up on his own in a field for goodness knows how long.'

'He doesn't want a girl,' Vicky answered him. 'He wants a cow.'

'That would seem reasonable, sir,' Creech agreed.

'Fussy sod,' Croom remarked. 'Still, that's an idea.'

Ysabel crept slowly along the corridor. The goats had failed to do their work, and her resistance had finally snapped. Her heart was hammering at the prospect of what Croom might do to her, but it was impossible to resist. Her bottom ached, and some of the worse cuts still stung, yet the compulsion to be punished and abused was stronger than ever. He wouldn't stop, she knew. In fact, her hurt was likely to further inspire his satanic cruelty, leading him to excesses that made her shiver with fright and need. She reached his door and pushed it gently open, her head spinning with images of tight bonds, of needles, of hot pokers used as branding irons.

The room was empty, the curtains open, soft moon-light playing over a neatly made-up bed. He was not there. That could mean only one thing. He was with another woman. She had watched him take Hecate upstairs, so knew it could be any of three, maybe all, one by one, spanked, fucked, buggered, humiliated and abused in every way.

The idea made her feelings stronger still. It was perfect, an ideal, that she should be last, and yet suffer the most. It made her lowest, a mere plaything for his cruel lust, while there was no doubt that the effort of bringing himself back to an excited state would mean long and painful torture for her.

Thinking to draw strength from the moon, she moved to the window. It hung as it had done the night before, a brilliant disc, now close to full, bathing the icy woods and fields in liquid silver. She muttered an incantation to Demeter, asking for the strength to bring her coming ordeal to true height.

As she finished she caught the flicker of light on the hillside opposite. For one instant a wild delight rose in her, only to fade at the realisation that it was no will-o'-the-wisp or spirit, but simply a man with a torch. For a moment she thought of the poachers Sir Gerard so hated, then of Croom and the fact that in all likelihood somewhere out in the grounds Blackman's legacy was hidden. Realising the truth, she turned, to run light-footed to Nich's room.

Dawn broke over Leicestershire. It was a dawn that Anderson Croom fervently hoped would be the last he saw for a very long time. Standing tired and shivering in the Temple of Pan-Vaunus, he prepared to put his shoulder to the crowbar. At the top of the field the Cynosure gave an occasional frustrated low, a frustration for which Croom felt he had a better sympathy following the events of the night. In the lane, Creech and Vicky led a Charolais cow patiently up and down, controlling the full attention of the great bull.

'Here goes,' Croom said to himself as his shoulder muscles bunched with the strain.

The slab creaked, began to lift, but shots of red heat were already running through his muscles, and he was forced to give in. The slab settled back with a dull thump.

'Maybe I could help you?' a dreadful voice sounded from behind him.

Croom let go of the crowbar and spun around. Nich, with a wicked smile on his face and Ysabel at his shoulder, was standing between two of the pillars that surrounded the temple.

'What are you doing here . . .?' he began to bluster and then realised that it was hopeless.

'Much the same as you are, I imagine,' Nich answered. 'This slab, I take it, conceals Julian Black-

216

man's legacy? Some time you must tell me how you worked out how to find it.'

Croom remained stubbornly silent, aware that there was very little he could do.

'Look, Anderson,' Ysabel said gently, 'I know greed is a part of your nature, and I respect that, but things can be shared.'

'Besides,' Nich added. 'You seem to be having a little difficulty with that slab.'

'With Vicky's help –'

'And another thing,' Nich interrupted him. 'What do you suppose Sir Gerard would make of your activities?'

'Blackmail now, is it?' Croom growled.

'Hardly that,' Nich answered, 'but I'm sure you'll agree that as his guest it would be my duty to report a theft, not to mention the seduction of his wife, spanking and sodomising his daughter . . .'

'Very well,' Anderson snarled. 'Seventy-thirty.'

'Let's just share,' Ysabel urged. 'Knowledge doesn't have to be parcelled out like so much meat!'

'Knowledge!' Croom snorted, and stopped. 'Hang on, you don't really mean to say you think the chamber under this slab will contain books and whatnot, honestly?'

'Yes, of course it will,' Nich answered. 'Blackman's published works barely scratch the probable extent of his knowledge!'

'Yes,' Croom answered, 'because Blackman was a fraud! He didn't have any knowledge, only what he made up!'

'Oh, for Grimm's sake!' Nich stormed. 'Stop trying to pretend you're a bloody innocent! Damn it, you admitted to Ysabel that you're a Satanist, and that your family has occult traditions dating back centuries!'

'No, I didn't,' Croom protested. 'I said we'd had a green man as a family crest for centuries. It's true; it was granted to an ancestor of mine in the fourteenth century.'

'An ancestor who must have been a secret pagan,' Nich hissed. 'Look, you can tell us. You won't get executed for it!'

'He was,' Croom admitted. 'Burned at the stake in 1396, I think. Anyway, you get plenty of green men in cathedrals and church architecture. It doesn't necessarily imply pagan beliefs.'

'Ah, but . . .' Nich began.

'Can we get on with it, please?' Ysabel put in.

Exchanging black looks, Croom and Nich applied themselves to the lever, Ysabel crouching down with a cold chisel to slip under the stone as soon as it cleared its neighbours. The great slab groaned as they took the strain, the crowbar clattering to the floor as it began to lift. An inch, then two inches of lip emerged, the men's muscles straining with the effort.

'I can see under it!' Ysabel exclaimed, jamming the chisel into the gap the instant it was wide enough.

'Stop!' Nich yelled suddenly. 'What if there's a ward, or a curse?'

'Don't talk nonsense!' Croom hissed through gritted teeth. 'Just lift!'

Nich had relaxed his hold, and Anderson was forced to do the same, allowing the slab to rest on the chisel.

'Look,' Croom panted. 'Enough mumbo-jumbo. You can't really believe we're going to be cursed, surely? Even if the concept wasn't inherently absurd, remember that Hecate was supposed to find the cache.'

'It could be guarded,' Nich insisted.

'It's ruddy stone!' Croom snapped back. 'What, do you think the temple roof's going to fall on us or something?'

'No,' Nich answered, 'not that. You've read the notebooks. Was there an incantation to go with lifting the slab?'

'Do you seriously mean to tell me,' Croom asked, 'that you believe that our failure to recite some hocus-pocus can alter what's under this stone?'

'Yes,' Nich urged. 'Of course it can. That's the very basis of chaos magic!'

'What absolute rubbish!' Croom exclaimed. 'Damn it, man, a physical object is either there or it's not, it can't just disappear because a man says a few words! Think of the physics involved! Don't you understand the law of conservation of energy?'

'But that's the art of chaos magic,' Nich insisted. 'To make a change by the careful balancing of natural forces. It's the very key to nature. In theory a skilled magician could cause a volcano to erupt on the far side of the world with a simple incantation!'

'My God, you talk drivel!' Croom answered. 'Come on, get on with lifting the slab.'

'There'll be nothing under it!' Nich persevered.

'Look, if it makes you any happier, there was no mention of an incantation,' Croom said.

'Did you read right through the notebooks?'

'No, but . . .'

'We'd better lift it,' Ysabel put in. 'Sir Gerard might come at any moment.'

'Exactly,' Croom answered. 'I'm glad one of you has some sense! Come on then, heave!'

Nich made a face and a quick sign across his forehead, but then put his back to the lever. Slowly, grinding as it came, the slab lifted. Ysabel jammed the chisel in deeper to support it. Croom and Nich changed their grip and finally toppled it over with a crash. All three of them peered into the octagonal hole beneath. It was empty.

'I told you so!' Nich sighed as he looked down at the smooth grey base of the hole, marked only by some crushed leaves and a black stain.

'Oh, for goodness' sake!' Croom began.

'Hang on, hang on,' Ysabel said. 'Look, acanthus leaves and a stain. The stain must be mixed wine and blood. It's the original dedication offering to Pan-Vaunus, there's no room for anything else.'

The three of them exchanged looks. It was true, nothing whatever could have fitted under the slab and beneath it was concrete. Nich tapped it hopefully with the chisel but received no hollow ring, only a solid thud.

'Better put it back, I suppose,' Ysabel said quietly.

Ten

Anderson Croom awoke to find Creech hovering with a tray laden with coffee, toast and other ingredients of a full breakfast. The world slowly came into focus after the first sip of the hot fluid. His brain had returned to full working order by the time he had finished his second slice of toast.

'What time is it, Creech?' he asked as he tucked into a sausage. 'And what's going on?'

'The time is shortly before eleven, sir,' Creech replied. 'The weather has ameliorated somewhat, and there was a brief flurry of rain earlier this morning. Lady Chealingham and Miss Persephone are in the drawing room, playing cribbage. Sir Gerard is out riding. Mr Mordaunt and Miss Ysabel are visiting one of the temples in the grounds.'

'Not the Temple of Pan-Vaunus, I take it? What a farrago! I suppose we're going to have to pinch everything back from Mad Nich, now.'

'So it would seem, sir, although after last night we might consider working with him rather than against him.'

'Point taken, Creech, especially if he's really fool enough to think it'll be books. Do you think he is?'

'I really could not say, sir.'

'Nor I. Still, they obviously haven't the faintest chance without the map, so today I have a different aim.'

221

'Indeed, sir?'

'Yes. Hecate and Sephany, two in hand.'

'Indeed, sir?'

'Stop saying "indeed, sir" like that, Creech. I couldn't tell you this earlier, not with Vicky around, but it seems that Hecate still spanks Sephany. She's agreed to do it in front of me, knickers down, if you please! Once Sephany's bum's warm, who knows where it will go?'

'Indeed, sir?' Creech queried.

'Yes, Creech, indeed,' Anderson answered. 'It's all agreed. Hecate will pick Sephany up on letting me ride Wellington down the tailings slope, start a row, and whoops, over she goes, down come her knicks and it's spankies time! God, the little minx'll hate it!'

'And you say Lady Chealingham has agreed to do this?' Creech asked.

'Yes,' Anderson declared with emphasis. 'Over the knee, bare bottom, it's all agreed. I expect I'll even be allowed to hold Sephany down if she kicks, and she's bound to. Like a mule, I expect!'

'If I may say so, sir,' Creech insisted, 'it seems a most peculiar thing for a mother to do.'

'Unusual, I grant you,' Croom answered. 'But the man who cries "impossible" when referring to human behaviour is a fool. Damn it, you have people going about making large holes in their genitals, hurling themselves off bridges with elastic bands around their ankles and even crucifying themselves. Offering to spank your own daughter in front of her boyfriend can hardly even be considered all that peculiar.'

'I follow your reasoning, sir,' Creech responded. 'Yet I must advise a degree of caution –'

'You're such a pessimist, Creech,' Anderson cut him off. 'This was after I'd given Hecate her own dose of the old Croom medicine, you know.'

'Nevertheless, sir . . .'

'Oh, don't be so wet, Creech. What could go wrong?

And, by God, once Sephany's warm we'll have some fun, won't we just! I think I'll spank them side by side, or make them watch each other while they get it. Better still, I'll do Sephany while her mother soothes her, perhaps cuddling her head . . . even suckling her at the breast. That would be something, wouldn't it?'

'Without question, sir,' Creech answered.

'In fact,' Croom went on, 'if Gerard's out riding, and Nich and Ysabel are playing silly buggers in the grounds, now would seem the ideal moment. Lay out some clothes, would you? And then if you could keep Vicky amused for a half-hour.'

'Ah, there you are,' Anderson announced as he entered the drawing room. 'I've been thinking, and really do feel I owe you an apology for running a risk like that with Wellington. It was unforgivable.'

'Not at all,' Hecate answered as she folded up the cribbage board. 'If I've told Sephany about that mine once, I've told her a dozen times. Gerard doesn't seem to mind, but –'

'Mummy!' Persephone interrupted.

'Well, you should be more responsible!' Hecate insisted. 'One of these days you'll cause an injury, maybe even to yourself.'

'But I didn't ride down the tailings,' Persephone protested, 'just down the side. It was Anderson –'

'Persephone!' Hecate cut in. 'Don't you dare be rude to your guest! And besides, you know very well it was your responsibility.'

'No, it was not!' Persephone responded hotly. 'You're just being a silly old –'

'Silly, am I?' Hecate snapped. 'I think an hour alone in your room would do you good, young lady.'

'Mummy! Now you are being silly!'

'Am I? We'll see about that, shall we? Up to your room, now.'

'No! Mummy!'

'To your room, now!'

'No, I won't and you can't make me!'

'Oh, can't I?'

She had stood, and marched quickly around the table, to take Persephone firmly by the ear. Persephone squealed in pain, and began to bat at her mother's arm as she was dragged to her feet and across the room.

'Stop it! Ow! Mummy, you're hurting me!' she wailed, but she went, only to suddenly lash her foot out, catching her mother's shin.

'Ow!' Hecate complain. 'You little bitch! Right, young lady, it's time you learned a little respect! I'm going to spank you.'

Anderson chuckled as the anger in Persephone's eyes turned to shock.

'You wouldn't . . .' Persephone was saying as she backed away from her angry mother. 'You couldn't, Mummy . . . stop it . . . That's enough! You're embarrassing me in front of Anderson!'

'Upstairs,' Hecate ordered. 'Now. Or I shall do in right here, whether or not Mr Croom is in the room.'

'No!' Sephany wailed, darting around a chair, and ran, only for her mother to block off her retreat.

She nipped back to the other door, only to find it locked. Before she could twist the key, Hecate had caught her. One swift motion and Persephone's arm had been twisted up into the small of her back.

'No . . . Mummy, please . . . not this . . . no . . .' she babbled as Hecate marched her smartly into the middle of the room. 'Not in front of Anderson . . . I'll be good . . . I promise . . . I swear! Make him go away!'

'Don't mind me,' Anderson remarked casually. After all, I've seen all there is to see already, but, er . . . it might be a little embarrassing were one of my servants to walk in, or Mad Nich . . . I mean, Nich Mordaunt or someone? Perhaps I could even help you take her upstairs.'

'You utter bastard!' Sephany yelled, kicking out backwards. 'Let go of me, you old bitch! I am not going to be spanked! I am not, I am not, I am not!'

'That does it!' Hecate snapped. 'Yes, Mr Croom, you may help me take her upstairs to her room.'

'No!' Persephone screamed. 'You won't! You can't!'

'My pleasure,' Anderson answered, stepping close to put Persephone in a tight arm lock.

'Ow!' Persephone protested. 'That hurts! Mummy, no, please . . . don't . . . you can't . . . you just can't!'

Hecate took no notice as Persephone was frogmarched out of the door and up the stairs, alternately pleading and protesting all the way. Croom held her close, her arms locked into the small of her back. His cock was hard in his trousers, and his heart was hammering at the prospect of what was going to be done to her. On the landing, he made straight for her bedroom, with her struggles and squeals growing wilder and louder as she was forced closer to where she was to be punished. Only when he had reached the door did he let go, sending her stumbling in with a push, to stand panting and dishevelled, her face glowing, not with fear or shame, but with triumph.

Anderson realised that something was wrong a fraction too late, as a loop of rope was pulled quickly down over his body and wrenched tight.

'What?' he demanded, jerking away, only to trip as Hecate neatly extended a foot.

He went sprawling. A desperate lunge saved his face from hitting the floor, and he was face down on Persephone's bed. She was on his back immediately. A sudden lurch threw her off, but he realised it had been a distraction as Hecate pulled a second cord tight around his legs. A moment later Persephone was astride his back again and his bonds were being tied off, Hecate using a twist of rope to pull her arms painfully tight behind his back. He twisted hard, again unseating her, but slipped from the bed, to land heavily on the floor.

'What are you doing?' he demanded, fear rising up as he realised that he was genuinely helpless. 'I ... I thought we were going to ... to ...'

He trailed off. Persephone had stood up and was smiling down at him, her arms folded across her chest. Hecate also looked thoroughly pleased with herself.

'To give Sephany a spanking?' Hecate finished his question for him. 'I'm afraid I lied.'

'Why?' he demanded, realising it was a stupid question even as it came out.

'Just to make sure you really deserved the little lesson that's coming to you,' Hecate said sweetly.

'Yes,' Sephany added as she went to turn the key in the lock of her door. 'I've never been spanked in my life, until you did it to me. You really are a beast, aren't you?'

'No ... no ... you don't understand,' Croom babbled, struggling to keep the note of panic out of his voice. 'It's not that at all! It's just that, sometimes, a girl needs to be ... needs to be, taken out of herself a little, to ... to learn to enjoy the finer points of er ... sex.'

'Such as being spanked until she's crying, and whipped with a riding crop?' Persephone demanded.

'Well, er ... yes,' Croom answered. 'I mean to say ... you enjoyed it, didn't you?'

'Yes,' she admitted, sullenly, 'but you hurt me ...'

'Just your pride, really ...'

'No, my bum! And my pride too.'

'Yes, Mr Croom,' Hecate stated firmly, 'so no more nonsense from you. Now, over my knee with, you I think, to learn to take what you give. A little spanking would do you a great deal of good.'

'Spanking?' Croom demanded in horror. 'Oh, come off it, Hecate, you can't ... No! I mean to say ... don't be silly! I'm a man, damn it!'

'And your point is?' Hecate queried.

226

'You simply can't!' he answered her, and stopped, realising that he was echoing Sephany's pathetic protests almost word for word, then went on, in desperation. 'Well . . . I mean to . . . damn it, girls get spanked, not men! I mean . . . you're designed for it . . . you, know, with fatter bottoms, and . . .'

'So we have fat bottoms now, do we?' Persephone asked sweetly.

'No, no, that's not what I meant!' Croom squealed. 'Fatter bottoms . . . fatter than men's, that is . . . better for spanking, and . . . damn it, you two, it's not natural to spank a man!'

'Oh, do be quiet, Mr Croom,' Hecate sighed.

'But it's not!' he went on, ignoring her in his growing panic. 'It's . . . it's just the way of things! Men spank women, not the other way around!'

'Would you pop off your knickers, please, Sephany dear?' Hecate asked.

Persephone responded quickly, reaching up under her dress to peel down a pair of large white panties decorated with pink polka dots. Croom could only stare in mounting horror as Hecate took her daughter's panties and bundled them into a tight ball.

'Open wide, Mr Croom,' Hecate instructed.

'No, not that, no . . .' he babbled, cut off abruptly as the balled panties were thrust at his mouth.

'Hold his nose,' Persephone suggested. 'That's what he does to girls.'

'I doubt that will be necessary,' Hecate replied. 'You see, Anderson dear, you have a choice. You may do as you are told, and all will be well. Sephany still wants you as her boyfriend, you know, just not when you seem to see yourself as some sort of master. Otherwise, I will untie you, about five minutes before I tell Sir Gerard that you sodomised and whipped his daughter.'

'He threatened to horsewhip my last boyfriend,' Persephone said proudly.

'And he has been known to take pot shots at people on the land,' Hecate added. 'Well over their heads, usually, but he dotes on Sephany.'

Anderson's mouth came open. The panties were pushed inside. Hecate sat down on the bed, smiling complacently as she patted her lap. Croom could only glare futilely as he struggled to his knees and shuffled around, already dizzy with humiliation, and wondering if all the girls he had spanked had felt as bad when put across his knee.

Hecate took hold of his arm and helped him as he pulled himself awkwardly across her lap. In position, she took a tight grip on the rope binding his waist and reached around him to fumble for his fly, speaking as she began to undress him.

'And naturally,' she said, 'it will be done bare, just as you did to me, and to poor Sephany, and, I'm sure I need not remind you, as you wanted me to do to her. Imagine that, Mr Croom, asking a mother to spank her own daughter, bare bottomed, in front of you. Really!'

Anderson slumped across her knee, his face set in deep consternation as he thought of what he had been expecting, Persephone in the same humiliating position he now occupied, and of all the other girls he had given the same treatment. His feelings grew sharply worse as his clothes were tugged smartly down, trousers and pants together. He felt the cool air on his balls and realised that he was making as rude a show as any of his victims.

'You see, Anderson,' Hecate went on as she adjusted his pants at half-mast, 'it's all very well teaching girls the joys of pain and of being made to feel humble, but there must be a balance. That is one thing of value my father taught me. So now I'm going to spank you, hard. Hairbrush, please, Sephany, dear.'

Croom's response was a gurgling sound made through Persephone's panties.

* * *

228

Persephone watched in giggling delight as Anderson Croom was spanked. He took it badly, kicking his legs and thrashing his body from side to side with no more restraint or dignity than she had shown herself in the same position. It was funny, yet it felt wrong, with a nagging voice at the back of her head telling her that she ought to be the one with a bare red bum.

Not that it stopped her watching as her mother laid smack after smack of the hairbrush across his buttocks. She had been aroused from the first, and it was growing, making her bolder, until she plucked up the courage to move position so that she could see his balls and cock as he was punished. As they came into view, she saw that he was fully erect and immediately burst into fresh giggles.

'Yes, my dear,' Hecate said, 'it is just the same for men as for women, but they do not like to admit it. Do you, Mr Croom?'

Anderson gave a frantic shake of his head, then jerked hard as the hairbrush landed across his bottom once more.

'But they do like their botties spanked, all the same,' Hecate went on, smacking vigorously away. 'Another fifty, I think, and we'll call him done.'

She tightened her grip, her mouth pursing in determination as she laid in, now applying the hairbrush with all her force. Croom immediately went into the same sort of wild, undignified tantrum Persephone had herself gone into over his lap and in the mine building. Satisfaction replaced amusement as she watched, thinking of how much her own punishments had hurt, and thoroughly pleased that her tormentor was getting the same treatment. There was still a nagging doubt in her mind, and her pussy was tingling urgently, but there was no question that revenge was sweet.

'May I, Mummy?' she said as Hecate finished off with a final vicious salvo across Croom's now purple buttocks.

'Of course, my dear,' Hecate puffed. 'Ah, that was most satisfying.'

Persephone took the brush and laid in, grinning as she beat him, and watching the way his erect penis waved under his belly in time to the smacks and the kicks of his bound legs. Soon she was laughing, just as he had when he beat her, and as his buttocks parted in his pain an idea for a wonderfully appropriate finale occurred to her.

She stopped, turned the hairbrush in her hand, pressed it between his buttocks, and pushed. Croom gave a muffled squeal of pain through her panties as his anus was penetrated.

'Sephany, really!' Hecate chided gently.

'He deserved it,' she answered.

'True,' Hecate admitted, and gave the hairbrush a brief waggle in his anus.

'So, what now?' Persephone asked cautiously. 'If we untie him, he might . . .'

'Oh, I don't think so,' Hecate answered. 'They're usually pretty obedient after a good spanking, but we haven't finished yet.'

'No?'

'No,' Hecate answered, and gave him another slap.

Persephone bit her lip, wondering if she dared ask her mother to leave so that she could take her pleasure on Anderson's cock, which she badly needed inside herself.

'Now, Anderson,' Hecate instructed, her voice firm and low. 'You will do just as you are told. Nod if you agree.'

She had slid a hand under his body, and squeezed his balls, digging her long nails into the sack, but he was already nodding with frantic urgency.

'Good boy,' she said sweetly.

Persephone felt a twinge of shock and jealousy as her mother's hand moved to her lover's cock.

'My,' Hecate remarked, 'but you are excited, aren't you? And such a big boy!'

230

'Croom gave an embarrassed squirm and looked round, to throw Persephone a pleading look that turned abruptly to shock as Hecate stood up, dumping him on the floor. He landed hard, on his side, grimacing in pain, and again as Hecate rolled him over with a heel, onto his back. Persephone put her hand to her mouth to stifle a fresh giggle at the sight of his cock, rigidly erect as it stuck up from his belly.

'Such a handsome cock too,' Hecate said. 'You are a lucky girl, Sephany.'

'Yes, Mummy,' Persephone replied. 'Would you mind if . . .?'

'I'm not sure he's really sorry yet,' Hecate interrupted. 'Now, Anderson, you're going to be a good boy, aren't you, and give Sephany a nice kiss to say sorry. Then I'll untie you.'

He gave a single, miserable nod.

'A kiss?' Persephone said. 'I was –'

'Not on your lips, dear,' Hecate cut her off. 'On your bottom hole.'

'My bottom hole!' she squeaked, the blood going straight to her face. 'Mummy!'

'You've no knickers on, you simply need to lift you skirt,' Hecate said. 'Don't be shy.'

Persephone made a face, embarrassment warring with need inside her, the thought of doing something so intimate in front of her mother appalling, yet her need for orgasm close to uncontrollable. Biting her lip, she looked to her mother, to Croom's straining erection, and back. She nodded, suddenly, but she was blushing and shaking as she cocked her leg over his head and began to settle, looking down. He spat out the panties, and for a moment his eyes showed, wide in shock, and then his face was hidden beneath her bottom. She reached down to pull up her skirt, then sat herself squarely down over his face, until her bottom was just touching.

231

'Now, Anderson,' Hecate said, 'a nice kiss, you know where.'

There was a pause. Persephone felt him move under her, then his lips touched her anus, a sensation so exquisite she let out an involuntary gasp of pleasure. The next instant his tongue had penetrated her hole and she was sighing in rapture as her bottom was licked for the first time in her life.

'Ah! He's licking me!' she sighed.

'He's a good boy, really,' Hecate said. 'Now, I shall leave you. Have fun, darling.'

Persephone nodded, and as her mother slipped quietly from the room she was able to bring the whole focus of her attention onto her pleasure. His tongue was wriggling in her bottom hole, a truly glorious feeling. She knew it would take her just moments to come if she touched her sex. Yet if the feel of a man's penis up her bottom could make her come, than maybe a tongue could too.

'Deeper, harder,' she moaned, and reached forwards to take hold of his straining cock. 'Make me come.'

She begun to use her nails on his cock, scarping them down the taut skin of his shaft. Immediately he was licking for all he was worth. She wiggled her bottom in his face splaying her cheeks in an effort to get her hole more firmly against his mouth.

'Oh, that's good!' she moaned. 'Oh, we can do this again, Anderson, lots . . . Um, lovely.'

His tongue pushed deeper still as she let herself go loose in his face. It was going to work, she knew, and she closed her eyes, focusing on just how deliciously rude it felt to have a man's tongue up her bottom, a man who had been spanked and humiliated, a man who had given her the same treatment . . . the first man to ever have the guts to take her knickers down and spank her . . . the first man to put his cock up her bottom hole and spunk in her . . .

She screamed as she came, indifferent to the fact that her fantasy had slipped to her own submission. The next moment she was face down on his cock, sucking in a desperate apologetic frenzy, to catch a mouthful of sperm almost the instant her lips met his foreskin.

Anderson struggled to make the best of a bad thing as he left Persephone's room. Both women were thoroughly pleased with themselves, and it was impossible to deny his own reaction to what had been done to him. He had kept his temper, even thanking Persephone when he was released, but for all the shaking in his hands as she gave him a reassuring hug, he was already plotting revenge.

Her change of heart as she had sucked his cock into her mouth didn't matter, he was determined to teach her a serious lesson, and what humiliation really meant. Tying her hands behind her back to have her spanked by Creech appealed, or possibly by Vicky, who she loved to boss around, and with Creech watching. Buggering her and making her suck his dirty cock also appealed, or pissing all over her as she masturbated after a whipping, or anything that would leave her in a state of grovelling humiliation . . .

'I feel much better now,' she said happily, breaking his train of thought as she took his arm. 'You see, Anderson, I don't mind, so long as it's fair.'

'Well, I suppose you're right,' he said, patting her hand as he wondered how she would look with her bare bottom in the air and her face pushed in one of the Cynosure's pats. 'Still, that was, er . . . enervating to say the least. A beer wouldn't go amiss, and it will soon be lunchtime.'

'Of course,' she answered as they reached the stairs to see Vicky and Creech standing in the hall below, talking.

'You, girl,' Persephone instructed, 'run along and fetch a beer. You know where the pantry is, don't you?'

'I . . .' Vicky began, and stopped, throwing a pleading look up at Anderson.

'If you would,' he said.

'Chop, chop,' Persephone added.

'I'm busy, actually,' Vicky answered. 'Nich and Ysabel promised to show me some of the temples.'

'For goodness' sake,' Persephone addressed Anderson, interrupting Vicky. 'Is she always like this? Look, you, you get paid, don't you? So do your work.'

'I will see to the beer,' Creech intoned gently.

'No,' Persephone said. 'Make her do it. She's so lazy! I don't think I've seen her do a single hand's turn since she got here. You're going to have to buck your ideas up if you want to keep your job, you know, Victoria.'

'No . . .' Vicky began, and stopped. 'I'm going now.'

She made for the front door. Persephone watched her go, mouth wide in outrage.

'Don't worry about it,' Croom said quickly. 'She gets like that sometimes. Wrong time of the month, I expect.'

'You can't let your servants treat you like that, Anderson,' Persephone replied. 'If we're going to be together, I'm not having some snotty maid who won't do as she's told. I'm sure she fancies you too. Sack her.'

Vicky had stopped in the doorway, her eyes blazing.

'He can't,' she said.

'Sack her, Anderson!' Persephone demanded.

'Go fuck your horse, you silly cow!' Vicky snapped, and walked out of the house.

'What did you say to me?' Persephone yelled, already clattering down the stairs. 'How dare you!'

'There's no need to make a fuss!' Anderson said desperately, dashing after her. 'Girls, please!'

'There is every need!' Persephone stormed as they reached the door. 'You're far too easy with her, Anderson. There are going to be some changes if –'

'I'm not a bloody maid!' Vicky shouted, turning from

where she had stopped in the middle of the carriageway. 'I'm his girlfriend!'

'Girlfriend?' Persephone queried. 'But . . .'

She stopped at the crunch of tyres on gravel. A car was pulling into the carriageway, a black BMW, about which Anderson sensed something familiar. He was already sidling past Persephone as it drew to a stop. The doors opened. Elizabeth Ferndale got out, then Tabitha, then Felicity Chatfield. Anderson Croom was running.

'Damn it, Vicky!' Anderson cursed as Creech placed a full pint glass on the table in front of him. 'Why did you have to lose your cool? You know I wouldn't leave you for Persephone, or anyone else.'

'No, I don't, not really,' Vicky answered sulkily, 'and anyway, that wasn't it at all. She's such a stuck-up bitch!'

'She thought you were a servant!'

'That's still no reason to treat me like that!'

Creech's discreet cough interrupted Anderson as he opened his mouth to reply.

'Sir, Miss Victoria, if I may say so, it is a little late for recriminations. Perhaps we should simply enjoy our lunch?'

'You're right,' Anderson answered. 'Is there anything good on the menu?'

'By the standards of a country pub, sir, yes,' Creech began, and stopped as Nich and Isabel appeared in the doorway.

'What the Hell are you doing here?' Croom demanded as they approached. 'Come to gloat, I suppose. I said you should have parked the Bentley somewhere less conspicuous, Creech.'

'Not at all,' Nich answered. 'We have come in order to make you see sense. Clearly you misinterpreted Blackman's riddle, and we, too, have had to admit defeat. Perhaps together?'

235

Croom sighed.

'And you still think it'll just be a few tomes full of mumbo-jumbo?'

'Julian Blackman's legacy of magic and theology,' Nich answered him, 'and I must point out that mumbo-jumbo is a technical term related to voodoo, but I suspect you know that?'

'I really couldn't give a damn,' Croom answered, 'but OK, so long as we're agreed. Tangible wealth goes to me, books and so forth or any other rubbish to do with the cult goes to you?'

'Done,' Nich answered immediately, extending his hand.

Anderson hesitated only a moment, then took Nich's hand. They shook.

'May as well make the best of it, then,' he said jovially. 'How about a spot of lunch?'

'Please, yes,' Ysabel answered before Nich could speak. 'We left Brooke House. They were all getting rather cross, and it seemed the only tactful thing to do.'

'Yes,' Croom agreed, 'very sensible. Anyway, let's find out where this damn cache is, if it exists at all. Creech, will you see to ordering. Steaks all round, yes?'

Nich glanced to Ysabel, shrugged and nodded. Placing his rucksack on the floor, he extracted the idol, the necklace, the spider and finally the notebooks, placing each on the table.

'First,' Ysabel said, 'have all curses been revoked, dolls deactivated, maledictions recanted, hexes taken off and anything else that might foul things up dealt with?'

'Yes,' Nich said with more than a tinge of regret.

'Anderson? Creech? Vicky?' Ysabel asked.

'I've never done anything of the sort!' Anderson protested.

'Neither, madam, have I,' Creech assured her.

'I don't even know what you're talking about,' Vicky put in.

'Right, then,' Nich said, turning to Croom, 'so show us how to understand Blackman's symbolic code.'

'Symbolic code?' Croom replied. 'No, no, it's a simple transposition cipher. I'll show you.'

He opened one of the books at random, flicking through until he found a piece of code.

'Here,' he went on, pointing at the book, 'this symbol, the little triangle . . .'

'The earth symbol, yes,' Ysabel put in, 'or maybe the symbol for the melancholic humour.'

'Eh?' Croom answered. 'No, it's just his symbol to indicate a break between words. That's why it comes up so often. Look, this crab sign is a "J", quite a rare letter, while the Aries symbol is an "N", which is much more common.'

'Oh,' Nich said, glancing at Ysabel with a wan smile.

'Never mind the details, though,' Croom continued. 'Most of it's just verbiage, anyway. Blackman never seems to have used one word where several hundred would do. He doesn't even tell us how to solve the riddle, not exactly.'

'What do we do, then?' Nich asked eagerly.

'How does the idol work?' Ysabel added.

'The jade teddy bear?' Croom continued. 'Oh, you don't need that, just the map that was hidden in its base.'

So saying, he produced the black vellum sheet from his pocket, spreading it out on the table for all to see. Nich exchanged a look with Ysabel and shook his head.

'It looks simple,' Croom stated. 'You simply place the plaque of the necklace onto the map in such a way that the contours of the map lie under certain parts of the necklace, thus . . .'

Croom took the plaque and laid it carefully on the map, its apparent lack of symmetry immediately becoming a rough mirror of parts of the map beneath it.

'. . . which leaves,' Croom continued, 'the central garnet directly over the house, and this hole over the

237

position of the cup on the carriage sweep. It's a bit out, and the garnet's not quite over the hall, but I don't see how the spider's leg can indicate anything other than the temple of Pan-Vaunus.'

'No,' Nich corrected him. 'The altar's been moved. It used to be in the centre of the hall, where else? After all, the hall was the principal temple.'

'Bugger!' Croom cursed. 'That means our calculation was completely wrong! Damn and blast!'

'Calm down,' Ysabel remarked as Anderson Croom began to thump the table with his fist.

'Sorry,' Croom said as he composed himself. 'It's been a trying day. That puts everything a little bit further north. Now, let's see . . . that way the big garnet fits the formal gardens. So, if we place seven of the spider's legs into their respective grooves on the plaque, the thorax lies over the hall instead of the carriage sweep and the eighth points to . . .'

'A point in a field,' Nich answered him.

'A point by a hedge,' Croom corrected him. 'Anyway, what's this little symbol next to it?'

'An oak leaf, I think,' Nich stated, scrutinising the tiny silver mark. 'If so, it should indicate the wildwood. That seems odd, in a field. It's quite inappropriate.'

'Each symbol represents a temple or shrine,' Croom said.

'Oh, yes,' Ysabel put in. 'There's one for Pan-Vaunus, and Vulcan-Thor-Hephastos, each slightly to the side of the spot that marks the temple.'

'There's a key in one of the books,' Croom said. 'The thinnest one.'

Creech passed the book across, Croom quickly locating the oak leaf symbol and decoding the line of sigils next to it.

'It's the Phane of the Spirits of the Wild,' he said after a while. 'Whoever they may be.'

'Of course!' Nich exclaimed. 'The one place that would never be disturbed!'

'Why not?' Croom asked.

'Any other shrine would be cleaned and repaired, but the essence of a dedication to the Spirits of the Wild is that any place sacred to them must be left overgrown! Of course, it's so obvious!'

'If you say so,' Croom replied. 'So it's in this phane thing, which is in a hedge. Unfortunately the hedge around the field in which the Cynosure is grazing.'

'We can get at it from the other side,' Ysabel said.

'OK, then,' Croom said, getting to his feet. 'This is what we do. There's not much chance of being seen, but we'd better take some elementary precautions. You've seen the old mine?'

'Yes. I was spying on you yesterday,' Nich admitted.

'When I buggered Sephany? I bet you took that out on Ysabel!'

'Perhaps,' Nich answered him coldly, Ysabel going abruptly pink as she glanced around at the crowded pub.

'Anyway,' Croom went on. 'We leave here separately, and meet up . . .'

'How do we know we can trust you?' Nich queried.

'Simple,' Croom answered. 'Take Vicky on the bike. Ysabel can come with us.'

Nich gave a slightly doubtful nod.

'We meet up in Melton Mowbray,' Croom went on. 'I'll hire a car. Creech drops us at the gates of the old mine and waits somewhere inconspicuous. We raid the phane, and off we go.'

'What if Sir Gerard sees us? Or notices that the phane had been robbed?'

'That's not likely, as long as we're careful. In any case, no one but us knows the phane is even there. Sir Gerard, yes, but I don't suppose he knows what it is. I certainly didn't notice it, did any of you?'

'No,' Nich admitted. Ysabel shook her head.

'So stop being pathetic. Of course there's a small risk, but the chances are the theft will go undetected. And if it doesn't, what will they find? An empty phane, which doesn't prove that anything's been taken out of it. Obviously we stash whatever we find somewhere safe until any fuss had blown over. We need gloves, and a few other bits of equipment, which we can get in Melton. Rely on me.'

'Fair enough,' Nich admitted. 'You seem very experienced at this sort of thing.'

'Life is sometimes dull for the rich,' Croom answered. 'I enlivened my teenage years with the occasional bit of skulduggery.'

'I might have guessed,' Nich snorted.

'I must say, you take the moral high ground very easily, for a Satanist,' Croom replied.

'I am not a Satanist!' Nich hissed through grated teeth. 'I am a pagan!'

'In that case,' Croom laughed, 'Won't you two be committing an act of desecration this evening?'

'You're right,' Ysabel replied. 'I suppose I'll just have to undergo expiation for it.'

'In my case,' Nich replied, 'I see Chaos as the supreme deity. Thus, any act that results in an increase in the overall entropy of the universe is acceptable. You should know that chaos is an essential element of the wild. One does not desecrate by enhancing.'

'Highly debatable,' Croom replied. 'One person's "enhance" is another's "despoil". Besides, you're entirely wrong. "The Wild", as you call it, merely represents a level of dynamic order beyond the immediate comprehension of the human mind. To assume that something is chaotic merely because it surpasses your mental capacity is surely an act of folly.'

'Chaos,' Nich retorted, 'may be defined in several ways: as unresolved primordial matter; as the eldest of all gods, sexless, but parent even to the basic human deities of mother and father, Blackman's Earth Mother and Hunter; or merely as utter confusion. The last

240

definition is effectively interchangeable with what you have just defined as "dynamic order".'

'I regard the last definition as trite,' Croom replied. 'The second is mere fantasy. The first correct. By the first definition nature is not chaotic. Indeed, it represents order at an extraordinarily high level.'

'To see chaos as divine is not mere fantasy,' Nich answered hotly. 'It is the basis of my beliefs!'

'Extraordinary,' Croom replied.

'Boys, boys, please,' Ysabel cut in. 'I thought we were going to be friends.'

'Yes,' Vicky added. 'This is no time to quarrel. Men!'

'Also,' Nich continued, ignoring the girls but in a less aggressive tone, 'this relates to the basic doctrinal difference between Julian Blackman, Ysabel and myself. To me chaos is the eldest and therefore supreme deity, all others being valid, but lesser. Both Blackman and Ysabel see chaos as inherently unworshippable. Ysabel, however, sees the Earth Mother as supreme. Blackman saw the male and female principles as inextricably linked opposites and worshipped the resultant combined deity.'

'Do you really believe that?' Croom asked Ysabel casually.

'Yes, I do,' Ysabel replied.

'Oh, well, I suppose it makes a lot more sense than a religion with two mutually contradictory creation myths.'

'That is in itself a simplistic statement,' Nich began, taking the bait. 'A pantheist recognises that any belief is inherently valid. Belief itself reflects divinity . . .'

'Hang on a moment,' Ysabel interrupted. 'Anderson, now that it's past the time for bullshit, what do you believe in?'

'Myself,' Anderson Croom replied.

'Gloves on, everyone?' Anderson Croom asked, speaking into the blackness of the mining building in which he had buggered Persephone Chealingham just the day before, although it seemed an eternity away.

'Yes,' Nich's voice answered him from one side, Vicky and Ysabel confirming a moment later.

'Good,' he went on. 'Has everybody checked that their foot rags cover the whole of their soles?'

Again there came three positive replies.

'OK, let's go, then,' he continued, speaking in a whisper despite being half a mile from the nearest house.

They moved slowly across the floor of the old workings. Around them the landscape was dimly lit by the now full moon, which provided just enough light to make torches unnecessary. Reaching the slope, they scrambled up it on hands and knees, quickly reaching the top. The overhanging trees of Pellow's Wood created deep shadow, and Croom flicked on his torch, the dull red light providing just enough light to see by.

Stalking slowly down the lane, Croom felt the old, familiar thrill of illicit activity. It worked on him like a drug, providing a pleasure close to that of sexual conquest. Thinking of the six women he had spanked and either fucked or buggered during the course of his hunt for Blackman's cache, he found himself grinning.

He turned off the torch as they emerged from the shadow of the wood, pausing for a moment to allow their eyes to adapt back to the moonlight. Ahead and down the slope was the bull's field, the Temple of Pan-Vaunus and its surrounding grove visible as a black smudge in the centre. Beyond that was the dark valley and the slope opposite, the shape of the Pentacle barely discernible in the dim light, Chealingham House a black block against the fractionally paler sky. Not a single light showed in the house, giving an added boost to his confidence.

There was no sign of the Cynosure as they passed along the top of the field, reaching the far end and finding the gate that led into the meadows. Croom unfastened it, letting the others pass through and then closing it gently behind him.

'Keep to the hedge!' he hissed as Nich started off at an angle across the meadows. 'Just in case.'

Nich obeyed, rejoining them to follow the line of the hedge back to the junction with the hedge that ringed the bull's field and then starting down the slope. Halfway down, Croom gave a glance at the house, turned his torch on and directed it into the hedge, illuminating a tangle of thorn, bare of leaves yet so dense that the other side was invisible.

His heart came up into his mouth as he began to move slowly along, peering into the hedge, expecting at any moment to reveal the regular shapes of stones. At nearly three-quarters of the way down the field the moment came; the light caught a low, roughly cubic structure built of unshaped blocks and topped by a single slab of shale. Sited in the very middle of the hedge, the phane was heavily overgrown, tangled branches masking it from all but the closest inspection.

'That'll be a bugger to get into,' Vicky whispered.

'So much for not creating a disturbance,' Nich added.

'Just pass me the big clippers,' Croom ordered. 'One of you use the saw.'

Fifteen minutes later the nearest face of the phane had been exposed. As they tried to force the heavy bar they had brought under the slab, a solid crash on the far side off the hedge sent all three sprawling.

'It's only the bull,' Croom managed, picking himself up from the wet grass. 'Get lost, you wretched animal!'

The Cynosure took no notice, instead pushing once more against the thick thorn but making no headway. A snort of frustration signalled his annoyance at having his hedge interfered with.

'Come on, quick,' Croom instructed.

Nich moved forwards, to help jam the bar hard under the shale slab.

'OK, on three,' Croom said. 'One ... Two ... Three ...'

They strained, the slab lifting, snapping thorn branches, keeling over to the side and then falling clear with a crackling of wood. All four of them pushed forwards, peering into the inside of the phane. Within sat a square metal box, some two feet to a side. The top fitted flush with the sides, held in place by clips but with no sign of a lock.

Croom reached forwards, grasping a catch even as Nich chose another, Ysabel holding the torch steadily on the lid. The catches snapped back. Croom's fingers began to tremble as he took a grip on the lid and lifted. It came loose with a little jerk, turning back on its hinges to reveal the interior.

'Bugger!' Croom cursed as his eyes fell on the rectangular shapes of books. 'Hell! I don't believe it!'

Neither Nich not Ysabel answered, instead staring at the contents of the chest with reverent awe. The books, solid, thick volumes obviously of considerable age, were piled up in the chest; dozens of them, leather bound and musty with age, gold leaf flaking off some, others with worn lettering still visible on the covers. On top of them lay a yellowing envelope, the legend 'To my darling Hecate' written across it in a bold, looping hand, the ink pale with age.

Nich's face was rapt with joy as he reached out for the upper volume, his fingers shaking visibly. Ysabel's face too was set in an expression of ecstasy, her mouth open and her eyes wide like a child staring at a much-yearned for present. Croom sat back on his haunches, heedless of the wet grass, a feeling of absolute despondency welling up inside him. He sighed, vaguely aware of Nich picking a book up and holding it up to Ysabel's torch.

'Let's see,' Nich whispered. 'It's so faint I can hardly read it. It must be ancient, nineteenth-century at least.

Yes! Look at the date, 1834! Let's see . . . that's a "B", yes, "Brooke" I think, shine the torch at a lower angle, yes, "Brooke House – Pig Register". "Brooke House Pig Register"! No, it must just be an old notebook, open it up.'

Croom leaned forwards again, oblivious to another snort and shove from the Cynosure.

'July twenty-four, Marshal Ney crossed with Rutland Lady. July thirty, Marshal Ney crossed with Meadow-sweet . . .' Nich was reading, his voice hoarse with disbelief.

Dredging out another book, Croom found the same format, only in a different hand and charting the breeding programme for sheep in the late eighteenth century. Another proved similar, and another. Nich and Ysabel were grabbing book after book, discarding each as it proved to be just another stock book. Vicky began to laugh, then Anderson as it became apparent that the chest contained nothing else, a fine prize for the owner of the estate, but virtually worthless for anybody else. Blackman had been clever indeed.

As he turned to speak to his companions, he saw the rear of Brooke House. A single light burned in the central window of the first floor.

'Jesus, Sir Gerard's awake!' he exclaimed.

'Who's there?' the baronet's voice sounded from the bottom of the meadow. 'Stay where you are or I'll fire!'

'Run!' Croom hissed, suiting action to words as he took off up the field.

An ear-splitting retort and the patter of shot signalled that Sir Gerard meant what he said. An instant later another shot sounded and a searing pain shot through Croom's left buttock.

'Come back here, whoever you are, damn you!' Sir Gerard was yelling. 'You thieving bastards! Set foot on my land, would you? Here, have some more!'

A double shot rang out, Sir Gerard's enthusiasm mercifully exceeding his aim. An instant later Croom made the gate, hurling himself over despite the pain and dashing away along the lane, crouched low to avoid Sir Gerard's volleys. Behind him he heard the metallic crash of the gate as the others came over.

Together they fled blindly down the lane, ignoring Sir Gerard's demands for them to stop and the occasional charge of shot whistling over their heads, Anderson Croom clutching his bleeding buttock.

NEXUS BACKLIST

This information is correct at time of printing. For up-to-date information, please visit our website at www.nexus-books.co.uk

All books are priced at £5.99 unless another price is given.

- - - - - - ✂ -

Please send me the books I have ticked above.

Name   ....

Address   ....

                  ....

                  ....

                  .... Post code ....

Send to: **Cash Sales, Nexus Books, Thames Wharf Studios, Rainville Road, London W6 9HA**

US customers: for prices and details of how to order books for delivery by mail, call 1-800-343-4499.

Please enclose a cheque or postal order, made payable to **Nexus Books Ltd**, to the value of the books you have ordered plus postage and packing costs as follows:
   UK and BFPO – £1.00 for the first book, 50p for each subsequent book.
   Overseas (including Republic of Ireland) – £2.00 for the first book, £1.00 for each subsequent book.

If you would prefer to pay by VISA, ACCESS/MASTERCARD, AMEX, DINERS CLUB or SWITCH, please write your card number and expiry date here:

....

Please allow up to 28 days for delivery.

Signature ....

Our privacy policy

We will not disclose information you supply us to any other parties. We will not disclose any information which identifies you personally to any person without your express consent.

From time to time we may send out information about Nexus books and special offers. Please tick here if you do *not* wish to receive Nexus information.   ☐

- - - - - - ✂ -